Murder in Morningside Heights

Center Point
Large Print

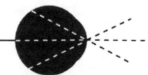

Murder in Morningside Heights

A GASLIGHT MYSTERY

VICTORIA THOMPSON

CENTER POINT LARGE PRINT
THORNDIKE, MAINE

17 Feb 6
Center Pt
35.95(21.57)

This Center Point Large Print edition
is published in the year 2016 by arrangement with
The Berkley Publishing Group, an imprint of Penguin
Publishing Group, a division of Random House LLC.

Copyright © 2016 by Victoria Thompson.

All rights reserved.

The text of this Large Print edition is unabridged.
In other aspects, this book may vary from the original edition.
Printed in the United States of America on permanent paper.
Set in 16-point Times New Roman type.

ISBN: 978-1-68324-042-6

Library of Congress Cataloging-in-Publication Data

Names: Thompson, Victoria (Victoria E.), author.
Title: Murder in Morningside Heights : a gaslight mystery / Victoria
Thompson.
Description: Center Point Large Print edition. | Thorndike, Maine :
Center Point Large Print, 2016. | ©2016
Identifiers: LCCN 2016014166 | ISBN 9781683240426
   (hardcover : alk. paper)
Subjects: LCSH: Brandt, Sarah (Fictitious character)—Fiction. | Malloy,
Frank (Fictitious character)—Fiction. | Private investigators—New York
(State)—New York—Fiction. | Murder—Investigation—Fiction. | Large
type books. | GSAFD: Mystery fiction. | Historical fiction.
Classification: LCC PS3570.H6442 M8653 2016b | DDC 813/.54—dc23
LC record available at http://lccn.loc.gov/2016014166

To my dear friend Roselyn O'Brien.
Thanks for giving me another career option
when this writing gig wasn't working out.

1

FRANK MALLOY, CONFIDENTIAL INQUIRIES.

Frank hesitated a moment to admire the sight of his name in gilt letters on the frosted glass of the office door. The "Confidential Inquiries" had been his mother-in-law's idea. Elizabeth Decker felt that "Detective Agency" was somehow undignified and might attract the wrong type of client. Frank wasn't sure what the wrong type of client might be for a private detective agency, but he was more than willing to give his new business at least a hint of respectability.

He turned the brass knob and stepped into the office.

His assistant, former police officer Gino Donatelli, instantly rose from behind his brand-new desk. "Here's Mr. Malloy now," he said to the respectable, middle-aged couple sitting in the row of wooden chairs lining the wall.

Frank removed his hat and went over to shake hands as Gino introduced him to Mr. and Mrs. Northrup. They both had the stunned look of people who had received one of life's harsher blows. Mr. Northrup covered his pain with bluster, the way men often did, but Mrs. Northrup could barely speak and looked as if she might shatter at the slightest touch.

"Gino, would you take the Northrups into my office?"

The slender young man hurried to escort them through the connecting door while Frank removed his tailored wool overcoat and hung it, along with his hat, on the wooden coat tree. Mrs. Decker had suggested a brass one, but Frank didn't want to look like he didn't need business, even though he didn't. He'd only consented to opening the agency because being a millionaire had turned out to be pretty boring for a former New York City Police detective. Since he didn't need the money, he also didn't want to scare off poorer clients who might well be the most interesting cases.

In the few weeks since he'd been open, he hadn't gotten any interesting cases at all. Unfortunately for them, the Northrups promised to break that streak.

Frank followed them into his modestly decorated office. The furniture in here was new, too, which couldn't be helped because the business was new, but it wasn't particularly expensive or ornate. The Northrups sat in the two wooden chairs placed in front of his plain, walnut desk. Frank sat down in a more comfortable chair behind it and pulled a pad of paper and a pencil from the drawer. Gino discreetly sat down on a chair in the corner behind the Northrups with his own pad and pencil to take notes, in case Frank missed anything.

"I'm very sorry to hear about your daughter,"

Frank said. "Mr. Donatelli told me a little bit about your case when he telephoned me."

Frank usually didn't bother coming to the office unless he needed to see a client, which hadn't been much of an issue until today.

"I don't know how much Mr. Donatelli told you," Mr. Northrup said uncertainly.

"Just that she was killed. Why don't you start at the beginning and tell me the whole story."

Mrs. Northrup made a small sound of distress and pressed a handkerchief to her lips. Northrup cleared his throat. "It's hard to know where to begin. Abigail is our only daughter. She was always so . . ." He gestured helplessly.

"Outstanding," Mrs. Northrup said almost defensively. "Outstanding in everything she did."

"Yes," Northrup said. "She excelled at her schoolwork, and she could sing beautifully and play the piano."

"And everyone loved her—don't forget that," Mrs. Northrup said. "She was like a . . . like a little star, always shining so brightly."

"She was too bright for Tarrytown, I'm afraid," Northrup said.

"Tarrytown?"

"That's where we live, you see. It's in Westchester County."

"I know where it is," Frank said, recalling the quiet little town north of the city. "If you live in Tarrytown, what was Abigail doing in the city?"

9

"Oh, she's lived here for years now, ever since she came here to attend college."

"I knew we shouldn't have let her come." Mrs. Northrup dabbed at tears. "If we'd kept her at home, she'd still be alive."

"Now, Mother, you know we couldn't have kept her in Tarrytown."

"She should've gotten married like her friends did. Why does a girl need to go to college anyway?"

Frank was getting a good picture of Abigail Northrup in his mind. She was a headstrong young woman, smart and ambitious. A New Woman. He knew all about them. He was married to one. "But she was too bright for Tarrytown," he said, echoing Northrup's own words.

They looked up at him in surprise.

"That's it exactly," Northrup said, obviously forgetting he'd given Frank that image. "She wanted to do something important with her life."

"Being a mother is important," Mrs. Northrup said.

Northrup ignored her. "She wanted an education."

"Where did she go to college?"

"The Normal School of Manhattan."

"The teacher's college," Frank said, picturing the impressive building in Morningside Heights.

"That's right. We investigated it very thoroughly before we allowed her to come, of course. All the girls live right there, together, in a dormitory, and they are well chaperoned. She couldn't have been safer in her own home."

"And that's where she should have been," Mrs. Northrup said, dabbing her eyes again. "We should have made her come home when she graduated instead of letting her stay in this awful city!"

"So she wasn't a student anymore?" Frank asked, a little confused now.

"Oh no," Northrup said. "I guess Mr. Donatelli didn't mention it. She graduated last spring, and they offered her a teaching job at the college, so she stayed on. It was quite an honor and she was very proud. I told you, she was an outstanding girl."

"And she still lived in the dormitory?"

"Oh no, she . . . Well, we would have preferred that, of course, and she could have become one of the chaperones who live there, I suppose, but she wanted to feel more grown-up, I think."

"She wanted to be *independent*," her mother said, as if the word left a bad taste in her mouth.

"One of the female professors offered to rent her a room in her own house," Northrup said. "Miss Wilson already shares her house with another professor, Miss Billingsly, so we thought . . ." His voice trailed off, but Frank knew what they'd thought. They'd thought their girl would be safe with two older women.

"So your daughter was teaching at the college?" Frank said to break the strained silence.

"Yes, since school started in the fall."

"She taught French," Mrs. Northrup said. "She spoke it beautifully. We sent her to France last summer as a graduation gift. She said it helped her perfect her accent, whatever that means."

Frank and his new bride had honeymooned in Europe. The one thing he hadn't liked about France was the French accents. Why couldn't they learn English? But he nodded his understanding. "She was teaching at the college and living with these two lady professors. Now tell me what happened the day she died."

Mrs. Northrup made that distressed sound again, and Northrup needed a moment to compose himself. "She . . . Well, nobody knows exactly what happened, of course. One of the students found her . . . her body. She was lying in this gazebo thing they have in the courtyard behind the college. It's a quiet place for the girls to sit, I guess."

"Do they know why she was there?"

"No. She taught her classes in the morning, and nobody remembers seeing her after that. Someone found her in the early afternoon. She'd been . . . stabbed."

"And what do the police say?"

Mrs. Northrup was sobbing quietly into her handkerchief by now, but Northrup's expression hardened. "They said she was probably killed by a stranger trying to rob her or something."

"On the grounds of the college?"

"That's what they said. They said it would be very difficult to find the killer."

The anger roiled in his chest in a hot ball, but he didn't let the Northrups see his reaction. The cops would have taken one look at the Northrups and figured them for bumpkins, which they were, of course. They were also bumpkins with money, which meant they'd be good for a substantial "reward," and nobody was going to exert themselves to find Abigail's killer until the reward was offered. "Do you know what they wanted?"

"Yes, they wanted a bribe, Mr. Malloy," Northrup said just as angrily as Frank could have hoped. "They made that pretty clear."

"You may find it shocking, but this is common practice in the city."

"And how common is it for them to actually find the killer in a case like this?"

Well, now, Mr. Northrup wasn't quite the bumpkin he appeared to be. "It could be difficult. If the killer really was a stranger, it could be impossible."

"And if the killer was someone my daughter knew, someone at the college, for example, how likely is it the police will be able to identify them?"

Frank tried to picture a bunch of hoity-toity college professors even giving the time of day to some red-faced Irish detective, much less confiding the kind of embarrassing information that might help identify a killer. Not very likely. "Why have you come to me then, Mr. Northrup?" Malloy was Irish, too, as Northrup could plainly see, and not very far from being a cop himself.

"You were recommended to me by a friend here in the city. I manage a bank in Tarrytown, and I have many business connections here. One of them belongs to the Knickerbocker Club, and he told me you handled a very sensitive matter for them."

Frank was always surprised at how his reputation had spread. "Is your daughter's death a sensitive matter?"

"It is to us, Mr. Malloy." Northrup drew a deep breath as if to fortify himself. "I know what the newspapers do when a beautiful young woman is murdered. I don't want to see my daughter's reputation destroyed just to sell newspapers. Her reputation is all she has left now, and I'd like her to be remembered for who she really was and not what some scandal sheet would make her."

Frank could understand that perfectly. He had children, too, and he'd do whatever he could to protect them.

"Will you help us, Mr. Malloy?"

"I will."

• • •

Sarah was lounging in the comfort of the brocade recamier they had bought in France and reading a novel when Malloy joined her in their private sitting room at home.

"Ah, a lady of leisure," he teased, giving her a kiss.

"I'm not having any trouble at all adapting to having servants, and you were right about this room." Their house had originally had adjoining bedrooms for the husband and wife, but Malloy had felt strongly that they needed only one bedroom to share and Sarah had happily agreed. They'd furnished the other as a sitting room where they could have some privacy in their very busy household.

He sank into the overstuffed chair on the other side of the fireplace and sighed in contentment. "I know. I like being right."

Sarah smiled. "Did you really get a case today?"

"Oh yes. Sadly, a young woman was murdered and her parents want me to find out who did it. They're worried about a scandal."

"As well they might be." Sarah sighed, remembering the sensational stories they'd seen over the past few years as Hearst and Pulitzer destroyed people's reputations trying to best each other in the newspaper business. "Can I help?" she asked hopefully. She didn't want to admit it just yet, but being a lady of leisure could be rather boring.

He frowned, and for a moment she thought he might say something ridiculous, like solving murders wasn't something a lady like her should be concerned with. But of course he knew better. "What do you know about college?"

"College? Why on earth do you want to know about that?"

"Because the girl . . . Well, I suppose I should call her a woman. The young woman who was murdered was a college professor."

He told her the story of how Abigail Northrup got from being an outstanding girl in Tarrytown to being a college professor in New York City.

"How awful," Sarah said when he'd finished. "Such a promising life cut short. And her poor parents."

"Which is why they want to keep this from becoming a scandal. Her memory is all they have left."

"You might not be able to prevent a scandal," she said. "Depending on who killed her and why. Anytime a young woman is killed, the reasons tend to be pretty sordid, even if a stranger did it."

"I know, but at least we'll try. The police won't. So what do you know about it?"

"Not a lot, I'm afraid. The girls in my social circle didn't go to college."

"I thought you had to be rich to go to college."

Sarah shrugged. "Poor children are lucky to get any education at all, that's true, and society families do often send their sons for higher education, but not their daughters. The girls go to Europe for a tour so they can polish their social skills and get their clothes made by the House of Worth in Paris."

"That's the place you got those dresses made that cost a fortune."

"Exactly."

"All right. If all the rich girls go to Paris, who are those girls at the Normal School?"

"Oh, their families might be wealthy, but they aren't society people. You said her father manages a bank. They're probably financially comfortable, but they won't be invited to Mrs. Astor's next ball."

"So her parents can afford to send her to college, but why would she want to go? Don't all girls just want to get married? She's not going to meet any eligible young men at a women's college."

Sarah smiled at that. "Surprisingly, no, not all girls just want to get married. This is the modern world, Malloy. The New Women are thinking about a career."

"Why would a New Woman want a career when she could . . . ?" He grinned, glancing meaningfully around the room. "When she could lie around reading all day?"

Sarah threw her book at him, which made him laugh, so she stuck out her tongue. "Not every woman has servants and a nursemaid to watch the children. Being a wife and mother is hard work, and it doesn't leave time for much of anything else. If a woman wants to do something important, like teach or be a nurse or a social worker or—"

"Or a midwife," he supplied, naming her former profession.

"Or a midwife. Well, not only does a woman who is married with children not have time for that, most of those professions won't even employ a married woman and certainly not a woman with children. On the other side of the coin, not every woman receives an offer of marriage in the first place and some wouldn't accept it even if they did."

"Why not?" he asked in genuine surprise.

She gave him a pitying smile. "Because not every woman wants to put her entire life in the hands of a man. You may find this shocking, but not all men are as kind and loving and wonderful as you."

He thought about this for a moment. "That's true."

"Good thing I don't have another book handy."

He grinned again. "So these women go to college so they can get a job and support themselves without a husband."

"Which is far preferable to the old system, where they'd be dependent on the charity of family members or be forced to sell themselves in the street."

"You're right. That is preferable to the old system." He thought for another moment. "I guess that tells me what I need to know about these lady professors, too."

"And what's that?"

"They're not society women, so I won't need your help getting them to talk to me."

Sarah winced under a crushing wave of disappointment, but then she saw the glint in his eye. "They may not be society women, but they're still women. You may feel the need for some feminine insight when you question them, and if you do, I'm sure I could spare the time to assist you."

Malloy glanced around the comfortable room again. "If you're willing to give all this up, then I'm sure I would appreciate the sacrifice."

She ignored his provocation. "When were you planning to see them?"

"Not until tomorrow, I think."

"What are you going to do in the meantime?"

"Go see Doc Haynes. He did the autopsy."

Doc Haynes looked up from behind the piles of paperwork littering his desk and glared at him with eyes that had seen far too much death. "I thought I'd seen the last of you when you struck it rich, Malloy."

"So did I, but you know how it is."

"No, I don't. How is it that a man who never has

to work another day in his life shows up at the city morgue looking for a dead body?"

"I've opened a private detective agency."

"Have you, now? And a good thing it is, too. I guess you'll be solving the cases the police can't."

"I couldn't possibly do that. I'm only one man, Doc."

Doc chuckled at the implied insult to the New York City Police Department. "So who is it you want to see today?"

"Abigail Northrup. She was killed at the Normal School."

"Oh yes. What a shame. So young, and you can still see how pretty she was."

"What do you mean?"

"Didn't they tell you? Oh, maybe her parents don't know. Somebody at the school identified her body, so there was no need for the parents to see her like that."

"Then she was beaten, too?"

"In a way." Haynes shuffled through a stack of folders until he found the right one. "She was stabbed in the face. Looks like it was three times."

"How did that kill her?"

"Let me finish. Three times before the final, fatal blow that went into her eye and then into her brain."

Frank muttered a curse. "What was she stabbed with?"

"A screwdriver."

20

Contrary to logic, the more information Frank got about this case, the less sense it made. "A screwdriver? Who kills somebody with a screwdriver?"

"I've seen it before," Haynes said, "but usually it's two fellows who get into a fight while they're working, and one of them grabs the closest thing to hand."

"So you think she was killed by some workman?" Frank didn't think college professors had much use for screwdrivers.

"I did ask, because it was so strange, and it seems the janitor was doing some repairs to the gazebo where she was found and had accidentally left it behind."

"Or so he said."

"Yes, well, figuring that out is not my job. What I *can* tell you is that somebody stabbed her in the face three times with the screwdriver and then put it through her eye, either by mistake or on purpose."

"And that killed her?"

"Obviously."

"How quick?"

"Not right away, but she didn't last long. It kind of looks like the killer tried to pull it back out and she was probably struggling, and well, there was a lot of damage. And a lot of blood."

Frank shook his head in wonder. "Was she interfered with?"

"No, and her clothes were all neat and tidy except for the blood. She was most likely still a virgin, too. You can't always tell, contrary to popular belief, but there was no sign of recent activity, and they watch those girls at the Normal School pretty close, I've heard."

"Jewelry?"

"A locket and a ring. I kept them in case her family wants them." Most jewelry and all the cash on a dead body would usually disappear long before the family came to claim the body.

"Valuable, do you think?"

"Not the crown jewels, but good quality."

"Then a thief would have taken them?"

"If she was being robbed, sure, but this wasn't a robbery."

"Of course it wasn't. In that neighborhood, in broad daylight, right on the school grounds? And the only things of value she had with her were left behind?" He didn't add that the killing had been much too personal. Thieves didn't stab people in the face. Frank sighed. "Can I take a look at the body?"

"Sure. I'll get Herman to take you down."

The dead room was as grim as its name, dark and dank and chilly on this wintry day. They ran cold water over the corpses to keep them fresh, even in February, so the sound of dripping water added to the bleakness. He didn't have to look far to find Abigail. Her lush white body stood out among the bloated and battered carcasses of the other dead. Seeing her lying there, completely exposed, was an abomination.

"Even with the cuts, she was a looker," the young man named Herman said, leering. "Wouldn't mind a piece of that when she was alive."

Frank gave him the glare he usually reserved for uncooperative criminals to frighten them into submission. It worked pretty well on Herman, too. He scurried away guiltily.

The wounds were worse than Frank had imagined. The eye, of course, was awful, but the other wounds were vicious, too, jagged and deep and probably inflicted by someone in a rage. If she had survived, she would have been scarred. Had that been the killer's original intention?

He checked her hands and saw that she'd tried to ward off the blows that had killed her, but bare hands weren't much help against a determined assailant with a weapon.

Even a woman could have done this.

With a sigh, he realized he'd just doubled his number of possible suspects.

Since he still had most of the afternoon left, he decided to take the elevated railroad up to Morningside Heights to look at the place where Abigail had been murdered and see if he could speak to the person in charge of the college. Would that be a dean or something? Frank realized how very little he knew about higher education.

He managed to get a hansom cab to carry him from Bellevue on First Avenue all the way over to Ninth Avenue, where he could catch the El up to Morningside Heights. The nine-block journey over to the El station took far longer than the ninety-block trip uptown to the Normal School on the El, since the El didn't have to stop for traffic at every intersection.

The trip gave Frank plenty of time to consider the various methods of transportation available in the city. His in-laws kept a carriage, which meant they had to keep horses and servants to tend the horses and drive the carriage. The electric trolleys were a big improvement over the old horsecars that used to carry passengers up and down the city, but they were always overcrowded and either too hot or too cold, depending on the season. They were still talking about a train system that would run underground, but Frank would believe it when he saw it. Meanwhile, he amused himself by watching the buildings flashing by outside the train and catching glimpses of the people living and working behind their windows.

He stepped out of the station at 118th Street into another world. Here trees graced the streets and traffic moved at a leisurely pace. Houses sat behind neatly tended front yards guarded by wrought iron fences. In summer, it would seem like the country, and even now, in the dead of winter, Frank could feel the relative peacefulness.

He'd been right. No thieves were stabbing young girls to death in broad daylight here, or even in the dead of night. He found the Normal School easily enough. In fact, no thieves or any other miscreants could get within a hundred feet of the building without being seen. It sat in the middle of what had been a field not too long ago, its U-shaped grandeur even more impressive because no other buildings competed with it. The entrance was columned and Frank stepped inside the impressive doors unchallenged. Inside, the entryway stretched upward to the domed roof three stories above, where a stained glass skylight filtered the feeble winter sun. An impressive staircase gave access to the floors above, and on either side of the foyer, doors opened into what Frank imagined were classrooms of some sort.

No one appeared to be assigned the task of welcoming visitors, so he glanced around, looking for the kind of directory one would see in a city office building. Before he could find one, two young women came out of one of the class-rooms. They wore the bell-shaped black skirts and starched white shirtwaists that seemed to be practically a uniform for young women today. They were chatting pleasantly until one of them noticed Frank standing in the middle of the foyer. She gave a shriek and both of them bolted back into the classroom and slammed the door.

Frank blinked in surprise, but then he figured they knew that one of their professors had been murdered just outside and seeing a strange man where he probably had no business being had made them fear for their own lives. This made him reconsider his plan to go wandering about until he found the dean's office. Luckily, before he had to decide what to do next, the classroom door opened again and an older woman wearing unrelieved black with a watch pinned to her ample bosom stepped cautiously out.

"Who are you and what do you want?" she demanded.

"I'm a detective investigating the death of Miss Abigail Northrup. I was wondering if you could direct me to the office of the head dean or whoever is in charge."

She seemed to relax just a bit, as if she wanted to believe him but didn't quite dare. "That would be President Hatch. His office is on the second floor."

Frank thanked her and hurried off up the grand staircase before he frightened anyone else. On the second floor he found an impressive set of double doors labeled President's Office and stepped inside into a wood-paneled room.

A young woman sitting at a desk worked a typewriter with a good deal of proficiency. She looked up in alarm, and Frank quickly identified himself before she could run away shrieking. "I'd like to speak with President Hatch if he's available."

As if struck dumb, she nodded quickly and scurried over to an interior door. She ducked inside and emerged after a few minutes, looking slightly less terrified. "President Hatch will see you."

She held the door for him and closed it behind him.

President Hatch sat behind a desk larger and more impressive than Frank had seen in any millionaire's office. Maybe a college president had to try harder to impress visitors. He was a slender man in his fifties with thinning gray hair plastered against his head and pince-nez glasses perched on his nose, probably to give him a scholarly look.

Hatch rose to his feet, but he didn't offer to shake hands. "I thought the police had finished their business with us."

"I'm not with the police."

"But Alice said—"

"I told her I was a detective. Maybe she got confused."

"Then if you're not with the police, who are you with?"

"I'm a private investigator." Frank tossed his card onto the massive desk. Hatch glanced at it

27

but made no move to pick it up. "Miss Northrup's parents hired me."

"To do what?"

"To find out who killed their daughter."

"I thought the police had settled that."

Frank gave him a pitying look. "Is that what you want to tell the parents of your students? That a young woman was stabbed to death by a wandering lunatic on the very grounds of your college?"

Angry color flooded Hatch's face, but he was far too civilized to shout or anything. "Really, Mr. . . ." He glanced down at the card again.

"Malloy," Frank said. "And I wouldn't want to send my daughter to a place where girls got murdered right in the front yard."

Hatch seemed to sag under his carefully tailored suit. "And yet that is what happened, Mr. Malloy, so I don't see how it matters who killed her. The damage has been done."

Now Frank saw the despair. Hatch envisioned his school failing in front of his eyes and had already given up hope. "That's true, but what if we can find the person who killed her and lock them up? Then you can tell the parents that your students are safe again." It wasn't much, but it was more hope than Hatch had a moment ago.

"How do I know you can do that? The police said—"

"I know what they said, but I can do it. I have

references, if you need them. Felix Decker, for one."

"Felix Decker? How would a man like that know a private detective?"

"I solved a murder for him at the Knickerbocker Club," Frank said, dropping another impressive name. "He also happens to be my father-in-law."

Hatch blinked several times, as Frank had expected. He needed a moment to reassess his opinion of Frank Malloy, and when he had, he said, "Perhaps you should have a seat, Mr. Malloy."

Frank took one of the leather wingback chairs that sat in front of Hatch's impressive desk. They were probably intended for rich parents, but he didn't mind.

Hatch sank into his own chair and sighed. He picked up Frank's card and looked closely. It was the engraved one that he used for wealthy clients, although Hatch didn't look overly impressed. Then he laid it down carefully, respectfully, pulled off his pince-nez, and rubbed his eyes. "And what can you do for us that the police can't?"

"It's more what I'll do that they *won't*, Mr. Hatch. I will actually try to find the killer, and I'm good at that. I will also do my best to keep the story away from the newspapers. Miss Northrup's parents were very concerned about scandal, and I'm sure you are, too."

"Of course I am, but I hardly think Miss Northrup was involved in anything scandalous."

"She was murdered at a respectable women's college, which alone is enough of a scandal for the newspapers. I won't be speaking to any reporters, and you should instruct everyone here to do the same. I'll also need your permission to speak with the other professors and some of the students, the ones who knew her."

"Is that really necessary? The young ladies are already nearly hysterical over what happened."

"They'll be a lot less hysterical if we catch the killer. I'd also like to look at the place where she was killed and see the place where she lived."

"You'll have to get permission from Miss Wilson for that. She lived at Miss Wilson's house, not here."

"Yes, with two other professors."

"Only Miss Wilson is a professor. In fact, she's the only female professor we have here. She was just elected this school year."

"I thought Abigail Northrup was a teacher here, too."

"She is . . . I mean was, but not a full professor. She was an instructor, as is Miss Billingsly and the other females who teach here."

"And you only have one real professor, this Miss Wilson?"

"Of course not. We have many male professors.

Miss Wilson just happens to be our first female."

Frank thought it odd that a college for women had only one female professor, but of course he didn't know much about colleges. "Can you tell me a little about your college?"

"I can tell you everything about the Normal School of Manhattan," Hatch said, a little defensively.

"How long have you worked here?"

"I started the school almost twenty-seven years ago." Here was a subject he felt confident of, and he straightened in his chair. "So many young men had been lost in the War between the States that a lot of young women found themselves with no prospect of marriage and no way to support themselves. Normal schools were opened all over the country to train them for professions."

"Why do you call them 'normal schools'?"

"Oh yes, I suppose that could sound odd to an outsider. The schools were established to train teachers and to establish normal teaching standards, so they were called normal schools."

"So you only train women to be teachers."

"That's right, although some of them choose other professions after they graduate, and still others marry. And before you ask, no, I don't think that means they have wasted their education. I think a generation of young men raised by educated mothers would be very good for our country, don't you?"

"I'm sure it would," Frank said quite sincerely.

Both men looked up when someone knocked on the door. Alice stuck her head in. "Excuse me, Mr. Hatch, but Tobias is here."

Hatch's expression soured. "Send him in."

Frank managed to feel offended that Hatch would interrupt their meeting in the minute it took for an older Negro man in work clothes to step tentatively into Hatch's office.

Tobias's apprehensive gaze darted between Frank and Hatch, finally settling on the president, who said, "Mr. Malloy, I'd like you to meet the man who killed Abigail Northrup."

2

After Malloy left to visit the coroner, Sarah tried to go back to her novel, but her mind kept wandering. He had only been teasing about her being a lady of leisure, but she was finding that she missed many things about the life she had led before their marriage. Back then, she'd made her living as a midwife, and every knock at the door could mean the challenge of bringing a baby safely into the world. Now she had a maid to answer the door and nobody ever summoned her to do anything interesting.

Malloy, too, had been chafing at his enforced retirement from the police department where he'd spent his entire adult life. Until he got this case, she hadn't seen him this interested in anything since they'd returned from their honeymoon just before Christmas. Opening the detective agency had been a wonderful idea . . . for him. Sarah's days still stretched out before her, full of deadly dull afternoons.

A tap on the door put a merciful end to her depressing thoughts. "Come in."

Her new maid, Hattie, came in with an envelope. "This just come for you, Mrs. Frank, from the Mission."

A message from the Daughters of Hope Mission, which Sarah had helped support for several years, usually meant a problem of some kind, so Sarah felt guilty for the tremor of excitement she experienced at the prospect of something meaningful to fill her afternoon.

She thanked Hattie and tore open the envelope. The note was from Mrs. Keller, the matron at the Mission. The Mission had been established years earlier as a refuge for girls who had been orphaned or abandoned by their families. It provided a safe place for them to live and get some education and training so they could make their way in the world.

Mrs. Keller hated to bother Sarah, the note said, but she had just learned that one of the girls who had come to the Mission a little over a month ago was with child. They had a policy of never accepting a pregnant girl, although many had come to them for shelter through the years. Caring for a destitute expectant mother was the mission of other charities, and after giving these girls a hot meal, someone from the Mission would escort her to one of the places where she could find the help she needed.

This situation was a little different in that the girl had already been living at the Mission and didn't want to leave for a place she might not like as well. Sarah was only too glad to provide whatever assistance Mrs. Keller needed.

• • •

Tobias's expression instantly changed from apprehensive to terrified. "I never done no such thing, Mr. Hatch, sir! I never would've touched a hair on that poor lady's head!"

From the way he looked at Frank, Tobias apparently thought he was here to take him into custody. Since Frank had instinctively jumped to his feet, he had silently confirmed this suspicion.

"Of course you wouldn't," Hatch said angrily, "but admit it—if you hadn't left your screwdriver behind, she'd still be alive."

Ah, so this was the janitor who had accidentally provided the murder weapon. Frank frowned, wondering why the cops hadn't jumped on him immediately as the killer. He was the perfect scapegoat since he was colored and his tool had killed her. Tobias was very lucky he wasn't sitting in a jail cell this very minute.

"Maybe you could take me out and show me where Miss Northrup was killed," Frank said.

"Ain't you here to arrest me?"

"Mr. Malloy is not with the police, Tobias," Hatch explained, still angry but not as much.

"He's a private detective investigating Miss Northrup's death. Take him outside and show him where you found her."

So Tobias had found the body in addition to providing the weapon. How interesting. "I'll have some questions, too."

"And answer Mr. Malloy's questions," Hatch added wearily.

Frank turned back to Hatch. "I'll need to see Miss Wilson and the others I mentioned."

Hatch sighed again. "I'll let them know to expect you and encourage them to tell you whatever they may know, although I'm sure it won't be much. Tomorrow is Saturday, so there are no classes. I'll have Alice make up a list of the faculty members and their addresses and a list of Miss Northrup's students. The students all live here in the dormitory wing. Men aren't permitted in there, but I'm sure we can find a room where you can meet with anyone you need to speak with. You can stop by here when you're finished outside and pick up the list."

Frank thought that questioning the students would be an excellent job for Gino. "Thank you for your help, Mr. Hatch."

Tobias, still looking terrified, stepped aside so Frank could precede him, but Hatch stopped him.

"Oh, and Mr. Malloy? Please keep me informed about what you find out."

Frank nodded, figuring Hatch would take that as agreement, although he had no such intention. He went out into the front office, where Alice had stopped her typing to stare at him warily. "Thanks very much for your help, miss," he said with what he hoped was a friendly smile. Sarah had told him that his friendly smiles weren't all that reassuring, but he still tried.

Alice didn't say a word, but Tobias followed him obediently out. When they were at the top of the stairs, Frank turned to him and said, "Where are we going, Tobias?"

Tobias swallowed nervously. "Is you sure you ain't here to arrest me, Mr. Malloy?"

"Absolutely. I couldn't arrest you even if I wanted to, and I don't. I would appreciate it if you'd show me where Miss Northrup was killed, though, and tell me everything you know about it."

This information didn't seem to cheer him much, but he said, "Downstairs and out back. I'll show you."

Tobias led the way down the massive staircase, moving slowly in the way old people did when their joints hurt. The short winter day was ending and the building was quiet.

"Where is everyone?"

"Classes is over for today, and a lot of the young ladies has gone home because of the trouble with Miss Northrup."

Hatch was right to be worried about the future of his school. "Tell me how you came to leave your screwdriver in the . . . what was it? A gazebo?"

"Yes, sir, that's what they calls it. Real nice place it is, too. The young ladies, they like to sit out there when the weather's nice. But you know how girls can be, sir, about bugs and things. They'd get right scared if a bee flew in, so a few years back, Mr. Hatch had us put screens up and a door. It don't keep the spiders out, but it works for most everything else."

"And you were working there on . . . What day was it?"

"Wednesday, sir. Yes, sir. On Wednesday morning. We had some wind the other night, and it set the door flapping. Tore it near off its hinges, it did. So I was putting it back."

"I know the night you mean, but that was almost a week ago. Why did you wait until Wednesday to fix it?"

Tobias looked at him in mild surprise. "Nobody else asked me that, Mr. Malloy. It was because that was the first nice day we'd had. The sun come out and it was warmer than it has been. My knees don't like the cold weather too much, so I try and stay inside when I can."

Frank remembered how mild the weather had been that day. "Even still, was it warm enough for somebody to sit outside in the gazebo?"

Tobias glanced up at where Frank stood above him on the staircase. "I wouldn't think so, no, sir."

That's what Frank had been thinking, too. So why was Abigail in the gazebo in the first place? That might be a question only the killer could answer.

"This way, sir," Tobias said when they reached the bottom of the stairs. He led Frank through the lobby to the opposite side from where he'd entered. They passed more closed doors to class-rooms or offices and finally came to an entrance door that was markedly less magnificent than the one in the front of the building. This one led to the courtyard formed by the sides of the U-shaped building.

Shielded from the wind off the Hudson River, the courtyard would provide a pleasant gathering spot in nicer weather. Frank judged the buildings to be about as old as Hatch said the college was, and through the years, someone had taken pains to plant trees and bushes here. The winter-brown grass would spring to life in another month or two and turn the area into a verdant field where young women could play croquet or that new game of lawn tennis and whatever other games rich girls enjoyed.

The gazebo was larger than Frank had envisioned and sat in the middle of the court-yard. A gravel path led from the door directly to it. Tobias didn't exactly drag his heels, but he couldn't have been more reluctant to go out there. Frank pitied him, but he needed information.

"Do you often leave your tools lying around?"

"Oh no, sir! I never . . ." He shook his head. "Well, I've done it a time or two lately. I'm get-ting forgetful in my old age. And . . ."

Frank looked more closely at the man walking beside him. "And you probably don't see as well as you used to."

"Please, sir, don't say nothing to Mr. Hatch. After all this, I reckon he's going to fire me anyways, but just in case . . ."

"I won't say a word. I don't intend to report anything at all to him, in fact."

"But you promised!"

Frank grinned. "No, I didn't. And Mr. Hatch didn't hire me. Miss Northrup's parents did. I report to them."

Tobias's eyes rounded in amazement. "You is a man to be reckoned with, Mr. Malloy."

Frank hoped so. "Did you see Miss Northrup that morning when you were fixing the door?"

"No, sir, I didn't see nobody. All the young ladies was in classes, and it was too cold to be out here for fun. I had the place all to myself."

"Any idea why she might've come out here?"

"No, sir. I been studying on it myself, and it just don't make no sense. If she was meeting somebody, why didn't she meet them inside where it was warm? There's always plenty of rooms empty, and usually nobody's in the library when the young ladies is in classes. Miss Northrup even had her own office where she could be private. She shared it with Professor Pelletier, but he would've let her talk private with somebody if she asked."

"Who's this Pelletier?"

"He's the French teacher, head of the depart-ment. Miss Northrup, she work under him."

"Did they get along well?"

Tobias looked up in surprise. "Far as I know. That ain't none of my business."

Of course it wasn't. Frank was being unfair to ask someone in Tobias's position to judge the professors. They'd reached the gazebo, and Frank saw it was just as Tobias had described. The original structure had been open to catch the breeze, but they'd installed screens. In this last month of winter, the screens were dirty and a bit rusty. Frank realized he couldn't really see inside even this close. "Hatch said you found her."

Tobias caught his breath at the memory. "Yes, sir, I did."

"Why did you come back?"

"Well, now, I noticed my screwdriver was missing. I recollected I probably left it here, so I come to get it."

"Did you notice anybody else around when you came back?"

"Oh no. It was just as quiet as it is now. A little earlier in the day, but still nobody was around."

"So you opened the door and what did you see?"

His breath caught again. "I didn't know what I seen at first. I thought maybe it was a bundle of rags or something. Not a person, not at first. Then I saw the blood. It was almost black by then. Dried up, it was, so I didn't even know it was

41

blood. My mind just couldn't make sense of it. Then I saw my screwdriver and it was sticking out of her poor face . . ."

Tears flooded his eyes and he covered his face with both hands. "It's all right, Tobias. I'm sorry you had to see that." Frank clapped his hand on the smaller man's shoulder. "You wait here. I want to take a look inside."

Frank pulled the door open, noticing it apparently worked fine now. Inside, the floor was weathered a dull gray, but he could see the stains from the blood that someone had scrubbed away. A bench seat ran all the way around the inside, providing seating for fifteen or twenty people. "Do they ever have classes in here?"

"Sometimes, in the spring when it gets real hot," he called from outside.

"I hate to ask, but can you show me how she was laying when you found her?"

To his credit, Tobias didn't hesitate, although he stopped short of actually entering the gazebo. He held the door open and stood just on the threshold. "Her head was there, where the stains are. She was on her back. There was blood on the bench there beside her, finger marks like she tried to grab hold and pull herself up. Probably wanted to go for help or something."

Judging from the size of the stain, she'd bled too fast for that. "Did you see anything else?"

"No, sir. I didn't stay long enough. Once I

realized what I saw, I took off running. Well, walking as fast as I can, I guess I should say. Went straight to Mr. Hatch's office and told him. I figured he'd know what to do."

"Thank you, Tobias." When Tobias stepped aside, Frank left the gazebo. He took a minute to look around, making note of how many windows overlooked this courtyard. The question was, had anyone been looking out any of them when Abigail Northrup was killed? And even if they had been, they probably couldn't have seen the crime itself through the dirty screens. At most, they might have seen Abigail and her killer arrive and the killer leave, but would anyone remember such a thing, even if someone had witnessed it?

"Let's go back inside where it's warm," Frank said, remembering what Tobias had said about his knees.

As they crunched along the gravel path, Frank said, "Why is it the police didn't arrest you for killing her?"

It was a fair question. Both of them knew that colored men were arrested every day in New York City simply for the crime of being unemployed and standing on a street corner. Tobias was actually involved to some extent in the murder of a white woman.

"Mr. Hatch wouldn't let them."

Frank didn't even try to hide his astonishment. Maybe he'd misjudged Hatch. "Why not?"

"First off, there wasn't no way I could've done it. Miss Northrup, she was teaching her classes until eleven o'clock. I finished up out here before that, and one of the maids comes to tell me the toilets was clogged up in the dormitory, on the second floor. I went up there and was working on them until nearly two o'clock. Lots of the young ladies saw me. They was all put out because they had to go to another floor to use the lavatory. It was when I was packing up from that when I noticed my screwdriver was missing, so I went back to get it. By then, Miss Northrup had been dead a long time, they said, an hour or more."

That was, Frank had to agree, an excellent alibi, but excellent alibis had never stopped the police from arresting someone if they saw an easy way to close a case. "And Mr. Hatch stood up for you and wouldn't let them arrest you?"

"Yes, sir. I was mighty proud of that."

Frank was sure he was. Poor Tobias probably thought Hatch did it out of gratitude to a long-time employee. Frank doubted that. He thought Hatch realized how bad it would look if one of his trusted employees, a man who worked right in the girls' dormitory at times, was charged with murder. No wonder he was so willing to blame a stranger.

They stepped into the building and took a minute to savor the warmth. "Can you show me Miss Northrup's office?"

"I can, but Professor Pelletier'll be gone by now, and he keeps it locked up. You'll have to get him to let you in."

"I don't suppose he lives in the building."

"Oh no, sir. No mens live here. He got his own place somewhere."

Frank thanked Tobias for his help and sent him on his way. Then he went back upstairs to see if Alice had the list prepared for him.

Mulberry Street ran through one of the worst slums in New York, even though Police Headquarters sat squarely on it as well. Sarah always made a point of noticing the filth and despair as she strode purposefully down this street, so she wouldn't forget how fortunate she was. How many of the children running barefoot along the sidewalk, in spite of the cold, had a real home and family? How many of them would be huddled together for warmth in a stairwell or doorway when night fell? The size of the problem would overwhelm her if she let herself think about it too long. She could not save them all, so she had to focus on the ones she could help.

Just up the street from Police Headquarters lay the Daughters of Hope Mission. The ramshackle house was usually crammed with girls who had no safe place to go. The child who was now Sarah's own daughter, Catherine, had once found shelter here, and Sarah had hired another of the girls,

Maeve, as Catherine's nursemaid. Many others had found refuge and a new life at the Mission. She could take some pride in that.

One of the girls answered Sarah's knock, smiling in recognition. "Mrs. Brandt . . . I mean Mrs. Malloy! So sorry! Please, come in." She wore a simple black skirt and shirtwaist, which had probably been made right there at the Mission by girls learning to use a sewing machine.

"That's all right, Matilda. Lots of people are still getting used to my new name, including me." As Sarah stepped into the entry, she saw several other girls peeking out from the various rooms that lined the hallway. Of course they'd be curious about any visitors. Sarah smiled at them. "Is Mrs. Keller busy?"

"She's always busy, but she'll have time for you," Matilda said.

Sarah was pleased to see the change in this girl who had come to them one dark night, starving and covered with bruises. The bruises had healed and regular meals had restored her health. More important, her time at the Mission had given her confidence and courage. She led Sarah back to the former butler's pantry, where Mrs. Keller had her office.

Mrs. Keller greeted her warmly. Sarah noticed her dress was a bit faded and frayed around the edges, even though the middle-aged matron was scrupulously neat and tidy. Sarah suspected she was spending her own meager salary on the girls instead of herself. She'd have to arrange for a new dress or two to be delivered anonymously to this wonderful lady.

Mrs. Keller urged Sarah to take a seat in one of the mismatched chairs crowded into the space in front of her cluttered desk. "I'm sorry to bother you, Mrs. Malloy, but this is a unique situation for me."

"From what you said in your note, you didn't know this girl was expecting until yesterday."

"That's right. Hannah is a large girl. Not fat, of course. She was nearly starved when she arrived, like most of the others. But she's large boned and tall. Her clothes fit loosely, so no one noticed anything out of the ordinary for almost two months. Then yesterday, two of the girls came to me with their suspicions. I questioned Hannah privately, and she finally confessed that she is with child. She apparently suspected this when she came to us, but lied about it so we would take her in."

"I don't suppose we can blame her for that." Sarah sighed. "Do you have any idea how far along she is?"

"Not more than six months, I'd guess, from what she told me."

"And the father?"

"Was a man who lived in the same building. He raped her, apparently."

"Oh dear, so that's another reason she came to us, I guess."

"Combined with the fact that her mother had just been evicted and told her she'd have to make her own way from now on. There were several younger children as well, I gather, and she couldn't feed them all."

It was an all-too-familiar story. "I suppose you explained to her that we don't usually accept girls who are expecting."

"Yes, but she . . ." Mrs. Keller frowned and shook her head as if silently chastening herself. When she met Sarah's gaze again, she looked almost angry. "You should have seen her, Mrs. Malloy. She was terrified. She must have gone to one of the charities that helps girls in her situation. They wouldn't take her in, of course, because she wasn't far enough along. That meant she'd have to live on the street for months, making money however she could in the meantime. We both know what she would have had to do to survive, and if she somehow managed to do that and didn't lose the baby and finally found a place that wasn't already full and would take her when her time came, they would probably pressure her to give her child up to an orphanage. So she came here and hid her condition for as long as she could."

"I guess she hoped to keep her secret at least until she was far enough along to be accepted into a maternity home," Sarah said.

"Yes, and if what she told me is true, that will just be another month or so. She's a good girl, Mrs. Malloy. She works hard and never complains or fights with the other girls, no matter how they provoke her, and heaven knows, the girls do provoke each other."

Sarah felt like the wicked stepmother in a fairy tale, but she had to say, "We have these rules for good reasons. You know that even better than I."

"Yes, I do." Mrs. Keller was even more angry now. "I know if our girls began producing babies, it would cause all kinds of rumors about this place. Our perfect reputation would be tarnished, and people would begin to wonder if we were a brothel in disguise, luring unsuspecting young women with false promises of protection."

"And as a result, the girls who leave here would always be under a shadow," Sarah said gently. "We've worked very hard to protect them up to now. I would hate to see that ruined."

This time Mrs. Keller sighed. "I know all that, and you're right, I know it even better than you do, because I see these girls every day. If only I didn't also know Hannah so well. It's much easier to turn away a stranger, isn't it? And she's right, she would have no place to go if we turn her out. I'm not suggesting that we change our rules, but just this one time, couldn't we let her stay a little longer so she doesn't end up on the streets?"

Sarah really hated sounding like the wicked stepmother in a fairy tale, so she decided not to. "I certainly don't want her to end up on the streets. How about if we let her stay for now, and in the meantime, I try to find a place for her at a maternity home? There might be someplace outside the city that would take her immediately."

"Oh, Mrs. Malloy, would you? That would be so kind."

"Letting her stay a week or two longer won't hurt anything, I'm sure. And if you don't mind, I'd like to meet Hannah and examine her to make sure she's in good health."

"Of course. I was hoping you would."

Just as Mrs. Keller had said, Hannah was a large girl. She'd probably filled out some since arriving at the Mission. The food here was plain but nourishing and regular, and Hannah had obviously thrived. She didn't smile when Mrs. Keller introduced her, and her brown eyes were wary. At Sarah's invitation, she sat down in the other "guest" chair and stared at Sarah.

"I'm a midwife, Hannah," Sarah explained gently. "I'd like to ask you a few questions and examine you, if you don't mind."

"Examine?" she echoed in alarm, instinctively laying a hand protectively on her stomach. Mrs. Keller had been correct. Sarah probably wouldn't have even guessed Hannah was with child yet. She wondered what had given the girl away.

"I'd like to listen to your heart, and to your baby's heart." Luckily, Sarah had thought to bring her medical bag with her.

"How do you do that?"

Sarah pulled her stethoscope from the bag and held up the little bell-shaped end. "I just put this against your stomach. I'll let you listen to it, too, if you like."

The girl's eyes widened, and she nodded eagerly.

Sarah asked the girl the usual questions about her menses and when she thought she had conceived and a few more about her general health. Then she looked in her mouth and ears and listened to her heart and lungs. Luckily, she found nothing amiss. Even the baby's heartbeat was strong and regular.

Hannah gasped in amazement when Sarah let her listen to it. "That's the babe?"

"Yes, it is."

The girl smiled for the first time, turning her broad, plain face almost beautiful.

"Do you mind if I touch your stomach?" Sarah asked when they'd both finished listening.

"What for?" Hannah asked, wary again.

"To see how big the baby is and what position he's in."

"Do you know it's a boy?" she asked in surprise.

"Of course not. I just don't like calling unborn babies 'it,' so I sometimes call them 'he' and other times 'she.' So, can I touch you?" Sarah held up her hand as if to lay it on the girl's stomach.

"I guess."

Sarah found the baby head down. He seemed a bit large for six months, but Hannah was a big girl, so Sarah would expect her child to be larger than average. "Everything seems fine. Mrs. Keller will explain what we have decided, but you don't have to be afraid of anything. We won't leave you on your own. Whatever happens, you and your baby will be safe."

"And I'll be able to keep him? Or her?"

"Yes, if that's what you decide."

"I've already decided. This baby is all I've got in the whole world."

Sarah nodded, not because she agreed with this decision but because she understood. The need for someone to love was strong, especially when a girl had been abandoned by her family. But if a pregnant girl found life in this city difficult, an unmarried mother with a tiny baby would find it even harder. She might be all right, though, if she found a job that could support them. She could leave her baby at the Salvation Army's crèche during the day, and then . . . Well, Sarah didn't want to look too far into the future.

Frank and Sarah set out for Morningside Heights the next morning. Miss Wilson lived a short distance from the college, so they decided to take the elevated train and then get a cab the rest of the way.

"This isn't a very elegant way to travel," Frank remarked as the train lurched to a stop at the next station. He was standing in the crowded car, holding on to the bar, while Sarah had perched on the last available seat.

"It's the fastest, though," she reminded him. "And you don't want to keep a carriage."

"If we had our own carriage, at least we could be warmer."

She smiled at that. The only advantage of the unheated El cars was that they were out of the wind. "You know what Gino would say."

Frank frowned. "I do. He wants me to get one of those motorcars."

"It would be a lot easier to keep than horses and a carriage."

"But then we'd need someone to drive it." Frank thought they already had enough servants with a maid and a cook.

"No, you wouldn't."

"Who would drive it, then?"

"You would."

The very thought of driving one of those mechanical monsters terrified him, but he couldn't admit that to Sarah. "I don't think you're supposed to drive your own motorcar."

"Gino could drive it, then. In fact, I'm sure that's his real plan in convincing you to buy one. I wouldn't mind learning to drive it myself."

"You? A woman could never drive one of those things."

He knew instantly from her expression that he'd made a mistake. "A woman can drive a team of horses. You see them all the time in Central Park. I don't know why she couldn't drive a motorcar."

This conversation was not going well at all. Fortunately, not many people had gotten off at this stop and a lot had gotten on, so Frank was squeezed down the aisle, too far away to continue their discussion.

At the 118th Street station, they found a cab that carried them to the pleasant street in Morningside Heights where Abigail Northrup had rented a room from the first lady professor the Normal School had ever had. Last night, in the privacy of their own sitting room, Frank had told Sarah everything he'd learned yesterday. Now, in the cab, they discussed the approach they were going to take with the two women they were about to visit. Frank was happy to let Sarah take the lead, since they were far more likely to be open with her than with him. He would be content to sit back and try not to remind them he was there so he could watch their reactions.

A mulatto maid, wearing a brightly colored turban in contrast to her severe black dress and white apron, answered the bell at the neat brick town house. She looked the Malloys up and down as if judging their worthiness. Before she could decide whether to admit them, Frank held out his card. "Mr. and Mrs. Malloy are here to see Miss Wilson. President Hatch sent us."

She examined the card closely, making Frank glad he'd given her one of the expensive ones. "Mr. Hatch didn't say nothing about no lady coming with you."

"That's unfortunate," Sarah said before he could give an answer he'd probably regret. "But I hope you aren't going to keep me standing on the front porch as a consequence." Her tone held a note of warning that her words did not.

The maid's eyes widened. Plainly, she hadn't expected a challenge from the wife of a lowly detective. "Of course not. Please come in." If she sounded less than welcoming, they pretended not to notice. "Miss Wilson said for you to join her in the living room."

How modern, Frank thought. Some people were starting to call their parlors "living rooms," although he'd noticed none of the old New York families had made the change yet. He supposed lady professors liked to be up to date, though.

A handsome woman, who looked to be about forty, stood when they entered. She wore a dark green dress, but no jewelry except a watch pinned to her bodice, much like the teacher he'd encountered at the college yesterday. He wondered if the teachers were required to wear watches.

The maid handed her Frank's card. "Mr. Malloy," she read.

"Thank you for seeing us, Miss Wilson. This is my wife. She sometimes assists me in investigations, and I thought you might prefer talking to a female."

"Why would you think that, Mr. Malloy?"

Frank needed a moment to think of an answer that didn't sound condescending. He'd expected Miss Wilson to be upset, if not hysterical, over the violent murder of a young woman whom she had taken into her own home. True, she'd had a few days to get used to the idea, but he hadn't expected her to be defensive.

Once again, Sarah rescued him. "Mr. Malloy was a police detective, Miss Wilson. He is more accustomed to questioning criminals than college professors, and he thought you would appreciate a gentler touch."

Now Miss Wilson was looking at Sarah the way the maid had a minute ago. "Then I suppose I should thank him for bringing you along, Mrs. Malloy. Won't you sit down? Bathsheba, please bring us some coffee."

Frank managed not to show his surprise at the maid's name, although he thought it probably fit. She did look like a sly one, and even though servants weren't supposed to have an opinion about whom their employers entertained, Bathsheba seemed to be muttering to herself as she set off for the kitchen.

The room was comfortably furnished with an overstuffed plush sofa and chairs. Delicate tables sat around, their tops cluttered with doilies and various figurines. Over the fireplace, which had been converted to a gas grate, hung a large painting of some Greek goddess in flowing robes that didn't really conceal much. He managed not to stare.

"We're so very sorry to hear about Miss Northrup's death," Sarah was saying. "It must have been a terrible shock."

For just a second, Miss Wilson's stoic façade cracked a bit, but only a bit. "Thank you. It was, of course. A shock, I mean. For everyone."

"Had you known her long?" Sarah asked.

Miss Wilson visibly gathered herself again. "Almost five years now, I suppose. She was a student at the college, you know."

"Was she one of your students?"

"Oh yes. I had her for several classes."

"And she was a good student?"

"One of the best I've ever had. Teaching her was a joy. She simply loved learning and couldn't get enough."

The sound of someone clattering down the stairway in the hall startled the three of them, and they all looked up as another woman appeared in the doorway that Bathsheba had left open. This woman was like a faded version of Miss Wilson, light brown hair where Miss Wilson's was dark, and pale, white skin while Miss Wilson's had a healthy glow. She also looked as if she'd just climbed out of bed, even though she was fully dressed. Her hair was half-down, with some of the pins sticking out at odd angles, and her eyes held the unfocused look of the newly awakened.

"Are you talking about her?" the woman demanded.

"Estelle," Miss Wilson said sharply, rising to her feet with conscious dignity. "We have guests."

"I can see that! And they're talking about her, aren't they?"

"This is Miss Billingsly," Miss Wilson said. "She also teaches at the college."

"And you," Miss Billingsly said to Frank. "You're the detective, aren't you?"

Frank was already on his feet, since a lady had entered the room, and he sketched her a little bow. "Frank Malloy. And my wife."

Miss Billingsly spared not a glance for Sarah. She had trained her unfocused gaze on Frank. "Do you want to know who killed her?" She took a step toward him, and then another. "Is that why you're here? Well, I'll tell you who killed her."

Frank watched in horrified fascination as Miss Billingsly took one last step toward him, tripped, and went crashing to the floor.

3

Sarah jumped up and hurried to where Miss Billingsly lay sprawled on the floor. Malloy was closer and had already knelt down beside her, but seemed reluctant to take any action.

"Miss Billingsly, are you hurt?" Sarah asked.

The woman's eyes fluttered and she frowned up at Sarah. "What happened?"

That's when Sarah smelled the alcohol and realized Miss Billingsly was drunk. "You fell. Are you hurt?"

"I . . . I don't think so." She pushed up on one elbow. "Who are you?"

"Bathsheba!" Miss Wilson called. She had made no move to help Miss Billingsly.

Sarah helped Miss Billingsly sit up, being careful not to look at Malloy, because she was afraid if she did, she'd see her own amazement of the absurdity of this situation reflected back, and neither of them would be able to keep their composure.

The maid had come running at the urgency of Miss Wilson's summons, but she stopped dead when she saw Miss Billingsly sitting on the floor with their guests hovering over her.

"Bathsheba, Miss Billingsly is ill. Would you help her back upstairs, please?"

"Excuse me, ma'am," Bathsheba said, shouldering Sarah out of the way so she could help Miss Billingsly to her feet.

"I fell down," Miss Billingsly told her with a drunkard's honesty.

"That's all right. You come with me now."

Bathsheba put her arm around Miss Billingsly's waist and led her from the room, but Miss Billingsly stopped when they reached the doorway and turned back to Miss Wilson.

"I'm sorry, Georgia. I didn't mean to—"

"That's all right," Miss Wilson said, cutting her off. "Go with Bathsheba now."

Miss Billingsly nodded and allowed herself to be taken away.

When their footsteps had receded up the stairs, Miss Wilson said, "I apologize. Abigail's death has upset her terribly."

Sarah wondered if Miss Billingsly drank regularly or if this was something new. "That's understandable," Sarah said, taking her seat beside Malloy on the sofa again. "Will she be all right, do you think?"

"Bathsheba will look after her, although we'll have to wait awhile for our coffee, I'm afraid. You were asking me about Abigail."

"Yes." Sarah tried to remember exactly where they were and realized she had learned precious little before being interrupted. "You said she was an excellent student. I suppose that's why Mr. Hatch hired her as a teacher."

"Of course it was."

"Was that common?" Malloy asked. "Hiring your students as teachers?"

"Not at all. Every graduate of the Normal School is a teacher, Mr. Malloy. If we hired even a few from every class, we'd very soon have more teachers than students."

"And you must have outstanding students in every class," Sarah guessed. "What set Abigail apart enough to be hired?"

Miss Wilson hesitated, making Sarah wonder if she was trying to decide whether to tell the truth or not. But maybe she was just trying to phrase her answer diplomatically. "As I said, Abigail was an excellent student, but more than that, she was naturally an excellent teacher. Not everyone is, even with training. But that alone would not have given her a place at the Normal School, since we pride ourselves on producing excellent teachers. She also happened to have excelled in French, and Professor Pelletier needed an assistant."

"Was it his idea to hire her?" Malloy asked.

Miss Wilson seemed annoyed by the question. "He agreed to accept her, if that's what you mean, but President Hatch makes the final decisions."

"And whose idea was it to make you the first female professor?" Malloy asked, surprising Sarah and annoying Miss Wilson even more.

"As I just said, President Hatch makes the final decisions."

Malloy pretended to think this over for a minute. "It just seems funny to me that a college for women didn't have any female professors for the first twenty-some years."

"How very progressive of you, Mr. Malloy. I couldn't agree more."

"Was Professor Pelletier happy with Miss Northrup's work?" Sarah asked, thinking they should get back on the subject they came to discuss. Malloy wasn't as progressive as all that, after all, and she didn't think Miss Wilson needed to know it.

"You'll have to ask him. He does not confide in me."

Sarah wondered if that meant the good professor *wasn't* pleased with Miss Northrup, and Miss Wilson didn't want to say so. "How did you come to have Miss Northrup boarding with you?"

Another brief hesitation. "She needed a place to live, and as a young, single female, her options were limited. It's customary for the female staff at the school to share living quarters in any case. For instance, Miss Billingsly and I have shared this house for over eighteen years. We had a spare room, so we offered it to Abigail."

"And did you enjoy having her here?" Sarah asked.

"Very much," Miss Wilson said, and for the first time Sarah felt she was telling the absolute truth.

"As I said, she was an exceptional young lady with a genuine thirst for knowledge. We spent many an evening in thoughtful discussion. Having her here was . . . exhilarating."

Sarah noted how Miss Wilson's voice had softened as she recalled Abigail Northrup. She had truly cared for the girl.

"Did Miss Billingsly like having her here?" Malloy asked, ruining the mood.

Miss Wilson's expression hardened again. "Of course she did. We both did."

Which meant, of course, that Miss Billingsly hadn't liked Abigail at all. How very interesting. Was that why she was drunk? "Unfortunately," Sarah said with a wistful sigh, "we're here to find out if you know anyone who *didn't* like Abigail or who might have been angry at her for some reason."

"Absolutely not. One or two of her students might have been disappointed in their grades, but students don't murder teachers over that. If they did, there would be no teachers left alive."

"You're right about that," Sarah said with a small smile. "What about her classmates, the other women she was in school with before she graduated? Were any of them jealous that she was selected to teach?"

"Some of them might have been, but once again, one doesn't kill over something like that."

"What about suitors?" Malloy said. "A girl as

accomplished as Miss Northrup must've had a lot of young men interested in her."

Miss Wilson stiffened and sent Malloy a murderous glare. "Miss Northrup was not interested in young men. She was a serious scholar who wanted to make teaching her life's work."

"That doesn't mean she wouldn't've had suitors," Malloy argued.

"It certainly would," Miss Wilson informed him tartly. "Married women are not permitted to teach at the Normal School or anyplace else. Abigail was far too serious about her career to entertain any thoughts of marriage."

But just because Miss Wilson thought so didn't mean it was true. Sarah knew a handsome young man could change a girl's mind in a moment, even a girl as *outstanding* as Abigail Northrup. What Sarah couldn't figure out was why Miss Wilson seemed so insulted at the suggestion Abigail might have had an admirer or two.

"I wonder if we might take a look at Abigail's room," Sarah said.

"Whatever for?"

"I don't know, but we might find something to indicate who might have killed her."

"I seriously doubt that."

Sarah knew better than to argue. She simply waited for Miss Wilson to figure out that she should have no objection to Sarah looking at Abigail's room.

After a few more moments, she said, "Well, I suppose that would be all right. Her parents haven't instructed us about what to do with her things yet, so nothing has been touched since she . . ." For the first time, Miss Wilson appeared to be fighting tears, but she quickly recovered. "Since she left it."

"Thank you. I know this must be very difficult for you, and we appreciate your help."

"I'll take you up."

Sarah was glad to see Malloy had sense enough to know he shouldn't try to accompany them upstairs. She was sure the maiden ladies who lived in this house would be scandalized to have a man go up to their bedrooms.

She followed Miss Wilson up the stairs. Only three doors opened off the hallway, and two were closed. The third led to a bathroom that was probably a recent addition to the house. Miss Wilson led her to the door at the back of the house and opened it to reveal a pleasant room. Flowered wallpaper covered the walls, and a brightly colored braided rug lay on the floor at the foot of the bed. The double bed was neatly made with a light green satin comforter spread over it. Abigail had kept her belongings in order or perhaps Bathsheba had straightened up behind her.

"What are you looking for?" Miss Wilson asked with some concern.

"I won't know until I find it." Sarah began with the dressing table, where she found the typical brushes and combs and hairpins along with a bottle of rosewater scent. The drawers contained nothing of interest. She moved to the dresser and quickly looked through the drawers there, finding nothing except neatly folded underclothes and shirtwaists, stockings and gloves. As Malloy had instructed her, she also checked the undersides of the drawers in case something had been concealed there. The wardrobe was next, and Sarah carefully felt each article of clothing hanging there in case Abigail had hidden something in a pocket or even the lining of a jacket. Finally, she searched the nightstand, where she found a novel in French that Abigail had apparently been reading. She picked it up to flip through it, as Malloy had instructed. People sometimes stuck letters in books, and sure enough, Abigail had done so. The return address was a female in Tarrytown, which seemed innocent enough. "Do you know a Miss Irene Raymond?"

"Oh yes, she and Abigail were in the same class. I believe they were childhood friends as well. Miss Raymond frequently writes to Abigail."

Sarah slipped the letter out of the book.

"You aren't taking that," Miss Wilson said in dismay.

"We'll return it to her parents when we've finished with it. They hired us to find out who killed her, so they won't object to our doing what we must."

Miss Wilson didn't like it, but she couldn't argue. She did, however, object to Sarah pulling the bedclothes off the bed. "What are you doing?"

"I'm searching the room." She tossed the pillows aside when she'd felt them to make sure they contained nothing but feathers. Then, wishing Malloy were here to do the heavy work, she lifted the mattress and looked under it. Sure enough, tucked into one of the springs near the center, where it wouldn't be noticed by someone who was just changing the bedclothes, was a stack of letters tied with a ribbon. Sarah let the mattress slide off the bed so she could reach it.

"What is it?" Miss Wilson asked when Sarah had pulled the bundle free of its hiding place.

"Looks like more letters from Miss Raymond." Indeed, when she flipped through them, they all bore the same name and address as the one she'd found in the book.

"Why did she keep them there?" Miss Wilson asked with a frown.

Sarah was wondering the very same thing. She would probably find out when she had the opportunity to read the letters. For now, she simply said, "You know how girls are about their privacy."

Miss Wilson looked offended. "She can't think Estelle or I would be interested in reading her private correspondence."

Sarah thought that might be exactly what she'd been afraid of, or perhaps she thought Bathsheba would be a snoop. In any case, she had hidden the letters, and now Sarah had found them. "Thank you for letting me look through her room. If you'll give me a hand, I'll put the mattress back."

"Don't worry about it. Bathsheba will put it to rights."

Just as they stepped out of the bedroom, the door at the other end of the hall opened, and Bathsheba emerged, giving Sarah a glimpse of Miss Billingsly lying motionless on a double bed. The maid closed the door behind her.

"How is she?" Miss Wilson asked.

"She sleeping now. Probably won't remember a thing when she wakes up. You still want that coffee served?" She eyed Sarah with disapproval.

"Don't go to any trouble for us," Sarah said. "Mr. Malloy and I are finished here."

"I see you found some letters," Malloy said when they were safely away from Miss Wilson's house.

"Yes. It looks like they're from a girlfriend, although I found one of them hidden in a book and the rest were under her mattress."

Malloy shook his head. "I would've thought a college girl could find a better place to hide her letters."

"In her defense, the room didn't offer many

alternatives, and I'm sure a maid like Bathsheba would consider it her duty to snoop."

"I'm glad we agree on that. And what about that name? *Bathsheba?*"

"It does seem to suit her," Sarah said with a grin.

"And pardon me for saying so, but was Miss Billingsly drunk?"

"I do believe she was."

"I wonder if that's a common condition for her."

"I was wondering the same thing, although she could just be upset over Abigail's murder."

"Even if she didn't like Abigail?" Malloy asked with a knowing grin.

"Oh, you caught that, too?"

"I did. It seems Miss Wilson adored her and Miss Billingsly did not. Why do you think that is?"

"Jealously, perhaps."

"Because Abigail was such an outstanding young lady?"

"More likely because Miss Wilson thought she was an outstanding young lady."

Malloy frowned as he considered this. "You mean Billingsly was jealous because Wilson liked Abigail better than her?"

"I think that may have been it."

"You make it sound like some kind of romance."

"It is, in a way, I suppose. Girls take their friendships very seriously."

"None of them are *girls,* not even Abigail, really."

"Well, women take their friendships very seriously, too. I'm assuming maiden ladies with no husband or children to distract them probably take them even more seriously."

"That's very interesting. Do women kill each other over these serious friendships the way people kill each other when they're jealous of a lover, for instance?"

"That's a very good question, Malloy. But we only have Miss Wilson's word that people don't kill teachers for giving them a bad grade or getting a teaching position they wanted, so those could be reasons, too."

"That's true. I've seen people get killed over a glass of beer, so being jealous of Abigail for getting the job at the Normal School seems like a pretty good motive to me."

"Well, maybe when we've read these letters, we'll know more."

Reading the letters had to wait, however. When they arrived back home, not only were their children eager for their attention, but Gino Donatelli had decided to pay them a visit.

"Just wanted to see if you had anything to tell me about the case," Gino whispered to Frank when he and Sarah had gotten their coats off.

But Frank wasn't fooled. Gino was far more interested in their nursemaid, Maeve, than he was in Abigail Northrup's murder.

Sarah's daughter, Catherine, and Frank's son, Brian, had been playing in his mother's private parlor while Gino and Maeve chatted in the formal parlor. Or at least Frank hoped they'd only been chatting. To Frank's relief, they'd looked perfectly innocent when they came out to greet Frank and Sarah.

"The girls are fixing lunch for everybody," Frank's mother informed them, referring to their cook and maid, who were relatively new additions to the household. Mrs. Malloy had never had servants before and insisted on referring to them as "the girls."

"And Gino can stay," Catherine reported. "We already asked him."

"How lovely," Sarah said with only a trace of irony.

Hattie, the maid, came to tell them lunch was ready, so they all trooped into the dining room and enjoyed a fine meal. When they were done, Mrs. Malloy said, "I'll take the children so you can go with them, Maeve."

For once Maeve looked a little disconcerted. She glanced at Sarah and then at Frank. "Is that all right?"

Frank grinned at her uncertainty. "Well, you did say you wanted to keep on being Catherine's nursemaid instead of coming to work for the agency, but I wouldn't mind hearing a young woman's opinion of all of this."

Maeve smiled radiantly and jumped up to help Mrs. Malloy wrangle the children before joining them in the parlor.

The parlor was a large, comfortable room that Frank had insisted not be so formal that the family couldn't enjoy it. Frank told Gino and Maeve what they'd learned while Sarah sorted the small stack of letters into order by date. When Frank had finished, she pulled the letter out of the first envelope, prepared to read it and pass it along so the rest of them could see it, but she stopped the instant she saw the letter itself.

"What is it?" he asked.

"The handwriting is different," she said, holding up the envelope to compare them. Then she turned the pages to look at the signature. She looked up and grinned. "It's not from Irene Raymond at all. It's from Cornelius Raymond."

"Who's Cornelius?" Maeve asked.

"Let's find out," Sarah said and started reading.

They soon had a system, based on the "ladies first" principle. Sarah read without betraying much in the way of judgment, but Maeve saw no reason not to reveal her feelings with exaggerated facial expressions before passing each missive on to Gino, who read with avid interest and usually just rolled his eyes when passing each one along to Frank.

"Poor Cornelius sounds like a desperate man," Frank said when he'd finished the last letter and placed it on top of the stack in his lap.

"I'm sorry I never got to meet Miss Northrup," Gino said, earning a scowl from Maeve.

"She was probably one of those stuck-up society girls who thinks she's too good for the likes of you," Maeve said.

"But not for Cornelius," Sarah said quickly. "She was plainly leading him on, making him think she would consider marrying him."

"Do you think she was just leading him on or could she have really been considering it?" Frank asked.

"We may never know for sure," Sarah said, "but I can't believe she wasn't at least considering it. Cornelius promises her a very comfortable life."

"But why go to all the trouble of hiding the fact that he was writing to her?" Gino asked.

"Malloy didn't mention the fact that the women Abigail lived with wouldn't have been happy to find out she had a suitor," Sarah said.

"Why not?" Maeve asked.

"Because married women can't be teachers," Malloy said, "so if she got married, she'd have to leave her job."

"But isn't that her business?" Maeve asked.

"Of course, but I gather it's rare to have an opening for a teacher at the school, and being hired is a great honor, especially for somebody who just graduated herself," Sarah said. "The women she lived with have dedicated their lives to teaching, so they'd be very put out with her if she threw it all away to get married."

"I thought all women wanted to get married," Gino said.

Maeve gave him another scowl, but Frank had come to understand that was the main reason Gino said such outrageous things.

"Getting married is one of the few ways for a woman to obtain security in this world, Gino, but a teaching job in a college would certainly be another," Sarah said.

"And maybe even a better one," Maeve said. "A teaching job isn't going to die or desert you, like a husband might."

"And the old maids might just be jealous because they never had a suitor themselves," Frank said, earning a scowl from Sarah, which he didn't enjoy at all. "Well, it's true."

"It might be," Sarah said. "At any rate, Abigail obviously understood her hostess wouldn't be happy to learn she was receiving letters from a young man, so she and Cornelius went to great lengths to conceal that information. According to Miss Wilson, this Irene Raymond was an old friend of Abigail's from home who also attended the Normal School."

"And from the letters, it appears Cornelius was her brother," Maeve said. "He must've had Irene address the envelopes. That's kind of romantic, I guess, getting your sister to keep your romance a secret. But do we think Abigail was going to leave the school and marry him?"

Frank shook his head. "From Cornelius's last letter, it sounds to me like she still hadn't made up her mind."

"And since it was dated a week ago, she probably had time to reply to it," Sarah said. "So if she said no, maybe he came to New York to see if he could change her mind. If he was very unhappy with her, well . . ."

"Do you want me to go to Tarrytown and find him?" Gino asked, obviously ready to leave immediately.

"Let's wait," Frank said. "If he did kill her, he can't imagine we even know about him, so he's not going anywhere. In the meantime, I'd like you to drop by Miss Wilson's house on Monday morning, when she and Miss Billingsly are at school, and talk to their maid, Bathsheba."

"Bathsheba? Is that really her name?" Gino asked.

"Do you think that's wise?" Sarah asked.

"Why wouldn't it be wise?" Gino asked.

"Sarah's afraid this Bathsheba will eat you alive," Frank said. "But I have confidence in your boyish charm."

"Boyish?" Gino echoed, insulted.

"Definitely boyish," Maeve said, earning a scowl from Gino, which she obviously savored.

"But the important part is 'charm,'" Sarah said,

trying not to grin. "Bathsheba is a tough lady, and I get the impression she isn't too impressed with her employers. She might be willing to gossip a bit if you show her some attention and flatter her."

"All right," Gino said, obviously feeling put-upon.

"And then I'd like you to interview the girls in Abigail's classes," Frank said, having saved the best for last.

He perked right up at that, although Frank saw at once that Maeve was none too pleased. "Do you think one of them did it?"

"I doubt it, but they might know something or have an idea about who didn't like Abigail."

"What do you want me to do?" Sarah asked.

"I'd like you to talk with Miss Billingsly, but I'm not sure how to do that without Miss Wilson knowing."

Sarah glanced at Gino. "Maybe you could find out from Bathsheba how we could arrange it."

"I'll see what I can do."

"And what will you do, Malloy?" Sarah asked.

"I'm going to take a look at Abigail's office and talk to the French professor she worked for, Mr. Pelletier."

"It doesn't sound as if we can do any of this until Monday, though," Sarah said. "Which means we should plan to do something with the children on Sunday afternoon. How about ice-skating in Central Park?"

• • •

Gino easily found the redbrick house where the lady professors lived. The neighborhood was peaceful early on a Monday morning. The men—and the single ladies who had careers—would have already left for the day. Monday was wash-day, as everyone knew, so wives and servants would be busy with that. He rounded the corner and found the alley running behind the house.

Counting the houses, he located the right gate and stepped inside the fence to find the woman he'd come to interview hanging wash on a clothesline strung the length of the yard. She was just as formidable as Malloy had described, although her turban was plain calico today, and the look she was giving him could've drawn blood on a boot.

"Good morning, miss," he said, pulling off his bowler hat.

"I ain't nobody's miss, and put your hat back on, boy. Your head'll freeze."

He resettled his hat but didn't let his smile fade. "I'm Gino Donatelli, and I work for Mr. Frank Malloy. I was wondering if I might ask you a few questions about Miss Northrup."

"I'm busy." She pulled the last garment from the laundry basket, a pair of ladies' drawers, and clothespinned them to the line.

"I can see that. I don't expect you to stop what you're doing just for me." Before she could move, he scooped up the basket in a silent offer to carry it inside for her.

She was still frowning, not sure what to make of him, but she let him carry the basket and follow her back into the steamy warmth of the kitchen, where a huge pot of water simmered, ready for the next load of wash.

He wiped his feet carefully before entering, knowing this would please his hostess.

"Put that basket down anywhere," she snapped as she pulled off her coat. "And close the door if you're staying."

He shut the back door against the wintry weather and set the basket down nearby.

"Ain't you a little young to be a detective?" she asked, eyeing him shrewdly.

"I'm young, but I was a police officer for almost two years, and I fought in Cuba with the Rough Riders."

She brightened slightly at this news. "My nephew Thomas fought in Cuba with the colored troops."

"They were very brave. They were right with us when we charged up San Juan Hill."

She sniffed at this, and Gino wasn't sure if she approved or not, but at least she hadn't asked him to leave yet.

"Take off your coat and sit yourself down. I gotta get this next load finished and on the line."

Gino made himself useful, carrying the hot water from the stove to the washer for her before finally taking a seat at the kitchen table while she churned the clothes in the wooden tub and then started fishing each piece out with a stick and running it through the mangle to squeeze out the excess water. He knew better than to offer to help with that. He didn't want to handle the ladies' clothes, but he also didn't want to get a finger crushed in the wringer.

Bathsheba cranked the first few items through before she said, "Why didn't that Malloy fellow come himself?"

"He thought you'd rather talk to me."

She grinned at that, showing a gold canine. "He was right about that. So what did you want to know? I ain't sayin' I'll answer, but you can ask whatever you want."

"Fair enough. I don't want to ask you to gossip about your employers—"

"Oh, of course you do. Don't lie, boy."

"All right, then," Gino said with a grin. "Seems kind of funny, three ladies living together in one house. Did they get along all right?"

"It ain't funny at all. It's necessary. A female can't live in a house by herself. It ain't proper and it ain't safe, not in a city like this."

"I didn't think of it that way."

"Of course not. You can live wherever you want and ain't nobody gonna bother you. A female alone, she gonna attract all kinda the wrong attention."

Gino supposed she was right.

"They also can't afford to live by themselves," she added without even being prodded.

"But aren't they all professors at that college?" Gino said, playing dumb.

"Only Miss Wilson is a full professor, and that just come real recent. Even still, they don't pay her the same salary they pay to the mens. She shares a house to save money."

Gino blinked at her honesty and stored that tidbit of information away for future reference. Of course, he knew that women usually got paid less than men, but that was because men had to support their families. Unmarried women had to support only themselves. It was only fair.

"I guess they were all good friends, then," Gino said, since she hadn't yet answered the part of the question he really cared about.

"Miss Wilson and Miss Billingsly, they lived here real nice for almost eighteen years now," she said, paying particular attention to the piece of clothing she was running through the mangle.

Gino didn't miss the implication. "I guess Miss Northrup coming kind of changed things."

Bathsheba made a rude noise.

"You didn't like her," he said.

"Ain't my place to like her or not."

"You're still entitled to your opinion. Why didn't you like her?"

Bathsheba turned her dark gaze on Gino. "Not for the reason you're thinking."

"I'm not thinking of any reasons at all," he claimed. "The only things I know about Miss Northrup are that she was real smart and got herself hired on at the college when nobody else could."

"That's true enough. She was pretty, too, which made it strange. Pretty girls don't have to work as hard as the rest of us, you know, but she always wanted to be the best. Pretty girls can usually get themselves a husband, too, so why did she want to teach school instead?"

"Maybe she liked teaching."

Bathsheba shook her head at such nonsense. "Nobody wants to work when they don't have to."

"So what's the real reason you didn't like her?"

For a minute, he thought she wouldn't answer. "She wasn't what everybody thought she was."

"What did they think she was?"

"A sweet young girl who loved everything and everybody. She only loved you if you could do something for her, and she never let anybody see what she was really thinking."

"Except you."

She sniffed. "She didn't think it mattered what I thought of her, but even still, she tried to pretend she was this gracious lady in front of me. I saw right through her, though."

"What about Miss Wilson and Miss Billingsly?"

"Miss Wilson never did. Miss Wilson thought she hung the moon."

"And Miss Billingsly?"

Bathsheba shook her head. "Poor lady. She never harmed anybody in her whole life. She didn't deserve what that girl done to her."

4

The lobby area of the Normal School was much busier on a Monday morning than it had been on Friday afternoon. Young ladies stood in clusters of three and four, speaking in hushed whispers, while others strolled purposefully by, probably on their way to something important. Every single one of them eyed Frank with suspicion, but at least none of them ran screaming up the stairs to report him to the president.

He climbed the stairs himself and found Professor Pelletier's office halfway down one of the wings. The room held two desks, some chairs, and some bookshelves filled with books. A window overlooked the courtyard where Abigail Northrup had died. The man was in, sitting at one of the desks and staring intently at something lying on it. Frank startled him with a knock on the doorframe.

He looked up and sighed. "Ah, you must be the detective Hatch told us about." He spoke with an accent. Frank hadn't expected that.

"Can I come in?"

"*Mais oui.*" He pushed himself to his feet and stuck out his hand to shake. He was tall with broad shoulders and erect posture, almost military in his stiffness. He wore his dark hair parted in the middle and smooth against his head and had trimmed his facial hair into a neat mustache and goatee. A set of pince-nez hung from a cord attached to a button on his vest. His suit, while cheap, was clean and neatly pressed. Since he'd come into money, Frank had become something of an expert in judging other men by their suits.

"Frank Malloy, Professor," Frank said as they shook hands.

"*Enchanté. S'il vous plaît*, sit down." He gestured to a wooden chair beside his desk. Frank imagined hundreds of anxious young ladies had sat in that chair to discuss whatever college girls discussed with their professors.

"You're French," Frank said.

"*Mais oui.* Is that a surprise to you?"

"Yes, although I guess it's easier to teach French if you already speak it."

"You are probably correct," he said with a small smile.

"Miss Northrup didn't already speak it, though, did she?"

His smile vanished, instantly transformed into an expression of painful but dignified grief. Frank imagined this was exactly the expression that would be proper for a man in Pelletier's position. "She spoke it very well, for an American, and she took great joy in teaching it to others."

"She must have for you to give her a job teaching here."

To his credit, Pelletier didn't even blink. "I know what you are probably thinking. When a man chooses a young, attractive female upon whom to bestow an honor, many people assume something is . . . improper."

That wasn't the word Frank would've chosen, but it would do. "I would think it's hard for a man to work with young females all the time."

Pelletier smiled ruefully. "You can have no idea, but not perhaps for the reasons you think. The young ladies can be silly and dramatic, and they can develop romantic attachments with the slightest provocation. A man must be constantly on his guard not to encourage such things. Rarely does the attraction go the other way, I assure you."

"Did Miss Northrup develop a romantic attachment to you?"

"*Pas du tout.*" He helpfully shook his head so Frank knew he meant "no." "You flatter me, Mr. Malloy. I have not had this problem with the young ladies for a few years now." He stroked his beard where some gray hairs mingled with the dark ones. "In truth, it was not my idea to hire Miss Northrup at all. Miss Wilson convinced President Hatch that I needed help, and she proposed Miss Northrup."

"And did you really need help?"

He shrugged the way Frank had noticed Frenchmen shrug when he'd been in France. He thought it made them look silly. "One grows weary of teaching the beginners, Mr. Malloy. I was glad to pass those duties to Miss Northrup."

"Did any of the other teachers resent her? I understand it was unusual for the school to hire somebody who had just graduated to teach here."

"I cannot speak for the others, but there is always a bit of jealousy when someone is chosen, is there not?"

"I don't have much experience with colleges, Professor. You tell me."

His smile looked a little bitter around the edges. "There is, I am afraid, but if you are thinking this is the reason someone attacked poor Miss Northrup, you will be wrong. If someone attacked Miss Wilson, then I would understand."

"Miss Wilson? What did she do?"

"She do what no female ever does here. She becomes a professor."

Gino hoped the surge of excitement he felt didn't show too much in his face. "What did Miss Northrup do to Miss Billingsly?"

Bathsheba stirred the washtub water with her stick and found no additional clothes to wring out. "Reckon I better get these things hung up."

She stood up and got her coat. Not to be deterred, Gino put his coat back on as well and picked up the laundry basket without being asked.

She acted as though she didn't even notice, but she let him follow her outside.

"Set it there." She pointed.

He did and stepped back, waiting because she was in charge and he knew better than to push her when she'd probably tell him everything in her own good time.

She pinned a few items to the rope before she said, "Miss Billingsly, she and Miss Wilson been friends since they first met. I never saw two womens get along like them two. They always talking about things together."

"What kind of things?"

"School things. Book things. I don't know. I never went to school, but they read books and get ideas about life and then they'd talk it over. I never understood much of it, but it was a comfort to hear them talk. They'd argue sometimes, because they didn't agree about something, but they'd never get mad. I couldn't understand that. I never saw peoples argue without getting mad at each other. It was a wonder."

Gino would like to see that himself. "But things changed when Miss Northrup moved in, I guess."

"Before that, even," she said with more than a trace of bitterness. "She started coming here long time ago and stirring up trouble."

"How long ago?"

"Since she first come to the school, I reckon. She was Miss Wilson's student, see. The two ladies would invite their favorite students over on a Sunday. Sometimes they'd read together or sometimes a visitor would give a talk. Then the ladies would all talk over what they learned. I never seen nothing like it. The young ladies—that's what they call the students—they never seen nothing like it either, I guess. They had more fun talking than I ever seen people have when they was at a party. Queerest thing you ever saw."

Gino was pretty sure she was right. "So Miss Northrup had already spent a lot of time here."

"She come real regular. Not like the other girls. They'd usually come for a year or maybe two, but she come for four years straight. It was plain to see she was up to no good."

"Why? What was she doing?"

Bathsheba pinned another garment to the line. "Wasn't what she was doing, exactly. It was how she was with Miss Wilson. It was like . . . I don't know how to describe it."

"Try."

Bathsheba cast him a dark look. "The teachers at the school, they have pet students."

"Pet students?"

"That's what they call them. Favorites, like."

Ah, Gino knew all about that. He'd seen it in his own school experience. The smart students who were well behaved and wore nice clothes. He'd never been a favorite. "I guess it's only natural for them to like some of their students more than others."

"I don't know nothing about that, but I do know they have different favorites every year. New girls come and the others move on. But Miss Northrup didn't move on. She just kept being Miss Wilson's favorite, and Miss Northrup made sure of it."

"How did she do that?"

"Oh, she was a clever one. She didn't do what you'd expect. You'd expect her to always agree with Miss Wilson and pay her compliments and such. Instead, she'd argue with her, like she didn't agree, and then she'd pretend Miss Wilson had convinced her and change her mind. Not every time, but often enough, you understand. Made Miss Wilson feel so important and smart. Made me feel sick."

"And what about Miss Billingsly?"

"I never knew if she saw through the girl or not, but she did know that Miss Wilson didn't argue with her no more. She only was interested in what Miss Northrup had to say about something. I was so glad when they said she was graduating. I figured we'd seen the last of her, but then I hear she's got hired by the college and she's coming to live here." She shook her head at such an unfortunate event.

"I guess Miss Billingsly wasn't too happy about that."

Bathsheba whirled to face him. "Don't you go thinking she killed that girl because she was jealous. She'd never do no such thing. She wouldn't hurt a fly, that one."

Gino nodded obediently, although he wasn't going to clear Miss Billingsly of suspicion just because her maid vouched for her. "But it must've been awkward when Miss Northrup moved in."

"Oh, it was. She'd just gotten home from France." Bathsheba said the word *France* as if it left a bad taste in her mouth. "She kept saying things in that Frenchy talk, like she expected people to understand her."

"And nobody did?"

"Miss Wilson did. She said she learned it in school, but Miss Northrup could talk it a lot better than she could. Miss Northrup said her accent wasn't right, and she'd learned to talk it right when she was in France, so they'd practice together, but . . ."

"But what?"

Bathsheba pulled the last article of clothing from the basket and pinned it with angry jabs. "Let's go inside."

She marched off, leaving the basket for Gino, who happily grabbed it and followed her back into the kitchen. By the time he got there, she'd removed her coat and started draining the wash-tub. The water on the stove had begun to boil, so she told him to pour it into the tub. Then she shaved some slivers of soap into it and stirred the whole thing with her stick until she was satisfied. Then she dropped in a bunch of bedsheets.

Before she could start turning the crank to agitate the load, he said, "Let me do that," and gently moved her out of the way. She sank down wearily into one of the kitchen chairs and watched him work.

She'd been silent for so long, Gino figured she'd forgotten what they were talking about, but she hadn't.

"They'd talk their Frenchy talk and giggle like they was little girls and then they'd look at poor Miss Billingsly who never learned to talk Frenchy, and you'd just know they was making fun of her. They could've said anything about her and nobody but them would've known. Made me sick to see it."

It must've made Miss Billingsly sick, too. And maybe it made her drink. Would it have made her mad enough to commit murder, though?

He knew better than to ask Bathsheba such a question. "There's nothing worse than having folks make fun of you right to your face and you can't even answer back."

"Well, there might be some things worse, but not many."

"How are the ladies now that Miss Northrup is gone? Do you think they'll make up?"

Bathsheba took her time answering him. "I don't know. I think it might be too late."

Frank studied Pelletier's smug expression. "Are you saying that the other female teachers would be angry that Miss Wilson became a professor?"

"Not only the female teachers. The male professors as well. She is taking a position a man could have filled. A man who needs to feed a family, you understand."

Frank understood perfectly. "Did they think she didn't deserve it?"

"That is not the question. Many of the female instructors deserve to be professors."

"And wouldn't they also resent Miss Northrup for taking an instructor position?"

"Of course, but perhaps not as much."

And yet Miss Northrup was the one dead. Frank studied the professor for a moment. "I could've used you a few months ago, when I was in France."

Frank had expected Pelletier to brighten at the mention of his home country. Frenchmen seemed inordinately proud of it, although Frank couldn't understand why. Instead, Pelletier stiffened slightly. "You visited France?"

"Yes. My wife and I took a European tour." He didn't mention it was their honeymoon.

"Where did you visit?"

"Paris. Some cities in the south. I don't

remember the names. We saw a lot of old things. Are you from Paris?"

"*Mais non*, I am from a tiny town in Bourgogne. You would not have visited it."

"Doesn't it have any old things?"

He smiled slightly at this. "All of France is old, but there is nothing of note in my hometown."

"I don't suppose you have any idea who might've killed Miss Northrup."

Pelletier sighed. "I wish that I did. Such a tragedy."

"It certainly is." Frank glanced over at the other desk. "I'm afraid I need to go through Miss Northrup's desk. I don't suppose you know where the key is." He remembered the coroner hadn't said anything about finding keys on Abigail's body.

Pelletier also glanced over at the desk. "I do not think it is locked."

Frank got up and went over. Sure enough, the drawers opened easily. He noticed that Pelletier had turned back to whatever had been fascinating him when Frank came in. Or maybe he was just unwilling to watch him search through the dead woman's belongings.

Frank wasn't satisfied with his conversation with Pelletier. He wasn't sure what had unsettled him, but he did know he'd probably be back with more questions very soon.

The search was brief. Abigail's desk contained

nothing personal or particularly interesting. He found a sheaf of papers that appeared to be student assignments that she was in the process of grading. They were all in French, though, so he had no idea what they said. The rest were just the normal supplies he'd expected to find. All except for one thing, which he did not find.

"Did she always keep her desk unlocked?"

Pelletier looked up in surprise. "*Mais oui*. We keep the office door always locked, and there is nothing here worthy of stealing, I think."

"Do you lock your own desk?"

"As I said, there is no need."

Then why was there a key in the lock on the professor's desk where Frank could plainly see it?

"Thank you for your help, Professor," Frank said, shaking the man's hand again. "If you happen to think of anything that might help, please let me know." He handed him one of his expensive cards.

"Of course, Monsieur Malloy. I wish you much luck in finding who killed the poor mademoiselle."

Gino had foolishly thought that Mr. Malloy was doing him a favor when he assigned him to question Abigail Northrup's students. After spending almost an hour interviewing them, he now understood that Malloy had merely fobbed off an unpleasant task to his underling. The girls were either openly hostile to a male they considered a dangerous interloper into their sacred sanctuary or they were too giggly and flirtatious to even make sense. Neither type had offered any useful information.

One of the other female teachers had helpfully gathered Abigail's classes together and sent them one by one into an empty classroom to meet with Gino. He had to leave the door open for propriety, but he'd set up his interviews as far from the door as possible to keep from being overheard by the teacher, who sat just outside as a chaperone. If only he'd heard anything worth overhearing. He was about to give up hope he ever would when the next student came in.

She sat down in the chair he'd placed in front of the student desk he'd commandeered. She was a plain girl with hair the color of carrots and a generous sprinkling of freckles. She peered at him suspiciously through her spectacles as he sat down and introduced himself.

"I'm Karen Oxley," she offered without either a giggle or a scowl. "I did see Tobias working in the lavatory on the second floor last Wednesday, and I didn't see anything outside. All the girls are talking, so I know what you're going to ask. I guess you've figured out by now that we don't spend a lot of time staring out the windows."

"It does seem like they keep you pretty busy." Not a single girl had admitted to so much as glancing outside on the day Abigail had died, although most of them knew the janitor had been working in the girls' dormitory.

"Of course we're busy. And I don't have any idea who might've killed Miss Northrup either." Her voice broke a bit, but she cleared her throat. "It's a terrible thing. She was a good teacher."

"You liked her, then?"

"Of course. We all liked her. None of us in our class knew a word of French when we came to her, and she made learning it fun."

"How did she do that?"

Miss Oxley smiled at the memory. "She'd teach us the grammar and the vocabulary, and then we'd do silly examples that would make us laugh but also remember."

"Like what?" Gino asked with genuine interest.

"Oh, we'd say something like, 'The bird sat on my head.' And then the next girl would try to think of something better, like, 'The bird ate my head.' By the end we'd be laughing so hard, we could hardly talk."

"And this isn't the usual way people learn French?"

"I don't know, because I never studied French before, but no teacher ever made me laugh except Miss Northrup. If she wasn't so young, she probably would've been my smash."

Gino blinked in surprise. "Your what?"

"My smash." Plainly, she thought he should know what that was.

"What's a smash?"

She registered a little surprise, but she said, "It's the teacher you . . . I'm not sure how to describe it. Love? But not romantically. Admire? Not strong enough." She frowned in concentration.

"But Miss Northrup was a female."

She gave him a pitying smile. "That's the whole point! None of us have ever met women like the teachers here. Nor have we ever been exposed to new ideas the way we are here. Talking about them and learning so much . . . it's intoxicating! And the females who teach here are so interesting. They're smart and educated, and they know so much about everything. Not like our mothers at all. When you meet them, it's like falling violently in love without having to worry about romance."

"Sort of like a crush?" Gino tried, still not sure he understood.

"Yes, in a way, only much more exciting because you don't have to be embarrassed or nervous or worry about a young man noticing you. All the freshmen girls have a smash, or most of us, anyway. They even call it the Freshman Disease," she added with a satisfied grin.

"And who's your smash?"

She wrinkled her nose at him. "None of your business, but not Miss Northrup. Like I said, she was too young. She was more like a friend than a teacher, I guess because she'd been a student herself just a few months ago."

But Abigail Northrup had probably had a smash of her own, and Gino knew exactly who it was.

Sarah had been waiting somewhat patiently for over half an hour in the living room of Miss Wilson's brick town house. She'd spent her morning trying to identify a charity that would take Hannah, the pregnant young woman at the Mission, but she hadn't had any luck. She only hoped her afternoon would be more rewarding. Finally, she heard the front door open. Bathsheba hurried down the hall to greet Miss Billingsly and tell her she had a visitor.

Sarah couldn't make out the exact words of the whispered conversation, but plainly, Miss Billingsly wasn't pleased. She spoke quickly, almost frantically, and Sarah knew a moment of guilt for having forced her presence on the distraught woman. Someone needed to speak with her, though, and Sarah knew she would be the most gentle. Bathsheba's tone was reasonable and persuasive. She'd welcomed Sarah a while ago without the slightest indication that she had set up this meeting by telling Gino when she expected Miss Billingsly to return home. Sarah had made no reference to it either.

After a few more whispered exchanges, Miss Billingsly came in through the open doorway. She was patting her hair into place after removing her hat and looked a bit flustered. Sarah rose from her chair and said, "I'm sorry to have imposed myself on you like this, but your maid said I should wait, that you'd be home shortly."

"That's perfectly all right," Miss Billingsly lied with a stiff little smile. "It's always pleasant to have company. I don't think we've met."

Sarah wasn't going to remind her of her unceremonious entrance the other day. "No, we haven't. I'm Sarah Malloy. My husband is the detective investigating Miss Northrup's death."

Miss Billingsly's stiff smile vanished. "Oh yes. Georgia told me about that. A frightful business."

Sarah wasn't sure if she meant the murder or the investigation. "We're trying to determine who might have attacked Miss Northrup, so we're speaking with all of her close friends."

Miss Billingsly frowned at that. "Close friends? I was hardly that."

"But she lived here, didn't she? And you knew her well."

"I knew her, yes," she admitted a bit reluctantly.

"And I'm sure you'd like to know her killer is locked up and unable to harm anyone else."

She couldn't possibly disagree with that, no matter how much she might have disliked Abigail Northrup, so she said, "Very well. Ask your questions."

She moved to the chair nearest Sarah's and sank wearily into it. Sarah took this as an invitation to sit down again herself, so she did.

Miss Billingsly looked her over. "Are you a detective, too?"

"Not professionally, no, but I sometimes help my husband. He thinks ladies respond better to me than to him."

"And do they?"

"Sometimes. How long had you known Miss Northrup?"

She sighed as if in relief. "That's an easy one. Going on five years now, I suppose. Since she first came to the Normal School as a student."

"Did you have her as a student?"

"I have all the young ladies at one time or another."

"What do you teach?"

"Geography."

"How interesting," Sarah said with genuine enthusiasm. "I always enjoyed geography."

Miss Billingsly's smile did not reach her eyes. "Yes, learning about all those countries you'll never see."

"I beg your pardon?"

"I always thought someday I'd travel. I wanted to ride a camel in Egypt and see the Roman Colosseum at night. I wanted to visit the Parthenon, but I'll never do any of that now, not on the salary of a normal school instructor. So I just tell other disappointed young women about the wonders they'll also never see."

Sarah had no answer for that, especially when

she remembered that Abigail had traveled to France during the summer between her graduation and when she started teaching. How jealous Miss Billingsly must have been of her opportunity. "Were you happy to have Miss Northrup living here?"

"Happy? Why should I be? This isn't a large house. We were already crowded before she came. And it made a lot more work for poor Bathsheba. No one even considered her."

"And yet you agreed to let her come."

"It's not my place to agree or disagree. It's Georgia's house. Miss Wilson's, I mean. She had a small inheritance when her mother died, and she bought it. I'm just a guest here."

"More than a guest, surely," Sarah said. "You and Miss Wilson have been friends for many years."

She pressed her lips together until they were no more than a straight line in her face, and Sarah slowly realized she was trying not to weep. After a few moments, she cleared her throat and said, "Yes, we have."

"Did you meet when you were students?"

"Oh no, not until I came here to teach. Georgia had been here for a year already. She took me under her wing, you see. She's like that, always making sure people feel welcome and included. That's why the young ladies love her so."

"And you became close friends."

Her whole body seemed to soften as she remembered. "I'd never had a friend like that before. I hardly dared believe that she felt the same until she bought this house and asked me to share it with her."

"You must have been very happy here."

"Yes, until . . ."

"Until Miss Northrup came?" Sarah said when she hesitated.

"I should have seen it," Miss Billingsly said softly.

"What should you have seen?" Sarah asked just as softly.

Miss Billingsly's expression hardened. "She would come to our Sunday Salons. That's what we call them. We'd invite a few of the young ladies, the more promising ones, to come for some literary discussions and a light supper. Georgia teaches English literature, and all the young ladies love that."

"Did you ever discuss geography?"

She shook her head impatiently. "We'd discuss other cultures and a woman's role in them. We'd discuss all sorts of things. Abigail was delightful in the beginning. She was so hungry for knowledge, and she admired Georgia so. All the girls did, of course. She was the one they came to see. I was just the one who filled their cups and passed around the cookies." Oddly, she didn't seem bitter about that at all.

"I'm sure you have your own admirers."

But Miss Billingsly didn't even seem to hear her. She was lost in her memories. "I was so blind. I should have guessed it was something more when Abigail continued to come. The girls usually lost interest after a year or two. The juniors and seniors formed their own friendships and cliques, and they didn't need us anymore, but not Abigail."

"Why do you think she kept coming?"

Miss Billingsly turned in her chair to meet Sarah's gaze squarely. "You wouldn't understand."

"Maybe I would. Help me."

"The girls fall in love with their teachers. Learning can be intoxicating to those who are being challenged for the first time in their lives, and in the beginning they look at us as the source of that knowledge. They think we're somehow special. After a year or two, they realize it's the knowledge they love, not the one who transmits it to them, but with Abigail . . . She loved Georgia at first, but I didn't think anything of it. Dozens of girls have loved her through the years, perhaps hundreds. But this was different."

"Different how?"

Her lips thinned down again, and this time her eyes flooded with tears. "Georgia loved her back."

Before Sarah could even register this remarkable statement, someone pounded on the front door.

"What on earth?" Miss Billingsly murmured.

They heard Bathsheba hurrying to answer it, and whoever was out there hammered on the door again before she could get there. As soon as she opened the door, a man's voice said, "I'm here to get my sister's things."

By then Miss Billingsly was on her feet and moving toward the doorway into the hall. Sarah was close behind her. When they reached it, they saw that a young man had pushed his way into the house in spite of Bathsheba's efforts to prevent him. He was a strapping youth with corn yellow hair and large ears that protruded just a bit from his head. At the moment, his handsome face was red with fury.

When he noticed the two women, he demanded, "Which one of you is Miss Wilson?"

"Neither of us. I'm Miss Billingsly. How may we help you, young man?"

Something in her tone, probably the natural authority of a longtime teacher used to managing her students, seemed to startle him a bit, and he lost some of his belligerence. "I'm Abigail's brother. Luther Northrup. I . . . I'm here to collect her things."

Sarah didn't know why she was surprised to learn Abigail had a brother. Malloy hadn't mentioned it, but surely her parents had told him.

"If you truly are her brother, then there's no need for you to be rude, young man," Miss

Billingsly said. "You have every right to Abigail's belongings."

"I . . . I'm sorry, miss. I just . . . I went to the school first and no one wanted to tell me where you lived. They acted like I'd done something wrong to go there. It took me hours to find you."

"Then you must be cold and tired. Come in and have a seat. Bathsheba, will you get Mr. Northrup some coffee? Or would you prefer tea?"

"Coffee, if you please."

Bathsheba didn't say any actual words, though her grunts and huffs made it perfectly clear how reluctant she was to serve this rude young man, but she headed for the kitchen.

"Shut the door and come in," Miss Billingsly said when he made no move to do so.

Miraculously, he obeyed her and followed them back into the living room. At Miss Billingsly's instruction, he perched on the sofa across from the two women. He still wore his overcoat. He couldn't quite meet their eyes and was probably feeling ashamed of his earlier behavior.

"I'm sorry you had so much trouble finding us," Miss Billingsly said with more kindness than Sarah could believe she felt. "I'm surprised you didn't have the address."

He looked up at that, and this time the color in his face was from embarrassment, not anger. "I . . . I copied it down wrong. My parents sent me to fetch her things since I was in the city already."

"Are you a student, too?"

He shook his head. "Oh no. Not a scholar. Not like Abby. Just here to . . . to see some friends."

That seemed an odd explanation, especially for a young man whose sister had just been murdered, but Sarah was more interested in his relationship with his dead sister than his current reason for being in the city. "Are you older or younger than Abigail?" she asked, earning a sharp look from Miss Billingsly.

"Older. By two years."

How very interesting. People usually spent their money educating their sons and giving them every possible advantage in life, but by his own admission, Luther Northrup was "no scholar." Instead, after being disappointed in their son, the parents had apparently chosen to educate their daughter, who was, by all accounts, "outstanding" in every way.

"I'm very sorry about your sister, Mr. Northrup," Sarah said quite sincerely. "Her death is a great loss to everyone who knew her."

Luther Northrup met her gaze for a long moment, the expression in his blue eyes unreadable. Then he turned back to Miss Billingsly. "Can I get Abby's things now?"

5

"They call it a smash," Gino explained.

"Why do they call it that?" Frank asked, glancing at Sarah to see if she knew, but she just shook her head.

The three of them had gathered in the empty classroom where Gino had interviewed the students. Sarah had walked over to the school to find them after she'd finished with Miss Billingsly.

"I don't know why they call it that, but it's so common, they also call it the Freshman Disease. All the girls fall in love with a teacher, or most of them do, anyway. But how can women fall in love with other women?"

Frank didn't think he wanted to discuss this in front of Sarah, but Gino had actually asked her the question. She gave him a gentle smile. "The same way a man can fall in love with another man."

Frank watched as Gino made the connection. His eyes widened. "Oh."

"But let's not jump to conclusions," Sarah said. "I don't think this is necessarily a romantic kind of love. Women are very emotional creatures, and we tend to love many different people in many different ways. Young girls often have close female friends whom they love dearly and with whom they remain close throughout their lives, even after they marry and have a family."

"Oh, like my aunt Stella," Gino said. "She and my mama were friends back in the old country, from the time they were little. I think they married brothers just so they could be sisters."

"And they're still close?" Sarah asked.

"We all live in the same tenement." He made a helpless gesture.

"So imagine your mother and your aunt as eighteen-year-old girls."

"Eighteen-year-old girls in love with a forty-year-old woman," Frank said.

"But it's usually only a temporary condition," Sarah reminded them. "Miss Billingsly told me the girls get over it by the time they're juniors, if not before. And didn't this Miss Oxley tell you it was really caused by a love of learning?"

"She called it 'intoxication,'" Gino said.

"Miss Billingsly used the same word. Going to college must be an incredible experience," Sarah said. "I'm sorry I missed it."

"Well, we're not sending Catherine," Frank said. "I think I'll marry her off when she's thirteen or something, just to be sure."

"I thought you weren't going to let any young men within a city block of her until she's thirty," Sarah reminded him.

"Maybe she'll join a convent," Gino said helpfully.

"All right," Frank said, trying to get them back on the subject of Abigail Northrup's murder. "We know that Miss Wilson was Abigail's smash."

"And Miss Wilson had a smash on her, too," Sarah said.

"What?" Gino said.

"Who told you that?" Frank asked.

"Miss Billingsly. She had just let it slip when Luther Northrup started pounding on the front door."

"Is that Abigail's father?" Gino asked.

"No, her brother."

"I didn't know she had a brother," Frank said. "Her parents didn't even mention him."

"Surely, they mentioned they had another child," Sarah said.

"I'm trying to remember. I don't know what they said exactly, but I got the impression she was their only one. They certainly never mentioned the name Luther. And what was he doing at that house?"

"He'd come to collect Abigail's belongings, I gathered. His parents had sent him."

"All the way from Tarrytown?"

"He said he was in the city visiting friends."

"While he's in mourning for his sister?" Frank asked, thoroughly confused.

"It didn't make sense to me either, but that's what he said. I didn't have much opportunity to question him, though, because Miss Billingsly sent me on my way shortly after he arrived. I think she was glad for the excuse to get rid of me, because she'd just admitted that Miss Wilson loved Abigail in return. So I never had an opportunity to find out more about that either."

"That would explain why Miss Wilson invited Abigail to live with them," Gino said. "And by the way, Bathsheba also told me Miss Wilson and Abigail were . . . Well, she didn't say they had a smash, but they were pretty fond of each other. Bathsheba said Abigail had been coming to the house ever since she started school there and making up to Miss Wilson all those years."

"And that would explain why Miss Billingsly didn't like her," Sarah said. "She was jealous and, I gather, heartbroken because Abigail had come between them."

"You mean Miss Billingsly and Miss Wilson had a smash on each other, too?" Gino asked.

"I know they were very close friends until Abigail came along, and Miss Billingsly blamed her for causing a rift."

"Are you sure about all this?" Frank asked. "Because Pelletier gave me another reason why Billingsly and the other teachers might've been jealous of Abigail."

"What's that?"

"Because there's a lot of jealousy among all the teachers over Abigail getting hired at the school. Maybe not as much as there was when Miss

Wilson was made a professor, but still a lot. It seems the men resent it when any woman gets hired because it's a job that could've gone to a man with a family to support."

"Women have to support themselves, too," Sarah said, just as he'd expected. After her first husband's death, she'd supported herself as a midwife.

"I'm just telling you what Pelletier told me. And apparently even the females were jealous of Abigail for getting the job at all. The school never hires their own students who just graduated."

"Why did they hire her, then?" Gino asked. "Besides the fact that she was so outstanding, I mean."

"I thought maybe Pelletier had taken a fancy to her," Frank said, "but he claims Miss Wilson was the one who decided he needed help and convinced the president to hire her."

"Which seems to support Miss Billingsly's and Bathsheba's theories that Miss Wilson loved Abigail. She'd want to keep her around after she graduated, and what better way than to get her a job at the college?" Sarah said. "Did Pelletier tell you anything else interesting?"

"He's French."

Sarah smiled at that. She knew his opinion of the French. "That's not too surprising, I guess. It must be wonderful learning a foreign language from someone who actually speaks it."

"Pelletier claims he was happy to let Abigail teach the beginners. He acted like he was too good to do that."

"Maybe he really was glad," Gino said. "Wouldn't it be boring for him, since he's an expert in it?"

"Or maybe he was insulted that they hired a girl with no teaching experience to teach his students," Sarah said. "Which one do you think it was, Malloy?"

"I honestly don't know. Pelletier is hard to read. But he did lie to me about one thing."

"What's that?" Gino asked, perking up.

"I asked him if he knew where the keys to Abigail's desk were, and he said she kept it unlocked."

"And you think that's a lie?" Sarah asked.

"He also said he kept his unlocked, too, but I saw a key with a fob on it sticking out of the lock on his desk. So unless he just keeps it hanging there all the time—and wouldn't it get in the way?—he wasn't telling me the truth."

"And was her desk unlocked?" Sarah asked.

"Yes, but there was nothing personal in it. If somebody wanted to take something out of it, they've had plenty of time to do it, since it wasn't locked. There's more to it than that, though. Pelletier said they didn't lock their desks because they kept the office locked. But we haven't found *any* keys belonging to Abigail. She must've had a key to her office, and probably one to Miss Wilson's house, too. Where are they?"

"Maybe somebody from the coroner's office stole them," Gino said.

"Doc Haynes said she still had her jewelry when he got to her, so why would somebody steal keys but not jewelry? And they weren't in the gazebo when she was found either."

"Maybe she lost them," Sarah said, "or left them somewhere."

"Or maybe the killer took them," Gino said.

"Why would the killer take them?" Frank asked.

Gino considered for a moment. "Because he wanted to get something out of her desk."

"That's what I'm thinking. But what?"

Of course, no one had an answer.

Frank and Gino went back to the office so Frank could telephone the Northrups and give them a report. He really had nothing to report, but he wanted to find out about Luther and why they'd sent him to the city, which meant he needed an excuse to speak with Mr. Northrup. Frank also wanted to know where to find Luther, so he could ask him a few questions.

The telephone wasn't the best method of communication, though. They both had to shout to be heard, and they knew operators at both ends were probably listening to every word. Finally, Northrup said he'd meet Frank at his office in a few hours, since he had to come to the city anyway.

When Northrup arrived late in the afternoon, his face was ashen. Frank ushered him into his office, sat him down, and pulled a bottle of whiskey and a glass out of his desk. He didn't know if Northrup was a teetotaler or not, but at the moment, he needed some medicinal alcohol.

Northrup gratefully swallowed the two fingers Frank poured for him.

"More?"

Northrup shook his head. "I . . . I went to that place to claim Abigail's . . . remains."

"I'm sorry. If you'd told me you were going there, I would've gone with you."

"I had no idea . . . What a horrible place. They'd just sent me word that we could bring her home, so I thought . . . Well, at least it's done now."

"I suppose you'll be having the funeral soon."

"Day after tomorrow."

"If you don't mind, I'd like to attend."

"Whatever for?"

"Don't worry, we won't disrupt anything. I'll bring my wife, and we'll look like ordinary mourners. I'd just like to see who attends the funeral and if anyone behaves strangely."

"Do you think the person who killed her will be there?" he asked in alarm.

Frank was almost sure of it, since he now felt certain she'd known her killer well, but he said,

"There's a small possibility, but even so, that person won't be doing anything to draw attention to himself. I'll also need to know if you see anyone you don't know."

"I'm sure people from the school will come. I don't know many of them."

"Then we'll look for anyone who seems out of place. At any rate, I'll be there in the unlikely event that there's a disturbance."

"I don't know if my wife could bear it if anything happened. She's already so distressed."

"Then we'll make sure nothing happens. I'll bring my associate with me, too. By the way, did you know your son, Luther, went to Miss Wilson's house to pick up Abigail's belongings?"

"Did he? I'm glad to hear it. I'd asked him to, but Luther can be . . . less than responsible sometimes."

"He said he was in town visiting friends."

Northrup didn't even blink, although they both knew how inappropriate this was under the circumstances. "He's a . . . restless boy, even at the best of times. Since we lost his sister, he's been even worse than usual. When he wanted to come to the city, I suggested he make himself useful, although I didn't really hold out much hope that he would."

"Who are these friends he's visiting?"

Northrup sighed. "I have no idea. They all belong to the New York Athletic Club. Apparently, young men can become very friendly indeed when they're boxing or lifting dumbbells."

"Do you at least know where he's staying?"

"He usually stays at the club. I told him we would need to reach him, so I hope that's where he is. I'd hate for him to miss his sister's funeral."

"Let me know if you can't reach him. I can try to locate him for you."

Northrup sighed again. "I don't suppose you've learned anything important yet."

"We've learned a lot, but as you say, nothing that points to anyone in particular. Which reminds me, do you know a young lady named Irene Raymond?"

"Irene? Of course I do. I've known her and her brother practically since they were born. Their parents are our neighbors. Irene attended the Normal School with Abigail, in fact." He frowned suddenly. "Good heavens, you don't think she had anything to do with Abigail's death, do you?"

"No, nothing like that. We just found some letters from her in Abigail's room," Frank said, not telling the entire truth.

"I'm not surprised. They're very close friends, or at least they were. They don't see much of each other since . . ." He caught himself as the memory of Abigail's death hit him again. "I mean, not since they graduated. Irene came home to Tarrytown. She wasn't really interested in teaching, and I hear she's going to become engaged soon."

"You mentioned her brother. Is he also a close friend of Abigail's?"

"Cornelius? I suppose so. He's Luther's age, I believe. Just a few years older than the girls."

"Was there ever anything romantic between him and Abigail?"

This startled Northrup, and he frowned. "Not that I know of. What makes you ask that?"

"I don't know," Frank lied. "I just thought if the families were so close, maybe you hoped the boys might marry the girls and bring them even closer."

"I suppose Cornelius was always fond of Abigail, but in a brotherly way. Luther and Irene never got along at all, though. If we'd ever entertained any thoughts of joining our families, the children themselves gave us no encouragement."

So Northrup didn't know about the romance brewing between Cornelius and his daughter. Why had they felt they had to keep it a secret? Surely, their parents would have approved. Maybe Abigail's letters would have the answers, but he didn't have Abigail's letters. He'd need Cornelius to tell him. "Do you know if Abigail was happy living at Miss Wilson's house?"

"She was thrilled when Miss Wilson made her the offer. The school wasn't paying her very much to start, you see, and she would've either had to live in a boardinghouse or been a matron in the dormitory. She felt she wouldn't get the proper amount of respect if she lived in the dormitory since she was so young herself."

"And as far as you knew, she got along well with Miss Wilson?"

"I believe they were very good friends."

"How about Miss Billingsly?"

"She hardly ever mentioned Miss Billingsly, at least to me. Maybe she said something to her mother."

Frank wasn't going to question Mrs. Northrup until after the funeral if she was as fragile as Northrup said. "Were there any girls . . . any students, I mean, that she didn't get along with?"

"Abigail never had a harsh word to say about anyone."

Frank doubted that, of course. When someone died, especially someone young and full of promise, her loved ones tended to forget any weaknesses or imperfections. "I'd like to speak with Miss Raymond. Abigail may have confided something to her that she didn't want to worry you with."

"Oh, I see. You think someone might have been bothering her or been hostile in some way."

"Yes," Frank said, glad he'd understood. "It might've even been someone Miss Raymond knew, so she'd sympathize."

"I hate to think she was having trouble and didn't confide in us," Northrup said.

"She probably didn't think it was serious or she would have," Frank lied again. Children were, in fact, most likely to keep secrets from their parents when it was a serious matter.

"Her mother is so distraught. She keeps saying we never should've let her come to the city, that she'd still be alive if we'd kept her at home."

Since she was right, Frank didn't have much to offer in the way of comfort. "We'll probably come up to Tarrytown tomorrow and see if we can call on Miss Raymond before the funeral."

"You'll take your wife with you?" he asked in surprise.

"Yes, she's much better with ladies than I am. I'll let you know where we're staying in case you want to contact me."

Northrup nodded. A few moments of silence passed as each man realized he had nothing else to say. Northrup started to rise but stopped himself suddenly. "I almost forgot. The coroner gave me this." He pulled something wrapped in brown paper from his pocket. It had been opened and clumsily wrapped up again. He handed it to Frank.

It was the jewelry Doc Haynes had told him they'd found on the body. "Is something missing?"

"Not that I know of. That's Abigail's locket. We gave it to her for her thirteenth birthday, I think. But the ring . . . I never saw it before."

Frank dumped the pieces on his desk and set

the paper aside. The locket was gold and rather ordinary, with a floral design etched on the face. The ring was gold, too, with a blue stone in a setting surrounded by tiny clear stones. Were they diamonds or glass? He had no way of knowing, although the gold seemed real enough. "Maybe she bought it for herself here in the city."

"She really didn't have the resources to buy something like this for herself, but if she did, then why hide it?"

"Hide it?"

"Yes. The coroner said it was on the chain with the locket, hanging around her neck and tucked inside her clothes so it wasn't visible."

Haynes hadn't told him that. No wonder nobody had stolen it before she got to the morgue. He examined the ring more closely. Engagement rings were all the style now for people who could afford them. Could this be one? Was Abigail secretly engaged to Cornelius Raymond? Or maybe to someone else entirely, which would explain why she wouldn't agree to marry him? "Would you mind if I hold on to the ring for a while? I can see if anybody recognizes it or knows where it came from."

"I suppose, but I'd like to take the locket home."

"Of course." Frank wrapped it back up in the paper and handed it to Northrup.

They took another minute to discuss hotels in Tarrytown where Frank and Sarah might stay, and then Northrup took his leave. He looked like a thoroughly beaten man.

"Poor fellow," Gino said from where he sat at his desk.

"What does this look like to you?" Frank asked, handing him the ring.

"A lady's ring. Where did it come from?"

Frank told him.

"I don't know a lot about women, but I do know they don't usually hang rings around their necks."

"No, they don't, especially one this pretty. A woman would want to show it off, even if she'd bought it for herself."

"And if a man had bought it for her, she'd want to show it off even more," Gino said.

"Exactly. Unless the woman worked at a school where she wasn't allowed to be married."

"And lived in a house where the other women would expect her to stay single. So you think this fellow she was writing letters to gave it to her?"

Gino handed the ring back to him. "If she was telling him she wasn't ready to get married—and from his letters, it sounded like that's what she was saying—then why would he give her a ring?"

"And why would she take it?"

"Those are exactly the questions I'm going to ask him when I see him tomorrow," Frank said.

Sarah examined the ring closely and then passed it to Maeve. They'd just put the children to bed and were enjoying a quiet evening in the formal parlor. Mrs. Malloy sat knitting near the fire, which they had lit even though they had central heat. Something about a fire just made everything seem more comfortable. She and Malloy had brought Maeve up to date on what was happening in the Northrup case.

Maeve looked at the ring. "It's a little too fancy to be something she bought herself."

"I thought so, but I wasn't sure what a younger woman would think," Sarah said.

"You're not that old," Maeve said with a grin.

"Maybe not, but I've been pinching pennies for too long to remember what it was like to be single with no one to worry about but myself."

"Northrup said Abigail wasn't being paid very much at the college," Malloy said. "He didn't think she could've afforded a ring like that."

"If the stones are real, you mean. Do you think they are?" Maeve asked.

Sarah took the ring back and examined it more closely. "The blue one could be a sapphire. If so, then the clear stones are probably diamond chips, and it's an expensive ring. It's definitely real gold at least."

"So an admirer gave it to her," Maeve said. "She must've been secretly engaged. Why else would she hide it?"

"Maybe she was ashamed," Mrs. Malloy said,

surprising them all. Sarah had almost forgotten she was in the room.

"Why would she be ashamed of a beautiful ring like this?" Maeve asked.

"Not the ring. What it stood for. Maybe she was ashamed of who gave it to her."

"I hadn't thought of that, Ma," Malloy said, not bothering to hide his admiration for her reasoning.

"Well, think of it. Don't let all those ideas of romance blind you."

Malloy bit back a smile and turned his head so she wouldn't see it.

"You're absolutely right, Mother Malloy," Sarah said. "We've forgotten that something was very wrong in her life or she wouldn't have been murdered."

"And because of this ring," Maeve said, "we know it could've had something to do with somebody who wanted to marry her."

"How many suitors did she have, though?" Sarah said. "It's not like she could've had gentlemen callers at her home."

Malloy grinned at the thought. "You're right. I can't imagine Miss Wilson or Miss Billingsly making them feel very welcome."

"What about that French professor?" Maeve said. "They must've spent a lot of time together in that office. And he's French . . ."

"What does that mean?" Mrs. Malloy asked with a disapproving frown.

"Frenchmen are supposed to be wildly romantic," Maeve said, not the least bit intimidated.

Sarah turned to Malloy. "How about it? Is this Pelletier wildly romantic?"

Malloy pulled a face. "Not that I noticed."

"Still, he's one of the few men she spent any time with," Maeve argued. "We have to consider him."

"And he did lie about the keys, or at least you're pretty sure he did," Sarah reminded him.

"But this Raymond fellow is a more likely prospect," he reminded her right back. "He's young and eligible, and we *know* he's wildly romantic from his letters."

"But he lives in Tarrytown," Maeve said.

"Which isn't far from here," he replied. "Luther Northrup apparently comes into the city all the time."

"It's too bad you didn't find him today," Sarah said.

"I know. I went right over to his club after Northrup left, but it didn't matter. They said he'd already left."

"Let's just hope he went home," Sarah said. "His parents will be devastated if he doesn't attend the funeral."

"If he didn't go home, I'll set Gino on his trail," Malloy said.

"I wish I could go with you tomorrow," Maeve said.

Malloy gave her a look of mock sternness. "You made your decision, young lady, and you decided to be a nursemaid."

"But I told you I'd help with your investigations whenever you needed me," she replied sweetly.

"And if we do need you, I'll let you know," he said just as sweetly.

"But won't Gino look odd coming to the funeral by himself? If I was with him—"

"He won't look odd," Malloy said.

Maeve sighed dramatically.

Sarah hoped she wasn't regretting her decision to continue as Catherine's nanny instead of going to work at Malloy's detective agency.

Then Maeve grinned. "Don't be surprised if Gino suggests that I go with him, though."

Malloy grinned back. "He already did."

Tarrytown seemed to be thriving. The broad, cobblestone streets were lined with four- and five-story buildings housing businesses and shops below and apartments above. Side streets held the comfortable homes of the business owners and their families, with large shade trees and sprawling porches. Out on the bluff over-looking the Hudson River, people with names like Rockefeller had mansions they used when they wanted to escape the city.

"The desk clerk told me they're building an automobile factory here," Frank told Sarah as he escorted her out of the hotel where they'd be staying.

"That'll be convenient when you decide to buy one," she replied with a knowing grin.

Why couldn't he convince her he had no intention of buying an automobile? "The clerk also looked up the Raymonds' address for me. He said it's just around the corner and down two blocks, if you'd like to walk."

"Walking sounds lovely after being on the train all morning."

They strolled along, enjoying the fresh air and the courtesy of the natives, who nodded and tipped their hats instead of rushing by without so much as a glance, as they would have in the city. They found the Raymond house with no trouble. It was a lovely Queen Anne style, surrounded by a wrought iron fence. Pots on either side of the front door had held flowers last summer. Winter had withered them nearly to dust.

A maid answered the door and stared doubtfully at Frank's card. "Mr. and Mrs. Raymond is not at home," she said.

"We'd like to see Miss Raymond, if we could," he said.

"Please tell her it concerns Miss Northrup," Sarah added helpfully.

"The one what just died?" the girl asked, even more dismayed.

"That's right," Frank said.

She shook her head, but she allowed them to step inside, out of the cold, while she made the proper inquiries. In only a few moments, a young woman emerged from one of the rooms at the back of the house and came hurrying down the hallway to where they waited. She was an attractive girl, even in her unrelieved black mourning. Her dark hair framed a pleasant face that was frowning at the moment.

When she reached them, she looked them over, then glanced at Frank's card, which she had apparently taken from the maid. "I don't understand who you are or why you're here."

"I'm a private investigator, Miss Raymond. Mr. Northrup hired me to look into his daughter's death."

"But when I heard they'd scheduled the funeral, I thought surely they had found out who . . . who did it."

"No, they haven't, I'm afraid."

"But why are you here? We don't know anything about what happened to poor Abigail." Her voice trembled a bit, and for a terrible moment, Frank thought she might cry, but of course she didn't. Society women didn't weep in front of strangers. They were made of sterner stuff than that.

"We're hoping you can answer some questions for us," Sarah said. "You knew her better than anyone, and we know you've been corresponding."

Her eyes widened at that, but she didn't deny it, which meant she knew about her brother hiding his letters behind her name.

"I don't think I can help you."

"You might be surprised at what you know," Sarah said. "And if you can't answer our questions, there's no harm done, is there? I know you want to do what you can to see her killer punished."

She still looked unconvinced, but she invited them into the front parlor. The maid took their coats while Miss Raymond opened the room. Frank and Sarah sat on a stiff, horsehair sofa and Miss Raymond took a chair opposite them. The parlor was the old-fashioned kind, crammed full of overstuffed furniture and tables cluttered with knickknacks and doilies.

"Can I get you something? Coffee or tea?"

"Thank you, no. We just had lunch," Sarah said.

"What is it you wanted to ask me?"

They had decided that Sarah would do most of the talking since she'd be less threatening than Frank. She smiled gently. "We know that you and Abigail were good friends since childhood."

"Yes, our parents have known each other all their lives as well. In fact my parents are with the Northrups today, helping them plan the . . . Abigail's service."

"You attended the Normal School with Abigail, didn't you?"

"You obviously know I did. We graduated last June."

"But you didn't want to teach?"

"Not as much as Abigail did, certainly. I . . . Well, I had met a young man, and he . . . We are planning to be married."

"How wonderful."

She smiled faintly. "I had thought so, but now . . . I feel guilty for being so happy about my own future."

"That's perfectly understandable, but I'm sure Abigail wouldn't want to spoil your happiness."

"You're right, of course, but still . . . I'm sorry. I shouldn't be talking about myself. What is it you want to know?"

"We believe that Abigail was killed by someone she knew."

"That's impossible. Everyone loved her. And I thought she was killed by a stranger. That's what everyone thinks."

"As I said, we don't believe that, and neither do her parents."

Poor Miss Raymond was growing more and more distressed. She glanced uncertainly at Frank and back at Sarah. "Excuse me, but why is a female involved in an investigation?"

"Oh, I'm sorry," Frank said quickly. "I should have introduced you. Miss Raymond, this is my wife. She assists me when"—he smiled apologetically—"when we're dealing with a gently bred female who might be offended by my bad manners."

"Your manners seem fine, Mr. Malloy. I'm sorry to question you, Mrs. Malloy, but I . . . I'm happy to say I've never known anyone who was murdered before, so this is all very new to me."

"New and distressing, I'm sure," Sarah said. "I'm sorry we have to upset you even more. What my husband didn't say is that gossip is what solves most murders, and I'm much better at coaxing it out of people than he is."

"Gossip?" she echoed in surprise.

"Well, perhaps that's too strong a word. But it's often the small, seemingly unimportant detail that is exactly the information we need to find the guilty party."

"And you think Abigail may have confided this detail to me."

"It's possible."

In the space of just a few seconds, Miss Raymond's whole demeanor had changed. She sat straighter, and she no longer looked as if she might burst into tears. "If that is the kind of information you want, then I most certainly will be able to help you. In fact, I may know exactly why she died."

6

Sarah blinked in surprise at Miss Raymond's sudden change in attitude. "What do you mean?"

Miss Raymond glanced over at the parlor door, which she'd left open, then quickly got up and closed it. When she was back in her chair again, she said, "Abigail told me she'd found out something terrible about someone at the school."

"You'd seen her, then?"

"Yes, when she came home for Christmas. She hinted that something was not quite right and that she was investigating."

"Investigating?" Frank echoed. "Is that the word she used?"

"Yes, it is, and I thought it was strange as well. She was very mysterious about the whole thing. She said she had to be sure, but when she was, well, everyone at the school was going to be shocked. And yes, *shocked* is the word she used."

"Did she give you any indication at all what she was investigating?" Sarah asked. "Or who? Or even if it was a student or a teacher?"

"No. She said she didn't want to start any rumors that might harm an innocent person."

Sarah glanced over at Malloy, but he looked as puzzled as she felt. "Do you recall any rumors about anyone from when you were at school?"

Miss Raymond shook her head. "Just the usual things. Girls can be very mean to each other, and they were always telling tales, trying to make someone look bad because they were jealous."

"What were they jealous of?" Sarah asked.

"A lot of the girls came from good families, but some were very poor and received scholarships. They were often the smartest ones, but the teachers didn't make pets of them very often. They preferred the company of girls like me and Abigail."

"And did the jealous girls tell tales about the other students or about the teachers?"

"The students. It wasn't a good idea to say bad things about the teachers, because if word got back to them . . . Well, you don't want them to think you're a troublemaker. You might find your grades aren't very good anymore or your scholarship isn't being renewed."

Before Sarah could think of another question, Miss Raymond stiffened at the sound of the front door opening.

"Excuse me, please." She jumped up and hurried out, closing the parlor door behind her.

"Maybe her parents are home," Sarah said.

Malloy nodded. "She probably doesn't want to involve them in this."

They waited, straining to hear, but no sounds reached them. Then the parlor door opened again, and Miss Raymond came in followed by a young man who looked so much like her, he could only be her brother.

Sarah and Malloy rose as Miss Raymond introduced them. Cornelius Raymond looked even more distressed to see them than his sister had.

"Why have you come here at a time like this?" he asked.

"Mr. Raymond," Malloy said. "We know you were corresponding with Abigail Northrup."

"How could you know that?" he demanded.

"We found your letters," Sarah said quickly, making her tone as gentle as possible. "Abigail had hidden them, but we had to search her room after she died."

"And you read them? You read my private letters to her?" He was furious now.

"I'm sorry, but her parents have hired us to find out who murdered her. She can't have secrets anymore."

"And you think I killed her?" he nearly shouted.

"Cory, please," his sister said. "They couldn't possibly think that."

Neither Sarah nor Malloy contradicted her.

"We know that you were corresponding with her," Malloy said, "but that your sister was addressing the envelopes so people would think the letters were from her."

"And the 'people' you're talking about were those old biddies she lived with," Raymond said.

Malloy slipped his hand into Sarah's and gave

it a little squeeze. She wasn't sure what message he was sending until he said, "Mr. Raymond, maybe you and I should discuss this privately. There's no sense in upsetting the ladies."

"That isn't really necessary," his sister tried, but Raymond cut her off.

"I think that would be a good idea. Come with me." Raymond strode purposefully out of the room, and Malloy followed, leaving the women gaping.

Miss Raymond turned back to Sarah, obviously mortified by her brother's behavior. "I'm so sorry. He's very upset about Abigail, as you can imagine."

"That's perfectly understandable," Sarah said. "And finding out strangers had read his letters to her must be devastating."

"I suppose you know he wanted to marry her."

Sarah hadn't planned to mention that, in case Miss Raymond didn't know. "Yes, we do, but we gathered that she hadn't accepted his proposal."

"No, she hadn't, but she wouldn't refuse him outright either. I was so angry with her. She just kept leading him on, refusing to say yes but not saying no, either, so he could get on with his life."

"It was probably a difficult decision for her. She'd been hired at the college, which was a great honor for a newly graduated student, and she really enjoyed teaching."

"But a very eligible young man had asked her to marry him," Miss Raymond said. "How could she refuse an opportunity like that so she could end up a fusty old maid like those women she lived with?"

Raymond led Frank down the hall to the room his sister had been in when they arrived. It turned out to be the rear parlor, the room the family used as their informal gathering place. The furniture here was more comfortable and inviting, and showed the wear of everyday use. Raymond closed the door behind them and whirled around to face Frank.

"Why do you think she wouldn't marry you?" Frank asked before Raymond could start his own argument.

As he'd hoped, the question shocked him, and as Frank watched, all the fight drained out of him, leaving him pale and shaken.

"Here, sit down, son," he said, taking Raymond's arm and leading him to the nearest chair.

He sank down wearily and covered his face with both hands.

"I'm sorry to do this to you," Frank continued, pretending not to notice the boy's distress. "But I know you want to see whoever did this to Abigail get punished."

Frank waited, and after a few moments, Raymond scrubbed his hands over his face and lowered them. He looked up at Frank with red-rimmed eyes. "You know I had proposed to her."

"Yes. As I said, we read your letters. I apologize for that, but we had to know if you had any reason to harm her."

"And now you know I didn't. I wanted to make her my wife."

Frank decided not to mention that her refusal could be considered a reason to harm her. "We didn't see her letters, of course."

"And you aren't going to."

Frank ignored that. "So I don't know what reason she gave for refusing you."

"What could that possibly matter?"

"It might give us a clue as to what else was going on in her life that might have made someone angry with her."

He considered this for a long moment. "She hadn't really refused me. Not outright, at least."

"What had she said?"

He had to clear his throat. "She said . . . She was very confused. She loved teaching, she said. She loved the young ladies she taught. I already knew she loved attending college. Irene enjoyed it, too, but not in the same way at all. I think Irene just enjoyed being away from home with a lot of girls her own age. She didn't mind the classes and the work. She was always good in school, so it came easily to her. But she wasn't one of these New Women. She didn't want a Life of the Mind or whatever they call it. She wanted a real life, with a home and a husband and children."

"And you thought Abigail would, too."

He looked up, his eyes dark. "Why wouldn't she? That's a woman's natural place in the world. I've been waiting for her for years, but I was patient. I waited until she was finished with college. She wouldn't even discuss it until then, at any rate. I proposed to her before she went to France last summer, as soon as she graduated, but they'd already offered her the teaching position. She wanted to try it. She wanted to be like those professors she admired so much."

"Miss Wilson?"

Raymond winced. "Yes, and the others. There were others, too. She told me how she enjoyed talking about ideas with them, but she'd already had four years of it. Shouldn't that have been enough?"

Frank had no answer for him. "Did she ever mention having any trouble with anyone?"

"Never, but she wouldn't, would she? Not to me. She couldn't admit anything was wrong because then she wouldn't have a reason not to marry me."

Frank hesitated, debating with himself the wisdom of asking him the final question. He decided he had nothing to lose. "If she hadn't accepted your proposal, why did she have this?"

He pulled the ring from his pocket and held it out for Raymond to see.

He looked at it for a long moment, then met Frank's gaze. "What are you talking about?"

Sarah shouldn't have been surprised that Miss Raymond didn't approve of Abigail's house-mates. Still . . . "Didn't you have a smash when you were a freshman, Miss Raymond?"

Her surprise was almost comical. "How do you know about that?"

"We've learned a lot in the past few days."

"You certainly have, and to answer your question, I suppose I did have a smash. Miss Cooper teaches history. She . . . Well, she loved all the girls."

"Loved?"

"I don't mean romantically. That would be silly. But she did care for us, even the ones who weren't as bright as the others. She always treated us with respect, and she'd invite a few of us to her rooms, and we'd make tea and toast and talk about the Roman Empire or the Renaissance or medieval England. She'd tell us what life was like for females back then, and we'd point out that we weren't much better off now. She tried to convince us we could change things, but after a while, I realized she was wrong. The world isn't going to change just because we want it to, so I stopped going to her gatherings."

"And you'd made your own friends, other students, by then."

"Yes," she said with a frown. "How did you know that?"

"It was just a guess. But Abigail never stopped going to Miss Wilson's salons."

Miss Raymond's pretty face pinched up in distaste. "No, she didn't. At first I was a little jealous. Miss Wilson was—well, I guess she still is—everyone's favorite teacher. Only the best girls were invited to her house."

"I guess Abigail was a particular favorite."

"Oh yes. The other girls would laugh about it, although I don't think they really thought it was funny. They were jealous, too. Not only was Miss Wilson the favorite teacher, but it was a chance to see a Boston marriage up close."

"A what?"

"A Boston marriage. The name comes from Henry James's book *The Bostonians*. A Boston marriage is when two women make a life for themselves together, without having to depend on a husband. We talked about this a lot when I was at school. It's very difficult for a woman to support herself if she doesn't marry, or at least it has been, historically speaking."

Sarah knew this only too well, but she simply nodded her encouragement.

"Women who graduate from college have a different experience, however. Many of them have found fulfilling occupations, so they don't need a husband to support them, which is fortunate because many of them would probably never have received an offer of marriage."

"And why was that, do you think?"

Miss Raymond gave her a pitying look. "Because they aren't attractive enough or pleasing or because they choose not to behave in a manner that appeals to men."

"I see." Sarah did, thinking how sad it was that women often had to change or at least disguise who they really were in order to be seen as marriageable. And of course many of them simply weren't born good-looking enough to catch a man's eye. "So they have one of these Boston marriages instead?"

"Some of them do. They choose to live together. For the companionship, you understand, and probably for economy as well. In New England, they've started calling that a Boston marriage."

Miss Wilson and Miss Billingsly obviously represented an example of this for the students at the Normal School. "Why do you suppose Miss Wilson and Miss Billingsly invited Abigail to live with them, then?"

"Miss Billingsly didn't invite her. It was all Miss Wilson's doing. She owns the house, you see."

"Do you think Miss Billingsly approved of the new arrangement?"

Miss Raymond started to reply and then caught

herself. "You don't think Miss Billingsly would have . . . That's insane!"

"Is it? You said there was a lot of jealousy at the school. Why wouldn't Miss Billingsly be jealous that a student moved into their marriage?"

"It's not a real marriage, not like a man and wife. It's just an expression."

Was it? Sarah wasn't so sure, but she said, "I suppose you're right. Did Abigail say how she liked living there?"

"She loved it, I'm sure."

"Did she say anything about it when you saw her at Christmas?"

"Not really. She was mostly thinking about the scandal she'd discovered, whatever it was. It upset me to think someone at the school was doing something shameful, but at least Abigail wouldn't have made her accusations publicly. I'm sure she would have been discreet."

But would she have? And did the person she was going to expose know that? And even if she was as discreet as possible, the person would most likely have lost her place at the school. Or his, she added mentally, since all but one of the professors were male.

"We know that you addressed the envelopes for your brother's letters to Abigail," Sarah said. "But did you correspond with her yourself?"

"Oh yes. Not as frequently as Cory did, but we did write."

"I didn't find any letters from you in her room."

"Really? That's odd. But maybe she didn't keep them."

No, Sarah thought, not keeping them would be odd. People rarely discarded letters from their close friends. She'd have to discuss this with Malloy.

No sooner had she thought of him than the parlor door opened and Mr. Raymond and Malloy came in. Mr. Raymond looked almost angry.

"Have you ever seen this before?" he asked his sister. He held out Abigail's ring for her to see.

She took it from him and examined it. "I don't think so."

"He said Abigail was wearing it when she died." He gestured toward Malloy, who stood by calmly, watching.

"It's very pretty," Miss Raymond offered, not sure what she was supposed to say.

"She wasn't exactly wearing it," Sarah clarified. "She had put it on the chain of a necklace she was wearing and tucked it inside her dress."

"Why would she do that?" Miss Raymond asked.

"Because she was hiding it," her brother said. "Don't you see? It's an engagement ring, and she was hiding it. That's why she wouldn't give me an answer. She was engaged to someone else."

"You don't know that," his sister said. "It's just a ring. How can you know it's an engagement ring?"

"Because nothing else makes sense. No girl hangs a ring around her neck and hides it."

"Do you have any idea who else might have proposed to Abigail?" Malloy asked.

Both of the Raymonds looked at him as if he were insane.

Sarah quickly added, "If she was involved with someone else, she was probably refusing to acknowledge him as well. He might have gotten angry and quarreled with her . . ."

Raymond's anger evaporated in shock, and he stumbled to the nearest chair before collapsing into it. "I . . . I didn't think . . ."

"Who could it have been?" Miss Raymond asked. "Think, Cory. Did she ever mention anyone?"

"Not to me, but she wouldn't, would she? You're the most likely one she would've confided in."

"What about that professor she worked with," Malloy tried. "Pelletier. Did she ever say anything about him?"

"*Monsieur Pelletier*?" Miss Raymond scoffed. She turned to Sarah. "Have you met him?"

Sarah shook her head.

"Abigail would never take him seriously. We always laughed at him behind his back."

"Did he know?" Malloy asked.

"He never let on if he did. Besides, what could he do about it? But I'll tell you, I was surprised when he gave Abigail a position. We all knew she was his best student, but I didn't think he was particularly fond of her. If anything, I got the impression he was glad to see her finish her studies."

"Then I guess you didn't know it was Miss Wilson who convinced President Hatch to hire her, not Pelletier," Malloy said.

"No, I didn't, but that makes perfect sense. I wonder how they got Pelletier to agree to accept her."

"What does it matter?" Raymond snapped. "None of this matters. Who else could have given Abigail that ring?"

Miss Raymond looked at the ring again and sighed. "I have no idea, and as for me being the person she would have confided in, I doubt it. I'm your sister, Cory. She'd never tell me she was keeping another man on the string at the same time she was leading you on."

She was right, of course. Sarah sighed and rose to her feet. "I think we've bothered you enough today. Thank you for your help." She put out her hand and Miss Raymond gave her the ring.

Malloy said, "If you think of anything else, please let us know."

"We will," Miss Raymond promised, rising to see them out.

Cory Raymond said nothing, nor did he even look up as they left.

When they were well away from the house, Sarah said, "Did we learn anything, do you think?"

"I learned that Cornelius Raymond is an angry young man."

"But was he angry before he knew about the ring?"

"Oh yes. He's been trying to court Abigail for years. She wouldn't discuss marriage until she graduated, and even knowing he was going to propose, she accepted the job teaching at the Normal School."

"She doesn't sound like a young lady in love, does she?"

"Well, she certainly wasn't anxious to get married."

Sarah smiled up at him. "Do you think that makes her strange?"

"It makes her unusual."

"Yes, it does, but society is changing. At the college, we've already met several women who have chosen to have a career instead of getting married."

"You're assuming they had the option to get married," Malloy said. "Somehow, I can't imagine Miss Billingsly having a long line of disappointed suitors."

"You may be right, but at least some of the teachers probably could have married if they'd chosen to. And we know Abigail had that choice."

"But you'll notice she hadn't turned the

Raymond boy down flat. If anything, she was purposely keeping him dangling."

"Yes, she was, and that makes me wonder why. If she was in love with him, she would've given up her idea of having a career without a qualm, I think."

"The way you did to marry me?" Malloy asked with a grin.

"Who said I've given up my career?" she replied with a grin of her own.

"Well, I don't see you going out to deliver babies anymore, and I have to admit, that surprises me a little."

"It does?"

"Yes. I thought after we got back from our honeymoon that you'd last about a month before you got bored and found something to do."

"I have the work at the Mission," she said.

"The Mission practically runs itself now. And you've got a dozen rich ladies who support it and spend time there. They don't need much from you."

This was true. "I guess I'm just not bored enough yet. You're keeping me busy being a detective, after all."

"Or maybe you just haven't figured out what you want to do."

"Malloy, you know me too well."

"I wish I did, but I know you well enough to know you need to be useful."

"All right. I'll try to make myself useful on this case. Where were we?"

"Giving up marriage to have a career."

Oh yes, which reminded her of her conversation with Irene Raymond. "Did you know there's a special name for the kind of household Miss Wilson and Miss Billingsly have?" She explained the concept of a Boston marriage to him.

"Maybe Abigail wanted to have a Boston marriage of her own," Malloy said.

"Then why was she keeping Cory Raymond on her string? Maybe she loved him and couldn't make up her mind between him and her teaching career."

"Or maybe she had another lover and was trying to decide which one was the better catch. That would explain the ring, at least."

"And she could have been trying to choose between the two men and the career. But she couldn't have been in love with either of her suitors, because that would have immediately eliminated the other one."

"Unless the one she didn't love was rich and the one she did love was poor."

"You're very cynical," she scolded.

"But very realistic."

"Unfortunately, the facts don't fit your theory. Cory Raymond isn't poor, and our mystery lover isn't either, judging from the ring he gave her."

"All right, so both suitors are equal, and she doesn't love either one."

"And she really loves teaching and knows she can support herself without a husband, so she doesn't need to marry at all," Sarah mused. "Why would she accept the ring, then? And why not just tell poor Cory Raymond she's not interested?"

"Let's not forget the scandal she told Irene Raymond about."

"Oh yes. In all the talk about suitors, I completely forgot the scandal. What on earth could it be?"

"All we know is she found out someone at the school was guilty of something unacceptable."

"A male teacher seducing a student?" Sarah said, stating what would be the most obvious type of scandal at a college for women.

"That's probably too easy."

"You're right, but what if Abigail was the one being seduced? What if the ring came from her seducer?"

"Do you think she'd be naïve enough for that?"

Sarah considered what they knew. "I wouldn't have thought so, but she was young and innocent. She might have believed this older, more experienced man. And maybe we're wrong about her being in love. If she loved this professor, she would have accepted the ring. She would have believed they were secretly engaged."

"Which would explain why she wore it but kept it hidden. But not why she didn't refuse Raymond's offer."

"Maybe she didn't trust this older man completely, and she wanted to keep all her options open. Or maybe she wanted to keep a suitor around in case someone suspected her romance with this teacher. If someone did, she could just point to poor Cory and say it was harmless gossip and she was spoken for or whatever."

"The whole thing sounds too complicated to me," Malloy said with mock despair. "Maybe if I'd gone to college, I could figure it out."

"Don't give up," Sarah said with a grin. "All we really have to figure out is who in this mess might have killed Abigail in a fit of rage."

"That's easy enough. Maybe Raymond found out she was just playing with him and got mad. Maybe this mysterious professor who seduced her and gave her the ring found out she had another lover—that would be Raymond—and got mad."

"Or maybe someone involved in a scandal that has nothing to do with Abigail's suitors got mad," Sarah said with a sigh. "This is giving me a headache."

"We should go back to our hotel and take a nap."

"A nap? I'm not tired."

"Neither am I," he told her with a provocative grin.

• • •

Luther Northrup was present for his sister's funeral, much to everyone's relief. He even looked appropriately grief stricken, although Frank thought he probably just had a hangover. Frank found he couldn't bear to look at her parents, however. Their grief was simply too profound to witness. He and Sarah had silently agreed to avoid the front parlor, where the family sat with Abigail's casket to receive the mourners. Instead, they stayed in the front hallway, where they could mingle with the arriving mourners and see who came in. Gino stood on the front porch, bundled up against the winter chill, so he could watch the street outside in case someone showed unnatural interest in the event without actually attending it.

The Northrups lived a block down from the Raymonds in a large, beautiful house. The Raymond parents had been at the Northrup home when Frank and Sarah arrived, and Mr. Northrup had introduced them. Mr. and Mrs. Raymond gave no indication their children had told them about their visit yesterday. Frank supposed that was good. He didn't want to cause the Northrups any extra distress on this difficult day.

When Irene and Cory Raymond came in, they pointedly ignored Frank and Sarah.

"I don't expect we'll hear any more from them, even if they happen to figure out who killed poor Abigail," Sarah whispered.

"Unless one of them decides to confess," he replied.

Her eyes widened at that. "You don't really think Irene could have done it, do you?"

"I wouldn't want to discount her just because she's female," he said, earning a swat.

Shortly before the service was to start, he was surprised to see Miss Wilson come in. Even more surprising, Miss Billingsly was with her. He supposed he should have expected to see them, though. Abigail had lived with them for months, and she had been their colleague and, before that, their student. Miss Wilson appeared to be controlling her emotions, whatever they were. Her expression was suitably grave, and she did not appear to have been weeping recently. Miss Billingsly, however, looked awful. Her eyes and nose were red, and her face pale. Even her hat looked like it was on crooked. She clung to Miss Wilson's arm as if she really needed support.

"Do you think she's been drinking?" Sarah asked him.

"I can't imagine Miss Wilson would bring her here if she has. Too much danger of a scene."

"I'll find out."

The maid was taking their coats, so Sarah made her way over and greeted them.

"Mrs. Malloy," Miss Wilson said without the slightest hint of warmth. "I'm surprised to see you here."

Frank noted that his wife refused to be baited and didn't even bat an eye. They probably taught society girls how to ignore barbed remarks before they even left the nursery. She merely smiled her gracious smile and asked Miss Billingsly how she was.

Miss Billingsly looked at her in surprise, obviously not used to being noticed. "It's just so terrible about poor Miss Northrup. I keep expecting her to come home and tell us it was all a horrible mistake."

"It *was* a horrible mistake, I'm sure," Miss Wilson said, although she sounded more angry than grieved. "No one who knew her could have wished her harm."

A man came in behind them, and when he removed his hat, Frank realized it was Pelletier. Frank stepped forward to greet him and introduce him to Sarah. The two female teachers moved past him with just the slightest nod of recognition, which suited him fine.

"Pelletier," he said by way of greeting. The two men shook hands, and Frank introduced the professor to Sarah, making careful note of her expression. She was too well-bred to let her real emotions show, of course. He'd have to wait until later to find out what her first impression had been.

"Please accept my condolences," she said. "It must be difficult to lose a fellow faculty member like that."

"*Mais oui, madame.* It is always tragic to lose one so young."

"It was kind of you to accompany Miss Wilson and Miss Billingsly."

"I did not accompany them," he said with a tiny smile. "We were on the same train and shared a cab only. Excuse me, please. I must make my respects to Miss Northrup's parents."

Frank didn't recognize any of the rest of the late arrivals, so he and Sarah retreated to the other end of the hallway while they shed their coats and made their way into the parlor.

"What did you think of him?" he asked.

"Pelletier? He's not exactly the stuff of young girls' daydreams, is he? Except for the accent, I mean. Many people think a French accent is appealing."

"Do you?"

She smiled. "On some men."

"So you agree with Irene Raymond that Abigail couldn't have been seduced by Pelletier?"

"Let's just say it seems very unlikely. Aren't you going to ask me if Miss Billingsly had been drinking?"

He'd almost forgotten. "Oh yes, has she?"

"I don't think so. I think she's just overcome with grief."

"That's funny, since she was the one who didn't like Abigail and didn't want her living in the house."

"Sometimes people react strangely when someone they don't like dies. It's like they feel guilty for disliking them in life and are trying to make amends."

"Or maybe they killed the person they didn't like and now they're feeling guilty," Frank said.

"Do you really think poor Miss Billingsly stuck a screwdriver in Abigail's eye?"

"I think women are just as capable of committing murder as men."

"How very modern of you, Malloy."

"You aren't the first person who remarked on that."

"Don't be too pleased with yourself," she said with a smirk. "It's not a compliment."

The minister saved him from having to reply by asking everyone to move into the parlor because the service was about to start.

7

The funeral service for Abigail Northrup was as heart-wrenching as Sarah had expected. While the minister enumerated her many accomplishments during her brief life, hardly any of those present had dry eyes and many of the women were sobbing.

She and Malloy had taken seats in the back so they could watch everyone else. Now Sarah wished they hadn't even come. Dabbing at her own tears, she saw even Malloy rubbing his eyes. Miss Billingsly wept quietly into her handkerchief, her shoulders shaking, while Miss Wilson only occasionally had to swipe at a tear with hers. Professor Pelletier had to blow his nose several times. The young Raymonds comforted each other. Cory put his arm around his sister and made no attempt to stem his own tears, allowing them to stream down his face. The only person apparently not overcome with grief was Luther Northrup. His parents clung to each other, seeming oblivious to him, and he appeared to be transfixed by the painting hanging above the fireplace.

In deference to the injuries to Abigail's face and the fact that so much time had passed since her death, the casket remained closed. No one needed to see her body to be reminded of her presence, however, because of the large portrait of her that hung in the place of prominence.

The artist hadn't been particularly skilled, and Sarah couldn't vouch for the likeness, having never seen the subject, but the picture of the blond girl in the powder blue gown definitely made her presence felt.

The minister offered the traditional words of comfort, promising the Northrups they would meet their daughter again in the next world, but that was little consolation for the many years they would spend in this world without her. They were quite obviously devastated, her mother hysterical and her father nearly so. Their son, however, just continued to stare at the painting of his dead sister, his expression unreadable.

Finally, the service was over, and the minister invited everyone to accompany them to the cemetery. Afterward, they would return here for a meal. The locals had their own transportation, of course, and the Northrups had hired carriages for those who did not. The process of getting coats and finding the proper conveyances took a while, and Frank and Sarah managed to be among the first outside so they could casually join the group they wanted to ride with.

When Miss Wilson and Miss Billingsly left the house, the Malloys fell in behind them.

"Do we have to go?" Miss Billingsly asked, sounding like a petulant child.

"Of course we do," Miss Wilson said.

"But it's cold."

Miss Wilson did not reply to that. They reached the next available hired carriage, and the driver helped them inside. Frank assisted Sarah and climbed in after her, and Frank slipped the driver a dollar and told him to follow the procession even though the carriage wasn't full yet.

"Hello again," Sarah said, pretending not to notice Miss Billingsly's alarm and Miss Wilson's disgruntled frown.

The carriage lurched into motion, startling them even more.

When neither woman spoke, Malloy said, "I didn't see President Hatch here today."

Miss Wilson waited a few moments to reply, making it clear she would prefer not to speak to Malloy at all. "He is organizing a memorial service at the school. He sent us in his place."

Sarah found that a little less than satisfactory. A teacher had been murdered on school grounds and the president didn't attend her funeral? The Northrups would be outraged.

"It was a lovely service," Sarah tried.

"Oh yes," Miss Billingsly quickly agreed. "Very lovely. Poor Abigail. Poor, poor Abigail."

"You must have been very fond of her," Sarah said, knowing this wasn't true.

Miss Billingsly's eyes widened with what might have been fear. "I . . . She was a lovely girl."

"We were both fond of her," Miss Wilson said, reminding Sarah that Miss Billingsly had said Miss Wilson had a smash on Abigail. "It was a delight having a young person in our home."

"Yes," Miss Billingsly said without much enthusiasm. "A delight. Like having a daughter."

Miss Wilson shot her a disapproving glance, but to Sarah's surprise, Miss Billingsly didn't wilt under it.

"Well, she could have been. She was young enough."

For some reason, this angered Miss Wilson, although she was much too well-bred to lose her temper in front of strangers.

"Teaching must be a very rewarding occupation," Sarah continued as if she didn't notice the tension between the two women.

"It can be," Miss Wilson said after a moment.

"But our efforts are wasted on many of the young ladies," Miss Billingsly said, her grief apparently forgotten.

"Estelle," Miss Wilson said in warning, but Miss Billingsly ignored her.

"We train them for a vitally important vocation, and then they throw their chances away by getting married."

"You don't consider marriage an important vocation for a woman?" Sarah asked with genuine interest.

"Of course—" Miss Wilson tried, but Miss Billingsly cut her off.

"For *some* women, those who can't do anything else."

"Estelle, you're insulting Mrs. Malloy," Miss Wilson snapped.

"No, she isn't," Malloy said. The twinkle in his eye told Sarah how much he was enjoying this conversation. "Mrs. Malloy is a midwife."

"Catering to married women," Miss Billingsly sniffed.

"Not all of my clients are married," Sarah couldn't resist saying.

Poor Malloy had to cough to cover a bark of laughter, while the two teachers just gaped.

"And if at least some women didn't marry and have children, you wouldn't have any young ladies to teach," Sarah added, not bothering to hide her own smile.

"I'm sure Estelle didn't mean to condemn marriage and motherhood as a legitimate calling for women," Miss Wilson said, giving Miss Billingsly another warning glance.

"Of course not. For *some* women," Miss Billingsly repeated, once again refusing to be cautioned.

"And President Hatch himself said he thinks a generation of young men raised by educated mothers would be very good for our country," Malloy said. Sarah knew he was being deliberately provocative and somehow managed not to grin.

"Of course he would say something like that," Miss Billingsly said. "He'd see nothing wrong with a woman wasting her education so long as she produced sons."

Sarah didn't know if that was a valid assessment of President Hatch's views or not, so she didn't bother to argue. "Your efforts weren't wasted on Abigail, though. You must have been gratified when she was chosen to teach at the college."

"I'm not sure 'gratified' correctly describes my feelings," Miss Wilson said.

"Doesn't it?" Sarah asked innocently. "I thought it was your personal efforts that convinced President Hatch to hire her."

"Who told you that?"

"Professor Pelletier," Malloy said helpfully. "I had thought maybe . . . But of course I was wrong."

"What did you think?" Miss Wilson demanded.

He glanced at Sarah, pretending he was too discreet to speak of the matter.

She happily rescued him. "When a man hires an attractive young woman to work with him, people sometimes assume their relationship is . . . close."

"What nonsense!" Miss Wilson said, flushing with anger. "Professor Pelletier's reputation is spotless, and Miss Northrup was above reproach."

"Was she?" Miss Billingsly asked with mock

innocence. "How can we be sure after what happened to her?"

"What do you mean by that, Estelle?"

"I mean she was murdered. Violently murdered. One might even say in the heat of passion."

"You know nothing about it," Miss Wilson said.

"No, I don't. Do you?" Miss Billingsly asked.

Miss Wilson flushed scarlet. "Of course not. How can you even suggest such a thing?"

Sarah half expected Miss Billingsly to apologize for her cruel accusation or to at least disclaim it. Instead she simply returned Miss Wilson's outraged glare with a cool one of her own.

After a long moment, Miss Wilson remembered they were not alone. She turned back to Sarah. "This is hardly an appropriate topic for conversation, under the circumstances. I'm afraid we're feeling entirely too emotional."

"That's understandable," Sarah said. "A young woman you cared for has died tragically. It would be a wonder if you weren't emotional."

"Mr. Malloy," Miss Billingsly said, "do you think you'll discover who was responsible for poor Abigail's death?"

"I hope so," he said, knowing better than to make promises.

"And what will happen to that person if you do catch him?"

"That depends. If the person confesses, they'll probably go to prison."

"For a long time?"

"Considering the violence of the crime, probably."

"And if they don't confess?"

"Then they'll go on trial, and it'll be up to a jury to decide their guilt or innocence."

Miss Billingsly frowned. "You mean the killer might get away without punishment?"

"It happens sometimes."

She glanced at Miss Wilson again. "So there's hope."

"Hope for what?" Miss Wilson asked, apparently confused.

If Miss Billingsly heard, she gave no indication. She looked back at Sarah and twisted her face into the semblance of a smile. "Are you really a midwife, Mrs. Malloy?"

"Of course I am."

"And your husband allows this?"

"So far, but we haven't been married very long."

"But you will allow it?" she asked Malloy with apparent interest.

"I don't think I could stop her," he admitted with satisfaction, confusing Miss Billingsly and making Miss Wilson frown.

"You are an unusual man, Mr. Malloy," Miss Wilson said.

He turned to Sarah. "Was that a compliment?"

"I don't think so," she replied.

The carriage slowed to turn, and Malloy glanced out the window. Sarah could see they were entering the cemetery.

"Did you find out what you wanted to?" Miss Billingsly asked suddenly.

"I beg your pardon?" he asked.

"You obviously rode in the same carriage so you could question us. Did you find out what you wanted to know?"

"I don't think we found out anything," Sarah said.

The carriage stopped, then sagged a bit as the driver climbed down.

"That's good," Miss Billingsly said just as the door opened.

The two teachers climbed out without another word. Miss Wilson's expression was stony. She was probably still angry at all of them for discussing Abigail and her murder. Miss Billingsly seemed thoughtful, or perhaps she was just worried. Sarah wished she knew why she'd be worried.

The driver helped Sarah down and Malloy followed. By then the two teachers had hurried off, following the other mourners to the ragged patch of earth where a hole had been prepared to receive Abigail's body. The Malloys strolled more slowly, in no hurry to see the end of Abigail's story.

"You lied to Miss Billingsly. We did learn that

Miss Billingsly is worried about something," Malloy said.

"Something that has to do with Miss Wilson. No question, she's jealous of Abigail."

"Even now that she's dead?"

"Apparently," Sarah said. "Something happened in that house that ruined their friendship."

"Ruined?"

"Well, damaged it, at least, and it most certainly involved Abigail."

"You already knew Miss Billingsly was jealous of her."

"This is more than just jealousy," Sarah said. "The problem is, neither one of them is likely to talk about it, especially to us."

They had almost reached the crowd gathered at the gravesite. "Maybe we should send Gino to talk to Bathsheba again."

Sarah smiled at that. "Or maybe you should go."

The graveside service was brief and heart-wrenching, as Abigail's casket was lowered into the ground. Stunned and weeping mourners filed back into their various conveyances in silence. Frank and Sarah were not surprised that the two teachers had chosen a different group of people for the return trip to the Northrups' home, squeezing into a nearly full carriage so Frank and Sarah couldn't possibly join them.

Back at the house, they decided to split up and

wander around in search of anyone behaving strangely or inappropriately. Frank found Gino, who had remained at the house during the graveside service to keep an eye on things there.

"Lots of people walked by," he reported, "but nobody seemed unnaturally interested and nobody tried to get inside."

"That's good. Go get yourself something to eat and keep your eyes open."

Frank decided to wait awhile before heading to the dining room, where a buffet had been set out. He glanced into the front parlor. The rows of folding chairs had been removed and the furniture arranged back into its normal position by efficient servants. The room was empty now except for one person.

Frank was surprised to see Luther Northrup sitting in there alone on a sofa. He was staring up at Abigail's portrait again, just as he had during the funeral. Frank walked in and sat down nearby.

"It must be hard to believe she's gone."

Luther looked up in surprise, as if he hadn't realized Frank was there. "Yes, it is."

Frank waited, but Luther had nothing else to add. He tried again. "Such a tragedy."

"That's what everybody says."

"You don't agree?"

"Oh, sure. She was . . . She was always the smart one. I guess you know. You're one of the professors from the school, aren't you?"

Frank didn't correct him. "You must be smart, too."

"Not book smart. I just . . . I prefer action."

"Are you a sportsman, then?"

His surprise was the first real emotion Frank had seen him display. "How'd you guess?"

Frank decided not to mention that his father had told him. "You look like one."

This pleased him. "I'm a passable gymnast."

"That takes a lot of practice."

"I've been doing it for years. I've won ribbons for it."

"You should come to the city. We probably have better equipment there in the athletic clubs."

"Oh, I already belong to the New York Athletic Club. They . . ." He glanced around to make sure they were still alone. "They've offered me a job."

"That's very impressive. Congratulations."

"Don't say anything to my parents. I don't . . . They don't want to think about me at a time like this." He glanced up at the portrait again.

"I'm sure they'll be pleased. It might even cheer them up a little."

But Luther shook his head. "They won't care. They just care about . . . well, books and things. But words and numbers, they never made much sense to me." He leaned forward and stared straight into Frank's eyes, as if determined to make him understand. "They said I was just lazy and didn't try, but I'm not lazy. I work really

166

hard at gymnastics. I know how to work. But it didn't matter how hard I tried. I just couldn't get it. Did you ever hear of anything like that?"

Frank remembered that Luther thought he was a professor. "Lots of people aren't good in school but are good at other things."

Luther nodded. "I knew it."

"Luther!" They both looked up to see Cornelius Raymond standing in the doorway, frowning in disapproval. "Your mother is asking for you."

Luther winced but he got to his feet. "Excuse me."

Frank nodded, then nodded to Raymond, who glared back. When Luther reached him, he said, "Why were you talking to him?"

Then they walked out and Frank didn't hear Luther's reply. Raymond was going to tell Luther who Frank was and make him feel bad for confiding in him. Frank was sorry for that, but not too sorry, because he now understood how frustrated Luther Northrup must have been all of his life to have his little sister excel at all the things he couldn't do. Could he have become so frustrated a week ago that he'd murdered her in the heat of passion, as Miss Billingsly had said so well?

Frank fervently hoped not.

Sarah had fixed herself a plate and was nibbling at it in a corner of the dining room when Irene

Raymond saw her. She wasn't happy. "Is it really necessary for you to be here?"

"Is it really any of your business?" Sarah replied as kindly as she could.

Irene flinched in surprise. Obviously, she hadn't expected a reply like that. "Abigail was my dearest friend."

"Then you should be glad someone is trying to find out who killed her."

"I am, of course, but you can't expect to find that person here. These are all the people who loved her."

Sarah thought of Miss Billingsly and Professor Pelletier, who certainly hadn't loved her, but she said, "People are murdered by their loved ones every day."

"What a terrible thing to say!" she said, trying to keep her voice low but not succeeding very well.

"Terrible but true. Miss Raymond, Mr. Malloy and I are trying very hard not to draw attention to ourselves or cause the Northrups any embarrassment, but you're making that difficult."

Irene clapped a hand over her mouth and glanced around. Sure enough, several people were looking at them curiously. "I . . . I'm sorry. It's just . . . It's so terrible . . ." Her voice broke and she began to weep.

Sarah hastily found a spot to set down her plate and put her arm around Irene. "It is terrible, and you have every right to be angry." She guided her out into the hallway, away from the curious onlookers.

Irene had pulled out her handkerchief and was making use of it. Sarah led her to a corner by the stairs, near the kitchen door, away from the crowd. "Do you want me to get someone for you?" Sarah asked.

Irene shook her head and blew her nose. "No, I'll be fine. I just . . . I'm so frightened."

"I really don't think you have anything to worry about. Whoever killed Abigail wouldn't—"

"I'm not afraid of being murdered," she snapped, angry again. "I'm afraid to find out who it is. In fact, the more I think about it, the surer I am that I don't want to know at all."

"Because you think it's someone you know?"

"Why can't it be a stranger? Someone who was trying to rob her or . . . or attack her or something?"

"Because she wasn't robbed, and she wasn't attacked, not that way."

Irene shook her head. "I know. I know all that. It's just . . ." She looked up at Sarah and grabbed her arm in a painful grip. "Abigail wasn't always . . . nice."

"What do you mean?"

"I mean she was rather . . . selfish. Not cruel, not really, but she had a strict idea of the way things should be, and she could be nasty when some-one didn't meet her standards."

Sarah felt sure Irene had borne the brunt of Abigail's nastiness a time or two. "And you think she might've made someone angry enough to . . . to do what they did?"

"I know she could. She's made me angry enough to throttle her, and if she did it to the wrong person . . ."

And Sarah was certain she had. "Thank you for telling me this."

"But if she drove that person to it . . . It wouldn't be that person's fault, would it? Not really."

"That isn't my decision to make."

"Please, Mrs. Malloy . . ."

But Sarah never learned what she was going to ask. Suddenly, her brother loomed over them. "What's going on here?"

"Nothing!" Irene said, and Sarah thought she almost sounded afraid.

"Your sister was upset. I brought her out here so she could compose herself."

"And you're probably the one who upset her," he said.

"No, she wasn't," Irene said. "I just started crying, thinking about poor Abigail, and I couldn't stop. Cory, will you take me home?"

Sarah stepped out of the way, earning a glare from Raymond, but he took his sister's arm tenderly. "Of course."

Irene gave her a beseeching glance as she

walked away. Sarah only wished she knew what it was for.

They caught the train back to the city that evening. Taking advantage of a nearly empty car, they flipped a seat back so Gino could sit facing them for the trip.

"I didn't see anything out of the ordinary," he reported. "I guess everybody in town knew about the funeral. A lot of folks made a point of walking by the house and some of them even stopped to get a better look, but it was mostly families or couples. Nobody who looked like he escaped from the asylum and was hunting for somebody else to murder."

"That's good to know, Gino," Frank said, not bothering to hide his grin.

"I saw you talking to the brother, though. What'd he have to say for himself?"

"You talked to Luther?" Sarah asked in surprise.

"Yeah. He's a sad case, I'm afraid."

"He didn't look very sad at the funeral," she said. "He was practically the only one in the room who wasn't crying."

"He might be glad she's gone. From what he said, his family thought he was a lazy bum, so compared to the outstanding Miss Abigail, he looked even worse."

"He did say he wasn't a scholar when I saw him at Miss Wilson's house the other day," she said.

"From what he told me, he's dumb as a post, at least when it comes to books and school."

"How did he happen to mention that?" Sarah asked.

"He thought I was one of the professors from the Normal School. He wanted to know if I'd ever heard of somebody who tried really hard but couldn't do well in school."

"What did you tell him?"

"I told him I did. I didn't do well in school myself."

She smiled at that. "Maybe he should become a detective."

"Too late. He's a gymnast."

"Is he?" Gino asked, obviously impressed. "Those fellows are really strong."

"Not only that, but the New York Athletic Club has offered him a job."

"Doing what?" she asked.

"Probably training fat rich men to be gymnasts."

"Not gymnasts," Gino said. "They train them to be physically fit, though. He'd probably know all about that."

"How do *you* know all about it?" Sarah asked.

"When I was in the army in Cuba, we had a lot of rich New York boys with us. They belong to clubs like that."

"Roosevelt recruited the sons of all his rich friends for the Rough Riders," Frank reminded her.

"And we had weeks and weeks of doing nothing but training to talk about things," Gino added.

"I see," Sarah said. "I guess that would be a good job for someone like Luther, then."

"Not something that would impress his parents, though," Frank said. "According to him, they're only impressed by academic accomplishments."

"So he had good reason to resent his sister," Gino said.

"And maybe he had good reason to hate her," Sarah said. "I had an interesting conversation with Irene Raymond. She told me that Abigail could be nasty to people who didn't meet her standards."

"Nasty?" Gino echoed in surprise.

"Her exact word. I didn't have any trouble believing her either. I've known women like that. They're usually bright and accomplished and do everything perfectly, and they don't have any patience for those who don't."

"Nobody else said anything about that," Frank said.

"Probably because people don't like to speak ill of the dead," Sarah said. "Especially when they've died tragically."

"I guess Bathsheba doesn't care about speaking ill of the dead, because she said something like that, too. I didn't think much of it at the time, because I thought she might've just imagined it since she hated Abigail so much, but she said Abigail only cared about people who could do something for her. She also thought Abigail made fun of Miss Billingsly when she was talking to Miss Wilson in French."

"Sounds like she was a piece of work. So maybe she was lording it over her brother for years, and he finally couldn't stand it anymore," Frank said.

"That's easy to imagine, isn't it?" Sarah said. "Irene even asked me if Abigail had goaded someone until they were angry enough to kill her, would it really be that person's fault?"

"What did you tell her?" Gino asked in amazement.

"That it wasn't my place to judge, of course, but it's an interesting question. She must also be thinking Luther could have done it."

"Maybe not," Frank said. "Don't forget, Irene's own brother also had a reason to be angry with Abigail, and Irene is more likely to be concerned about him than Luther."

"So the first thing we should do is find out where Luther and Raymond were on the day Abigail was killed," Gino said.

Frank nodded his approval. "It should be easy enough to check the New York Athletic Club and find out if Luther was staying there last Wednesday."

"I can do that tomorrow," Gino said.

"How will you find out about Cory Raymond?" Sarah asked.

"That'll be harder. He must have a job some-where. We could check with his office to see if he was at work that day."

"I think he mentioned the name of the company he worked for in one of the letters we found," Sarah said. "I'll find it when we get home."

"Give the name to Gino, then," Frank said. "He can go back up to Tarrytown and sniff around."

Gino's smile threatened to split his face.

"But let's not forget about Miss Wilson and Miss Billingsly," Sarah said. "Miss Billingsly was behaving very strangely today. We had a conversation with them on the way to the cemetery," she added for Gino's benefit.

"What did they say?"

"It was more how they were acting. I didn't expect Miss Billingsly to be sad about Abigail's death, and yet she was the one who cried the most during the funeral."

"Maybe she's the killer and she was crying because she feels guilty," Gino said.

"That certainly crossed my mind," Sarah said, "but when we were in the carriage, she seemed to be baiting Miss Wilson. Is that what it seemed like to you?" she asked Frank.

"Yeah, it did. What was all that about Abigail being like a daughter to them?"

"Miss Billingsly said having Abigail in their house was like having a daughter," Sarah explained to Gino.

"That would make sense, considering their ages," Gino said.

"But Miss Wilson took offense for some reason," Sarah said. "She actually seemed angry."

"She took offense at most of what Miss Billingsly said," Frank said. "What do you think was going on?"

"Something private, certainly," Sarah said. "Something only they understood. Malloy and I believe that having Abigail there somehow ruined their long friendship."

"Bathsheba thought it did. Like I told you, she thought Abigail set out on purpose to win Miss Wilson over and come between her and Miss Billingsly," Gino said.

"They certainly don't seem close now," Sarah said. "Miss Wilson was appalled that Miss Billingsly was subjecting her to her veiled abuse in front of us. And now that I've had time to think about it more, I get the oddest feeling that she was afraid."

"Who, Miss Billingsly?" Frank asked.

"Yes."

"Afraid of us?"

"I didn't get that impression, since she was baiting Miss Wilson right in front of us, and not afraid of Miss Wilson either, but . . . I just don't know, which is why I'm so confused. What would she be afraid of?"

"The killer?" Gino asked.

"Or maybe finding out who the killer is," Frank said, thinking back to the conversation. "It seems like that's what everybody's afraid of."

"The killer would be afraid of that, of course, but why would anyone else?" Sarah asked.

"Maybe because they're afraid it's someone they care about," Gino said.

"But didn't they all care about Abigail, too?" she argued. "Except for Miss Billingsly, and she's one of the frightened ones, so she's probably not the killer."

"Unless she's afraid we'll find out it's her," Frank said.

Sarah sighed. "As I said, it's very confusing. Did either of you get a chance to speak to Pelletier?"

Gino shook his head, and Frank said, "No, I never saw him after we went back to the house. I think he left."

"That was rude," Sarah said. "Hardly anyone from the school was there in the first place."

"They probably think the memorial service at the school is enough," Frank said.

"Will her family be invited?" Gino asked.

"I hope so, although I wonder if her parents will want to attend," Sarah said. "Being in the place where she was murdered would be very difficult for them, I'm sure."

"Maybe they'll send Luther," Frank said, earning a scowl from Sarah.

They spent some time telling Gino about their visit with the Raymonds the day before.

"So now we don't have any idea where Abigail got that ring," Gino said when they were finished.

"No, although we haven't shown it to her mother yet," Sarah said. "I wouldn't expect her father to know much about what jewelry she owned, but her mother probably would. We should show it to her before we start coming up with any more wild theories."

"How do you propose to do that?" Frank asked.

"I was thinking I'd wait a few days and then visit her."

"Let's hope we have this solved before then," Frank said. "Meanwhile, Gino will find out if Luther and Cory were in New York the day Abigail was killed."

"And what are you going to do?" Gino asked.

Frank sighed. "I'm going to visit Bathsheba and see if I can find out more about what's going on in that house."

8

"Your hair is getting very long," Mrs. Ellsworth told Catherine. Their neighbor had come by earlier, and Sarah had been visiting with her in her private parlor when Maeve brought Catherine in to join them.

"Maeve says it's straggly," Catherine said. "She's going to cut it today."

"Oh my," Mrs. Ellsworth said, looking over at Maeve in alarm. "You can't cut her hair today."

"Why not?" Maeve said with perfect innocence, although Sarah noted she didn't so much as glance in Sarah's direction, knowing they would both probably burst out laughing at what was most certainly one of Mrs. Ellsworth's strange superstitions.

"Because you can only cut a person's hair on Monday, Tuesday, or Wednesday."

"Do barbers know this?" Maeve asked, still not meeting Sarah's gaze.

Mrs. Ellsworth waved the question away. "If you cut someone's hair on Thursday, Friday, or Saturday, you will never grow rich."

"Oh, so I'm the one who has to be careful," Maeve said. "But what about Sunday?"

" 'Best never be born than Sunday shorn,' " Mrs. Ellsworth quoted. "And you must burn the hair clippings so . . ." She glanced at Catherine, who was staring up at her, wide-eyed. She obviously decided not to explain in front of the child the potentially dire consequences of leaving hair clippings unburned. "So they don't make a mess."

"Burn them?" Maeve made a face. "Have you ever smelled burning hair?"

"Of course I have."

Sarah had to assume Mrs. Ellsworth had been burning hair clippings her entire life. "You could burn them outside," she said just to tease Maeve.

Maeve was too fond of Mrs. Ellsworth to actually roll her eyes right in front of the woman, so she said, "I suppose I could."

"I'd recommend it, dear," Mrs. Ellsworth said in all seriousness. "And what are you and Maeve planning to do today, Miss Catherine?"

"Play inside. It's too cold to go for a walk."

"Then why don't you come over to my house. I was going to make cookies."

Catherine's eyes lit up. "I love cookies."

"I know you do, dear."

"May I go, Mama?"

"Of course you may," Sarah said with a smile, "if it's all right with Maeve."

"It's certainly all right with Maeve," Maeve said with a grin. "I love cookies, too, and I'm going with you."

"Well, then, just give your mother and me a few

more minutes to finish our conversation, and we'll go," Mrs. Ellsworth said.

Catherine obediently jumped to her feet. "Thank you very much, Mrs. Ellsworth." She scurried over and gave Sarah a kiss, and Maeve escorted her back to the nursery.

"She's growing into a lovely young lady," Mrs. Ellsworth said when they were gone.

"Yes, she is. We've been trying to decide where to send her to school."

"Oh, speaking of school, Maeve told me you're investigating a murder at the Normal School."

"Mr. Malloy is investigating," Sarah clarified.

"But you're helping, surely. You attended the poor young lady's funeral yesterday, I understand."

Nothing happened on Bank Street that Mrs. Ellsworth didn't know all about. "Yes. It's so sad. She had a promising future ahead of her."

"As a teacher, you mean?"

"I suppose she would have become a professor eventually. The lady she lived with had recently become the first female professor at the college."

"Times are certainly changing. Did you say it was the lady she lived with?"

"Yes, she was renting a room in the house where two of the other female instructors lived."

"It was a rooming house, then."

"No, Miss Wilson, the professor, owns the house. She shared it with Miss Billingsly, and Abigail had recently joined them."

"Are these two ladies related?"

"Not that I know of."

"Oh my, times really are changing! My father would never have let me live on my own with people who were no relation. If I hadn't married, I would probably still be living in his house."

"I'm sure her parents thought she'd be well chaperoned by the two older ladies."

"I don't think I've ever heard of such a thing before, two unmarried, unrelated females living together in their own home."

"It isn't often that unmarried females can afford to have their own home," Sarah said. "They call it a Boston marriage."

"Really? Why on earth do they call it that?"

"Because Mr. Henry James talked about it in one of his novels that was set in Boston."

"I've heard they do strange things in Boston."

Sarah bit back a smile. "Women's colleges are changing a lot of things."

"I suppose so. They train young ladies to be teachers, don't they?"

"And for other professions as well. Social work, for instance. And you'll even see female doctors now."

"That can only be an improvement," Mrs. Ellsworth said. "So this poor girl who was murdered was living with these two female professors."

Sarah decided not to bother explaining that

Miss Billingsly wasn't a full professor. "That's right. They had a spare bedroom, and when . . ."

"Is something wrong?" Mrs. Ellsworth asked when Sarah hesitated.

"What? Oh no, I just . . . I just remembered something I noticed when I was visiting that house. I didn't think anything of it at the time, but now it seems . . . odd."

"How odd?" Mrs. Ellsworth asked with interest.

"Oh, not odd really," Sarah said quickly to deflect her interest. "I was exaggerating. It was just unusual, I suppose. What kind of cookies are you going to make? Malloy is partial to the shortbread, you know."

During his many years as an Irish police detective, Frank had often been sent around to the back door when he called on the wealthier residents of the city. He didn't think Miss Wilson and Miss Billingsly qualified as wealthy, but he also knew he'd probably find their maid a little more friendly if he saved her the walk to the front door.

Bathsheba answered his knock wearing a disgruntled frown that deepened when she recognized him. "The ladies ain't home."

"I know. I came to see you." When she looked as if she was going to slam the door in his face, he held up the box he carried. "I brought you something."

She eyed the small white box suspiciously. "What is it?"

"Bonbons."

"What's that?"

"Chocolate candy."

"For me?"

"All of it, if you let me in so we can have a little chat."

She sniffed derisively, but she stepped back to let him inside.

He wiped his feet and went in. The warmth of the kitchen enveloped him, and he couldn't help his sigh of relief.

"Cold out there, is it?" she asked. "Give me your coat."

She took it and hung it over a chair. Then she accepted the box that he presented to her. "Don't think this'll make any difference in what I tell you. Nothing that happens in this house is your business."

"Do things happen in this house you don't want to talk about?"

"Course not!" she snapped, irritated now.

"Well, then, you shouldn't mind talking to me. Can I sit down?"

"Suit yourself," she said, jerking her chin toward the kitchen table. "I wouldn't mind sitting for a while myself. You'll want some coffee, I expect."

She poured them each a cup, then took the chair

at right angles to his. She set the box down right in front of her but made no move to open it. "I would've thought that young fella you sent already found out what you needed to know."

"He's young and hasn't been doing this long, and I didn't realize how important you were until after he was here."

This pleased her, although she tried to pretend she was offended. "I'm just the maid."

"Which means you know more about your people than they do. We know a little more about Miss Northrup now than we did when Gino was here, too. For instance, I know she wasn't always nice to people."

"Who told you that?"

"A good friend of hers, so we believed it."

"I told your boy the same thing. Didn't you believe me?" she challenged.

She had him there. "Let's just say we thought you had good reason not to like her, but her friend didn't. This friend said she had high standards and wasn't very . . . *understanding* if someone didn't meet them."

"Oh, that. Can't fault a person for wanting things done right, can you?" she asked with a sly grin.

"I don't suppose you can, but . . . Well, did she have a temper?"

"Do you mean did she get mad easy? No, she didn't. She had good manners, that one. Knew how to act and how to hide what she was really feeling."

"I guess that does take good manners," Frank said, sipping his coffee. "I'm still working on that one myself."

Bathsheba grinned knowingly. "Me, too."

"But you think she sometimes hid what she was really feeling."

"Everybody does, don't they? But her, she always looked like butter wouldn't melt in her mouth."

"Did she ever get mad at Miss Wilson or Miss Billingsly?"

"If she did, she never let on," she said carefully.

"Are they hard to get along with?"

"Not at all! There was never a harsh word said in this house until—"

Frank waited but she pressed her lips together, determined not to finish her sentence. "Until Miss Northrup came," he guessed. "So if Miss Northrup didn't get mad at them, did they get mad at her?"

"They's ladies, Mr. Malloy. Fine ladies. They don't yell at each other like they do in the tenements."

"But Miss Billingsly wasn't happy to have her here, was she?"

"You'd have to ask her that."

"We did, and she said she wasn't. She said it made more work for you."

Bathsheba seemed genuinely surprised. "She did? Ain't that nice of her."

"And she was jealous, wasn't she?" Frank said, taking a chance.

"What'd she have to be jealous about?" Bathsheba said, although he could see his question had shaken her.

"Of Miss Wilson's affections. You told Gino she and Miss Billingsly were close friends all those years, living here happily until Miss Northrup arrived. She came between them, didn't she?"

"I don't know what you mean," Bathsheba said with a frown.

"Yes, you do. Miss Wilson liked her better than she liked Miss Billingsly. That's why Miss Billingsly started drinking, isn't it?"

"You don't know nothing about it," she tried, but he could see the alarm flaring in her eyes.

"I know Miss Northrup caused trouble. You said she didn't argue with Miss Billingsly, and you said Miss Billingsly and Miss Wilson didn't argue with each other, but . . . wait, it was Miss Northrup and Miss Wilson, wasn't it? They were the ones who argued."

"No, it wasn't like that. They wasn't fighting, not like you think."

"How was it, then?"

Bathsheba was angry now, aware that he had tricked her. "They had words one time. They wasn't yelling. Ladies like them, they didn't raise their voices, but they was both upset. You could tell that."

"What were they arguing about?"

"I told you, it wasn't like that. They . . . I couldn't hear much. Like I said, they didn't raise their voices, but it was something about a letter."

"Do you know what letter it was?"

"No."

Had Miss Wilson discovered Abigail's secret correspondence with Cornelius Raymond? That certainly could have made her angry enough to attack Abigail. "One of the letters my wife found when she was here?"

Bathsheba shrugged and fiddled with her coffee cup. "I reckon."

He could see she knew something she didn't want to tell him. "We know she got other letters that we didn't find. If we find out you're hiding them . . ."

"I ain't hiding nothing, and if you mean those French letters, I don't know nothing about them."

Frank gaped at her. *"French letters?"*

Bathsheba winced, and for a moment he thought she'd realized she'd used the slang term for condoms in front of a strange man, but that wasn't it at all. "She got some letters that was written in French," she reluctantly admitted.

Frank didn't bother to feel relieved. "You're sure it was French?"

"Well, I don't know for sure. The handwriting

was all foreign-looking, and the name of the person who sent it was right strange. I couldn't read the name of the town neither, and she told me it was in France. She was real happy to get it."

"Did she get a lot of letters from France?"

"A few, since she's been here. She visited France in the summer, she told me. She said . . ."

"What did she say?"

Bathsheba frowned. "She said she never really knew how to talk French until she went there. But that's silly. She learned how to talk it in school, didn't she? She learned it so good, she was hired to teach it."

Frank had no idea how to answer that. "Do you know what happened to those letters? The ones in French?"

"No. Your wife, she looked all over Miss Northrup's room, and all she found was the ones under the mattress. I never did figure out why Miss Northrup'd hide letters from her friend under the mattress."

Frank wasn't going to enlighten her. "Would you mind if I took another look in her old room? Maybe she had a hiding spot Mrs. Malloy didn't find."

Bathsheba frowned again. "No, sir. Miss Billingsly, she done moved into that room now, and I don't reckon she'd want no man poking around in her things."

He didn't suppose she would, but how strange.

Why had Miss Billingsly moved from the room she'd had for years into the one Abigail had used? If it was a nicer room, why hadn't she chosen it in the first place? He didn't suppose Miss Billingsly would tell him the answers to those questions, and he was sure Bathsheba wouldn't, even if she knew, but maybe Sarah could figure it out. "Well, if you happen to find anything, would you let me know?"

He gave her one of his expensive cards, because he wanted her to feel flattered. He thanked her for her help.

"She had a room at the school," Bathsheba said as he rose from his chair. "An office. Maybe she kept the letters there."

Frank figured she was just trying to distract him from wanting to search the house, but he actually thought it was a possibility. He had already looked through her desk, but if this letter was so important, she might have hidden it well. He hadn't really searched the rest of the room either. "That's a good suggestion."

Gino looked up at the imposing eight-story gray stone building that took up the entire block at 55th Street and Sixth Avenue. The New York Athletic Club counted many of the city's elite among its members, and they demanded the best facilities. Inside, the lobby seemed more like a hotel than a place men went to sweat. A smartly dressed young man greeted him with cool reserve. Gino knew the fellow had judged his clothes as tailor-made, which meant he was successful, but he couldn't do anything about his Italian face, which meant he wouldn't usually be welcome at a club like this.

Pretending he didn't notice the lukewarm reception, Gino stepped up to the counter and gave the young fellow a big smile. "I'm supposed to meet a friend here, Luther Northrup. Is he around?"

"I don't believe he is."

"Donnie, is that you?" a voice nearly shouted.

Gino turned to find Fred Vander Hooten grinning at him. "Vandy, how are you?"

Vandy pumped his hand and slapped him on the back a few times while they exchanged greetings. "This fellow was in the Rough Riders with me," Vandy informed the man behind the desk. "Are you a member here now?" he asked Gino.

"They wouldn't let me in here," Gino said with a grin, as if it were a joke.

"We'll see about that. Rudy, this is Gino Donatelli. Gino, Rudy Ledbetter here is the man to see about whatever you might need. Rudy, you can sign Mr. Donatelli in as my guest. Come on, let me buy you lunch, Donnie."

Lunch was an elaborate affair in a dining room with wood-paneled walls and a crystal chandelier. The waiters wore uniforms and white gloves. Vandy was the son of one of the old Knickerbocker families, so he had a lot of time to spend at clubs like this one. He was fascinated to learn that Gino was a private investigator now and working on a case.

"Luther Northrup, eh? Terrible thing about his sister."

"You know him, then?"

"Not well, but everybody was talking about it. She was a teacher or something, wasn't she?"

"Yes, at the Normal School. What do you know about him?"

"Good gymnast. An expert on the rings. You can't imagine how hard that is."

"Yes, I can! Did you know the club offered him a job?"

"They did? Bully! Maybe I can get him to train me."

"He'd like that, I'm sure. Does he spend much time here?"

"Oh yes. He keeps a room here, I think. His family lives upstate somewhere, and it's too far to go back and forth every day."

"He must've been pretty upset about his sister."

"I expect so. Wouldn't know it to look at him, though. He's the manly sort."

Gino had noticed that. "Would somebody know what days he was here and what days he wasn't?"

"I expect so. What days are you interested in?"

"Last Wednesday."

Vandy scratched his head. "I couldn't tell you. I

was probably here. I'm here most days, but I don't keep track. Rudy would probably know, though. Tell him I said he should help you. You should think about joining the club. A lot of the other fellows are here. Have to keep strong in case the old man gets us into another war," he said with a laugh.

"Roosevelt's just a governor, and governors don't start wars, so I think we're safe," Gino said.

"How long do you think Roosevelt's going to be satisfied in Albany? You better sign up here so you're ready. I'd be glad to sponsor you."

Gino had to promise to think about it, even though he was pretty sure they wouldn't admit an Italian detective to a club like this. After lunch, he sent Vandy off to throw around some Indian clubs and went back to the front desk.

Ledbetter was much friendlier this time. "Mr. Northrup hasn't come in yet."

"He must've forgotten we were supposed to meet. Say, can you tell me if he was here last Wednesday?"

Ledbetter's smile slipped a few notches. "Why would you need to know that?"

Gino pretended to look around to make sure they weren't overheard, then he leaned in closer. "I've got a bet going, and I need to know where Northrup was that day. I know he keeps a room here. Do you have a record of what nights he uses it?"

Gino had put his hand in his pocket and now he pulled it out with a folded dollar bill in his palm, which he made sure Ledbetter saw. A dollar would be a day's pay for someone like him.

"We're not allowed to talk about the habits of our members, you understand," he said as he pulled a ledger book out from underneath the counter. Then he opened it and flipped the pages until he found the one he wanted. He laid the book down on the countertop, turned it slightly so Gino could read it, then walked away to greet a member who had just come in.

Gino glanced at the book and saw it was a register of sorts where guests signed in for the sleeping rooms. He easily found Luther Northrup's name. He'd come in on Monday of last week and stayed over Tuesday night. He hadn't stayed on Wednesday night, though. He'd probably gone home after hearing of his sister's murder.

But he'd been in the city on the morning she'd died, at least.

He tucked the dollar bill into the book and closed it, then wished Ledbetter a good afternoon and left.

Frank waited until the afternoon to visit Abigail's former office. He'd noticed that the classes were mostly in the morning and the building was much quieter in the afternoon. The fewer students he saw, the less panic he would cause, he reasoned.

He did encounter a handful of young ladies who were startled at first and then quickly scurried away, whispering urgently to each other. At last he came to the office and was pleased to see Pelletier was there.

"Malloy, I am glad to see you," he said, rising to his feet and shaking Frank's hand like they were old friends. "The strangest thing happened."

"What's that?"

"Well, I come back to my office a few minutes ago, and the door, it was not locked."

"Maybe you forgot to lock it when you left the last time."

"*Mais non*, I am sure I lock it. I have been *très prudent* after . . . Well, after poor Miss Northrup . . . I remember I lock it this morning, because I drop the key and almost drop the books I carry when I try to pick it up. Then when I return . . ." He gave one of his Frenchy shrugs.

He did look a little distressed.

Frank remembered Tobias telling him that first day that he didn't have a key to this room, but he decided to test Pelletier. "Maybe the janitor cleaned while you were gone and forgot to lock it."

"*Au contraire*, only two keys exist, one to me and one to Miss Northrup. I insist to open the door for the janitor myself. I do not like anyone to access my things. The person who opened the door must have her key. Do you know who that could be?"

A little frisson of excitement shivered down Frank's spine. "Her keys haven't been found, at least not that I know of. We think the killer took them."

Now he really did look distressed. "*Mon Dieu*, that is a horrible thought. He has been with the keys all this time. He might have . . ." He gestured helplessly.

"Yes, he might've," Frank agreed, thinking there was a key to Miss Wilson's house among them, too. "Is anything missing?"

"I do not think so. My desk, he is locked always, of course. Nothing else was disturbed, I do not think. I did not look in the desk of Miss Northrup. I did not want to presume, and I would not know if anything was missing, *non*?"

Frank well remembered how Pelletier had insisted he didn't normally lock his desk, but he didn't mention it. "I came today to pack up her things for her parents," Frank said, indicating the wooden crate he carried under one arm, "so I'll be glad to check to see if anything is missing."

"But how would you . . . ? Ah, *mais oui*, I remember. You look in her desk when you are here before."

"And I didn't see anything of value or even of interest then. Nothing worth stealing, at least, but I'll notice if anything is gone." Without waiting to be invited, Frank set the crate on the floor and plopped himself down in the chair at Abigail's desk. Everything looked the same as it had on Monday, so if the killer really had come in, he'd been very neat.

Frank wanted to search the room thoroughly, and he didn't want to do it in front of Pelletier. He considered asking him to leave, but that would probably make Pelletier suspicious and more likely to stay. Frank decided to be obnoxious instead. He started to hum tunelessly and earned a frown from Pelletier, which he pretended not to notice. Then he scooted his chair back abruptly and bumped into Pelletier's. "Oh, sorry. There's not much room in here, is there?"

"Miss Northrup, she is much smaller," he said coldly, turning back to his papers.

"Are these her books?" Frank asked, indicating the shelf over her desk.

Pelletier looked up from his work again, clearly annoyed. "Everything on that side is hers."

"Thanks." Frank started pulling the books down off the shelf and slapping them onto the desktop as loudly as possible.

Pelletier rose from his seat and gathered up the papers he'd been reading. "I will leave you now. I will be in the library. If you will please to let me know when you are finished."

"Oh, sure. Hope I'm not driving you off."

Pelletier gave him a sour smile and left. Frank waited until his footsteps had died away, and then he started searching the desk. Or at least that had been his intention, but when he opened the top drawer, he stopped dead. In the drawer were several things that had not been there three days ago. The first thing he saw was the last thing he'd expected: Abigail's keys. Or at least someone's keys, and he was pretty sure they would prove to be hers.

Sure enough, when he tried the smallest key on her desk, it worked perfectly. One of the others worked on the office door. The third one would probably fit Miss Wilson's house. A long brown ribbon was attached to the ring, probably so she could wear them round her neck if she chose. Ladies often didn't have convenient pockets for such things. The other thing he found in the drawer was a packet of letters tied with a ribbon similar to the one securing the letters Sarah had found under Abigail's mattress.

He was sure neither the letters nor the keys had been in the desk on Monday when he'd searched it. This meant that whoever had taken Abigail's keys—and it was most likely her killer—had probably come into the office at some time after her death and taken the letters. Then this person had returned both the letters and the keys today, probably because they didn't want to be caught with them. He'd left the door unlocked because he had to leave the key in the desk.

But why go to all this trouble? Letters could be

burned, and the keys could have been tossed into the river or somewhere else where they'd never be found. Was the killer too naïve to think of this? Had he simply returned them because he didn't know what else to do with them? Sarah would probably tell him it was just good manners to return someone else's property. He supposed he'd have to get used to well-mannered killers if he was going to deal with society.

He slipped the ribbon off the letters and flipped through them. Some of them were from Irene Raymond. He pulled one out of its envelope and saw it was in her handwriting, so these would be the letters she told them she'd written herself to Abigail. He also saw a few from other females, probably more friends of Abigail's. No letters from any other young men, however; but to his delight, he saw that several of them were from France.

Just as Bathsheba had described, the return addresses were in French, the spidery handwriting almost too ornate to read. He pulled a couple of them from their envelopes, but the letters were also written in French. He'd have to find someone to read them. For one fleeting moment he considered Pelletier; but no, he was too close to the murdered girl. He might even lie about what the letters said if he thought it would embarrass the school or someone who worked there. He might even try to protect Abigail. Frank would have to find someone who hadn't even known Abigail or anyone else involved with her.

After tucking the letters into the crate, Frank began his systematic search of the desk, emptying every drawer and then checking to make sure nothing was underneath or behind it and that he hadn't missed any secret compartments. He even looked under the desk and pulled it away from the wall to check the back side. He found nothing else that hadn't been there the last time he'd searched. Finally, he looked at each of the books he'd pulled from her shelf and left lying on top of the desk when Pelletier had gone.

He fanned the pages and felt the bindings to see if she'd hidden anything in any of them. He found it in the third book he picked up, a thick volume that was probably a dictionary except it was in French, so he couldn't tell for sure. When he fanned the pages, three more letters that had been tucked inside slipped out. The paper was expensive and delicate, making it thin enough to hide in the large, heavy book. Unfortunately, these letters were also in French.

Maybe they were simply messages from friends she'd made while she was visiting France last summer, but why would she have hidden these particular letters? Maybe they were from a lover, possibly the one who had given her the ring. If she was secretly engaged to a Frenchman, she'd certainly want to keep that a secret. But he wouldn't know for sure about anything until he found someone who could read the letters.

Maybe Sarah's parents knew someone French.

"This is making me wish I'd paid more attention when I studied French in school," Sarah said, frowning over the letters. She and Malloy were in their private sitting room at home, where they could talk without the children interrupting them.

"You said the same thing when we were in France," Malloy said.

"I know, but this time it's really important. I'm trying to think if I know anyone who speaks French well, and I can't."

"Do you think your mother would?"

"Oh, what a good idea. She probably does, and she'll be thrilled to help you on a case. Even my father can't object since it's not the least bit dangerous."

"Unless the person she knows is some slippery French count who wants to seduce her."

Sarah smiled at the memory from their honeymoon. "He wasn't really a count, and I'm sure he wasn't trying to seduce me."

"Well, I'm not."

Sarah laughed at his disgruntled frown. "Anyway, he's far away now, and I can't imagine my mother knows any counts, slippery or otherwise. But she might know someone French. I'll telephone and ask her."

"Good."

"I still can't help wondering why the killer took the other letters from Abigail's desk." They had read through the ones in English, the ones from Irene Raymond and Abigail's other friends, and found nothing of interest. The French ones in the desk were probably equally unimportant, since Abigail had made no effort to conceal them, but the hidden ones were another story.

"We don't know for sure that it was the killer who took them," Malloy said. "All we know is someone had her keys and borrowed the letters."

"But whatever they were looking for wasn't in those letters or they wouldn't have returned them. And you're sure whoever it was hadn't found these other ones?"

"As sure as I can be. If they had, they obviously decided what's in them isn't important either and returned them, but why bother to put them back in the book? Just throw them in the drawer with the others."

"And they were well hidden, I guess."

"You had to be searching the book on purpose to find them, so Abigail didn't want anyone to see them. I guess when we find out what they say, we'll know why."

"That could take a while. What are you going to do in the meantime?"

"I haven't decided yet."

"While you're thinking, I remembered something today when I was talking to Mrs. Ellsworth."

Malloy grinned. "Ah, Mrs. Ellsworth! I hope you didn't do anything that'll bring us bad luck."

"It was a near thing!" she said with mock horror. "Did you know you should only cut someone's hair on Monday, Tuesday, or Wednesday?"

"I had no idea."

"And Maeve was going to cut Catherine's hair today. If she had, she would never be rich."

"Then it *was* a near thing. Thank heaven Mrs. Ellsworth warns us about these things," he said, making her smile. "So what did she make you remember?"

"When we were at Miss Wilson's house and I went upstairs to search Abigail's room, remember?"

"Yes. Miss Billingsly had already gone up because she was stinking drunk."

"Malloy, ladies do not get stinking drunk. She was merely indisposed."

"She was *very* indisposed."

"And Bathsheba had put her to bed. I didn't think about it at the time, but there are only two bedrooms upstairs."

She gave him a minute to think that over, but he only needed a few seconds. "That's why Miss Billingsly moved into Abigail's room, then!"

9

Sarah frowned, obviously confused. "What do you mean, she moved into Abigail's room?"

"When I was questioning Bathsheba today and she told me about the letters Abigail had gotten from France, I started wondering if maybe she had a hiding place you'd missed, like loose floorboards or something. I asked if I could search the room again, but Bathsheba told me Miss Billingsly had moved into that room and she wouldn't want me going through her things. I couldn't figure out why she'd move from her room into Abigail's room."

"But she didn't have a room," Sarah said, still frowning. "At least not one of her own. She and Miss Wilson shared a room."

Frank considered this, trying to make sense of it. "Doesn't that seem strange? Wouldn't a grown woman who was sharing a house with someone want a room of her own?"

"I'm sure she would. So why would they be sharing for all those years when there was another bedroom available? Unless . . ."

"Unless what?"

"Unless Miss Billingsly had been using that room until Abigail came. Maybe Miss Billingsly moved in with Miss Wilson and gave her old room to Abigail," she said with a grin.

Frank grinned back. "That would've been very nice of her."

"Yes, considering she didn't like her and wasn't happy she moved in. And why would Miss Wilson inconvenience herself in her own house just to make room for Abigail?"

"Maybe you should ask her."

"Ask who? Miss Wilson?"

"Yes."

Sarah smiled sadly. "I can't imagine she'll want to talk to me again."

"Maybe not, but you have something she'll want."

"What's that?"

He pulled it out of his vest pocket. "Abigail's key to her house."

Sarah and her mother had spent most of the morning in the nursery being served imaginary tea by Catherine. When it was time for Catherine's lunch, they withdrew to Sarah's private parlor to visit.

"Are you ever going to tell me why you wanted to see me today?" her mother asked as soon as they were alone.

"Of course. I told you on the telephone, it's nothing for you to be concerned about."

Her mother took a seat on the sofa beside the

fireplace. "But it does concern a case you're working on, doesn't it?"

Sarah walked over to the cabinet and took out the slim packet of letters. "Yes, but I'm afraid you're going to be disappointed. I don't need you to question anyone or anything like that."

"You're right, I'm already disappointed, but you know I'll help, no matter what it is."

"We're investigating the murder of a young woman at the Normal School. Perhaps you read about it in the newspapers?"

"You know I only read the society pages in the newspapers," her mother said, eyeing the letters curiously. "But I may have noticed something about it. I thought it was a robbery."

"That's what the police decided when no one offered them any incentive to investigate."

"Ah, I see nothing has changed since Frank left the police department."

"Not much," Sarah agreed. "At any rate, her parents wanted to find out the truth, but they were afraid of a scandal in the press if the police were involved."

"So they hired Frank," her mother said, delighted. "And what have you found out?"

"Only that she was loved by all and no one could possibly have a reason to kill her."

Her mother sighed. "Isn't that always the case? One wonders how anyone gets themselves murdered, and yet they do, with alarming regularity."

Sarah didn't bother to hide her smile. "Yes, they do."

"So how can I help?"

"I'm not sure you can, but you were the only person Malloy and I could think of who might be able to. Do you know anyone who speaks French?"

"Most of the women I know studied it in school, and so did I, but that was a long time ago. I don't think any of us could speak it today."

"I know. I studied it, too, but that wasn't much help to me when we were in France. It certainly wasn't any help to me in figuring out what these letters say."

Sarah handed her the packet and she examined them briefly.

"They're in French."

Sarah smiled. "Yes, they are. I'm thinking we'll need someone who is a native of France to tell us what they say."

"And you think what they say will help you figure out who killed this young woman?"

"We hope so, but we can't be sure until we know what they say."

Her mother returned her smile. "Now I see your problem. And if the letters contain something scandalous, you also need the person who reads them to be discreet."

"Exactly right. Whatever is in these letters might very well be scandalous but have nothing at all to do with Miss Northrup's murder. We wouldn't want any stray gossip to ruin someone's reputation for no reason."

"Well, then," her mother said with satisfaction, "you've set me a very challenging task. This should keep me from being bored for days!"

That morning, Gino caught the train up to Tarrytown. He had to admit, it was a pretty place. A little quiet for his tastes, of course, but for people who hadn't ever lived in the city, he supposed it was all right. The air was sweeter, too. Oh, he could still smell the ever-present scent of horse manure, but they did a better job of keeping the streets clean here, so it wasn't bad at all. The main thing he noticed was the place didn't smell like garbage.

He found the building he was looking for easily. A three-story brick that took up the entire block, it housed several businesses. The first floor was entirely devoted to the Raymond family's company, however. He stepped into the office and to his surprise, he found a very responsible-looking girl secretary sitting at a desk just inside the small lobby. She looked up at him through wire-rimmed spectacles and smiled a greeting.

"May I help you?" She wore a white shirtwaist and paper guards on her cuffs to protect them from stains.

"I'd like to see Mr. Cornelius Raymond, if he's in."

"Cornelius, you said?" she asked with a tiny frown.

"Yes." He waited, knowing better than to explain anything. He didn't want to tell more lies than absolutely necessary.

"I'm afraid he's not in today."

"Will he be in later? I can wait."

"Did you have an appointment?"

"No, but he said just to stop in when I was in town." Gino gave her his most innocent smile.

She glanced around to make sure they were alone. "Mr. Cornelius Raymond doesn't keep regular hours here."

Since she looked uncomfortable sharing this information, Gino figured she meant more than she was actually saying. "And where does he keep regular hours?"

She smiled a little at this. "Well, he often goes to New York City."

"He's got a lady friend there, I think," Gino tried.

Her smile vanished. "He did, but . . . It was a terrible tragedy. She died, you see."

"Died? That is a tragedy. Poor Raymond! I feel terrible that I didn't know. How did it happen?"

She glanced around again, then leaned forward and whispered, "She was murdered."

Gino feigned shock. "How awful! But I guess things like that happen every day in a place like New York."

"Oh dear, I hope not!" she replied.

"Well, maybe not every day. Raymond must feel pretty bad. Was he in the city when it happened?"

"I suppose so. He was there all last week."

"You're sure of that?"

Her eyes widened in surprise, and Gino realized he'd been a little too eager with his question.

"I mean, he must feel terrible if it happened while he was there. Because he couldn't protect her."

"He did feel terrible, I know," she hedged.

"Do you know where he stays when he's in the city? I'd like to look him up and pay my condolences."

"I couldn't possibly give out that information," she said, no longer returning his smile.

"Oh, wait, it's the New York Athletic Club, isn't it? I think I've seen him there."

"Then perhaps you'll see him there again. Now, if you don't have any further business . . ."

Gino thanked her with all the charm he could muster, but she wasn't going to be charmed anymore. She turned back to her typing, silently dismissing him. He stepped out onto the sidewalk. The town had lost some of its appeal, and he wouldn't be sorry to leave it again. He tried to think if there was anyone else in town he could talk to. He didn't really have anything new to tell Abigail's parents, and he felt certain

Irene Raymond wouldn't be happy to see him.

But maybe if he went back to the New York Athletic Club, he could find someone.

After her mother left, Sarah waited until mid-afternoon to call on Miss Wilson, remembering that Miss Billingsly hadn't gotten home until after lunch the day Sarah had visited her. Bathsheba frowned when she opened the front door, but Sarah wasn't sure if her displeasure was personal or if she greeted all visitors that way.

"I'd like to see Miss Wilson, if she's at home. I have something to give her."

Bathsheba looked her up and down, probably noticing that she didn't seem to be carrying anything. The key, of course, was in her purse, but she wasn't going to explain anything to a maid, and she matched Bathsheba's intimidating stare with one of her own.

"Miss Wilson, you said?"

"That's right."

"I'll see if she's at home." Then she closed the door in Sarah's face.

Determined not to lose her temper, she waited patiently until Bathsheba opened the door again. She'd kept her waiting in the cold for a good ten minutes, far longer than the task of asking Miss Wilson if she was willing to see her visitor would have taken. Sarah knew it and Bathsheba knew she knew, and she didn't care. Without a word, she led Sarah to the parlor and closed the parlor door behind her.

"Didn't she even take your coat?" Miss Wilson asked in dismay. "I'll have to speak to her, I'm afraid. Please, allow me."

Sarah removed her coat and Miss Wilson laid it over a chair while Sarah went to the gas grate to warm her hands.

"I'm sorry to bother you," Sarah said. "But I wanted you to know that we found Miss Northrup's keys."

"Did you?" she asked stiffly. "I didn't know they were missing."

Which was a lie, if Miss Wilson had them all this time. "They were. She didn't have them when she was found, and they weren't in her office or her room here."

"Where did you find them?"

"Oddly enough, in her desk in her office."

"But you said—"

"Yes, Mr. Malloy had searched her desk on Monday, and they weren't there, although the desk was unlocked. Yesterday, when he returned to empty it, he found the keys and some letters that hadn't been there before. We think the killer took the letters and read them, then put them back again, along with the keys."

Miss Wilson held her face very still, revealing nothing. "How very strange."

"Yes, it is."

"And why do you think the . . . why would someone have done that?"

"We aren't sure, but we think it may have been to see what the letters said. Abigail told a friend that she'd discovered a scandal of some sort."

Alarm flared in Miss Wilson's eyes, but she managed to keep her composure. "What sort of scandal?"

"Abigail didn't say."

"And you didn't find anything in the letters?"

"Nothing important, no."

Miss Wilson's hands were clenched in white-knuckled fists, even though her face remained frozen. "Who were the letters from, do you know?"

"Some women who appeared to be school friends."

"Were any of the letters from someone in . . . in France?"

Sarah's mind was racing. So Miss Wilson knew about the letters Abigail had received from France, and if she was the killer, she'd know the answer to that question. Unless she was trying to learn if Malloy had found them where she had failed. How would Malloy answer her? Sarah had to think he'd be bold. "As a matter of fact, they were."

Alarm flickered across her entire face this time. "And yet, after reading them, you don't know what the scandal was?"

Sarah felt a shiver of excitement. Miss Wilson obviously believed the scandal was mentioned in the letters from France. "No. They were written in French. We haven't translated them yet."

Miss Wilson smiled bitterly. "Pelletier could read them for you."

Sarah managed an ironic smile. "I know he could."

The two women stared at each other for another long moment. Sarah had the impression Miss Wilson was taking her measure and wishing she could read Sarah's mind. Finally she said, "You must know, Mrs. Malloy, that I find discussing Abigail very distressing. If you have something for me, please give it to me and be on your way."

Sarah reached into her purse and pulled out the key. "I believe this is a key to your house."

Miss Wilson stared at it in surprise. If she was acting, she was very good. "Was this with her other keys?"

Sarah nodded.

Miss Wilson drew an unsteady breath. "When you said they were missing, I didn't realize . . ."

"Yes, and we believe the killer had it all this time, along with the keys to her desk and her office."

Miss Wilson continued to stare at the key for a long moment, until she realized Sarah was offering it to her and she needed to accept it. "Thank you," she said, taking it. "I just . . . I keep thinking someone could have walked into our home at any time."

Certainly a disturbing thought, and yet no one had. "Miss Wilson, could we sit down for a few minutes? There's something I need to ask you."

Miss Wilson was instantly on her guard again but too well mannered to refuse a civil request from a guest. "Of course." She gestured toward the sofa.

Sarah sat down on one end, and Miss Wilson perched tentatively on the other, as if prepared to jump up and flee if Sarah's question proved too disturbing.

Sarah reached into her purse again and pulled out a handkerchief that had been loosely knotted. She carefully untied it to reveal the ring Abigail Northrup had been wearing around her neck. "Have you ever seen this before?"

Miss Wilson gasped. "Where did you find that?"

"Then you have seen it."

"Answer me," she said, angry now. "Where did you find it?"

"Abigail was wearing it on a chain around her neck."

"When she died? She was wearing it when she died?" Miss Wilson asked, her eyes flooding with tears.

Before Sarah could reply, the parlor door burst open and Miss Billingsly cried, "What's going on here?"

Miss Wilson sprang to her feet. "Nothing that concerns you, Estelle."

But Miss Billingsly didn't even glance at her. She was too busy glaring at Sarah. "What do you want with her? Haven't you and your husband caused enough trouble?" She came toward Sarah now, her eyes red-rimmed and her cheeks flushed, and Sarah realized she'd been drinking.

Feeling vulnerable, Sarah rose, too, still clutching the handkerchief with the ring in it.

"What's that?" Miss Billingsly asked. "What have you got there?"

"Nothing," Miss Wilson said. "Estelle, you aren't well. You need to—"

"I'm perfectly well. What are you hiding from me?"

Sarah decided to take a chance. "It's Abigail's ring."

Miss Billingsly stopped dead and her whole body stiffened. "Abigail didn't wear a ring."

"Not on her hands, but she wore this one on a chain around her neck. Hidden under her clothing. Have you ever seen it before?" Sarah held it out to her.

"Estelle, this doesn't concern you," Miss Wilson tried again, desperate this time, but Miss Billingsly was staring at the ring in horror.

When neither woman spoke, Sarah decided to provoke them. "I thought it looked like an engagement ring."

Miss Billingsly let out an agonized cry, and for the first time she turned her fierce gaze on Miss Wilson. "You gave it to her, didn't you? You said it didn't mean anything, but I knew when you started sleeping in her room—"

"Estelle! Stop it! You're drunk. You don't know what you're saying."

"You gave her a *ring!*" Miss Billingsly nearly screamed, snatching it from Sarah's hand. "Eighteen years! I lived with you for eighteen years, and she comes along and you give her a *ring!*" She flung the ring at Miss Wilson with a strangled cry. It hit her in the chest and bounced off, but Miss Wilson just stood like a statue, her cheeks crimson.

"Bathsheba!" she called, but the maid was already there.

Bathsheba wrapped her arm around Miss Billingsly. "What's all this shouting about now? That ain't no way to act, is it? What kinda example you setting for the young ladies?"

"She gave that girl a *ring,*" Miss Billingsly informed her, tears flooding her eyes and running unchecked down her cheeks as she allowed Bathsheba to lead her away. "And then she killed her!"

Miss Wilson gasped and turned to Sarah. "She doesn't know what she's saying. She . . . she drinks, and you can't believe anything she says."

"Of course," Sarah said, walking over to pick up

the ring. "But you did give this ring to Abigail, didn't you?"

"We were friends. I . . . I loved her dearly."

Sarah looked at the ring and then back at Miss Wilson's anguished face. "Did you love her the same way you used to love Miss Billingsly?"

Her expression froze. "I think you should leave now, Mrs. Malloy."

Sarah agreed. She started to wrap the ring back up in her handkerchief.

"Wait!" Miss Wilson said, reaching for it. "Could I . . . ?"

Sarah tied it up. "I'm afraid not. It could be evidence."

"Evidence of what? That I loved her?" she asked bitterly.

Sarah tucked it back into her purse. "Did you know a young man had proposed to her?"

Miss Wilson flinched. "She'd refused him. She'd never give herself to a man." She didn't sound very confident about it, though.

Sarah smiled sadly. "I think you know she hadn't refused him. In fact, they were corresponding, and he believed she intended to marry him."

Miss Wilson shook her head in silent denial, but Sarah could see she knew it was true.

"That must have made you very angry."

"I didn't hurt her. I would never have hurt her."

Sarah didn't know what to say to that. She picked up her coat and left.

"She actually said Miss Wilson killed Abigail?" Gino asked.

"Yes, but don't forget, Miss Billingsly had been drinking," Sarah said. "And she was very upset after seeing the ring."

"Because Sarah had goaded her by calling it an engagement ring," Frank added, grinning when she scowled at him. He loved making her scowl.

The three of them had gathered in the Malloys' formal parlor after supper while Maeve and Mrs. Malloy put the children to bed.

"I admit I was a little harsh with her," Sarah said. "But it's so hard to get information out of those two."

"The real question is, could it be true?" Frank asked. "Could Miss Wilson really have killed Abigail?"

"Why would she, though?" Sarah asked. "She obviously loved her."

"People kill people they love all the time," Malloy reminded her. "Don't forget, this wasn't a carefully planned murder. This was someone who was probably arguing with Abigail and got so mad he—or she—picked up the first thing that came to hand and jammed it into her face." Sarah winced, and he was instantly contrite. "Sorry. I didn't mean to—"

"No, you're right. This killing was the result of sudden anger."

Frank continued. "And the question is, did Miss Wilson have a reason to be that angry with Abigail?"

"I'd expect Miss Billingsly would have more reason to be angry," Gino said. "She's the one who didn't like Abigail."

"And she had good reason to be jealous of her, too," Frank said.

"Yes, she did," Sarah said. "You should have seen her face when she realized Miss Wilson had given Abigail a ring."

"That's what I don't understand," Gino said. "Why would a woman give another woman a ring?"

Frank and Sarah exchanged a knowing look. "For the same reason a man gives a woman a ring," he said.

They waited while he worked this through. After a few moments, his eyes grew wide and he said, "Oh." Then after another moment, he said, "But a woman can't marry another woman."

"Only if it's a Boston marriage," Sarah said. "Apparently, Miss Wilson and Miss Billingsly had that and more. They'd lived together happily for eighteen years, according to Miss Billingsly."

"Sharing a bedroom, like a married couple," Frank added, earning another scowl from Sarah. "Well, that's important, because according to Bathsheba, they're not sharing a bedroom anymore."

"And from what Miss Billingsly said, Miss Wilson had been sharing Abigail's room before she died," Sarah said.

"Really?" Gino asked in astonishment. "With Miss Billingsly still in the same house and everything?"

"I know. Miss Wilson behaved very badly."

"But if she loved Abigail, why would she have killed her?" Frank asked, hoping Sarah had the answer.

"Perhaps because she found out Abigail had decided to marry Cornelius Raymond."

"Did she?" Gino asked.

"We don't know for sure, but from my conversation with her today, Miss Wilson apparently knew Abigail had a suitor. We do know Abigail hadn't given Mr. Raymond a definite answer yet, but if she told Miss Wilson she intended to accept him, that probably would have made Miss Wilson furious."

"So Miss Wilson could have had a reason to kill Abigail," Frank said.

"And Miss Billingsly could have, too, if she was jealous," Sarah said. "But she seems certain Miss Wilson did it."

"Maybe she's trying to throw suspicion off herself," Gino said.

"That could be, although she doesn't seem clever enough to have thought of that," Frank said.

"She's a college professor," Sarah reminded him. "Well, not a full professor, but the next best thing. She's very intelligent."

"I didn't mean she wasn't smart," Frank said. "I meant she doesn't seem devious enough to try to implicate somebody else."

"So you think Miss Wilson is the more likely killer?" Sarah challenged.

Frank wanted to kiss that smirk off her lovely mouth. If only Gino weren't there.

"Well, before you arrest Miss Wilson," Gino said as if prompted, "I should tell you what I found out about Luther and Cornelius Raymond. They were both in the city the day Abigail was killed."

"How do you know that?" Frank asked.

"Luther keeps a room at the athletic club, and he used it Tuesday night. The club keeps records. He might have an alibi for the day she died, of course, but I haven't seen him yet to ask him. I went to Tarrytown today to see Cory Raymond, and I found out he doesn't spend much time working at his father's business. He also has a room at the athletic club, and the secretary in Tarrytown told me he was in the city last week, and she hinted he's here now, too."

"Raymond might also have an alibi," Frank said.

"I know. I went by the club to see them both this

afternoon, when I got back from Tarrytown, but neither of them was in, so I'm going back in the morning early, before they have a chance to go out."

"Don't forget, we don't know exactly when Abigail was killed, so they'll have to account for several hours," Sarah said.

"Maybe I should go with you," Frank said. "They might not be too friendly, and one of them might've killed Abigail."

Gino waved away his concern. "We won't be alone. The club has hundreds of members."

"I just wish we knew why Abigail went out to the gazebo in the first place," Sarah said with a sigh. "Why did she go outside on a cold day when she had an office?"

"And lots of other places inside the school where she could meet people," Frank said. "When Gino needed to interview students, they had lots of empty rooms."

"Well, when we find the killer, we'll ask him," Gino said.

"Or her," Frank added.

Gino found Ledbetter behind the front desk at the New York Athletic Club again the next morning, and this time his smile of greeting was genuine. "Good afternoon, Mr. Donatelli. Still looking for Mr. Northrup?"

"I sure am."

"Then you're finally in luck. He's here. I'll see if I can find him."

Gino slipped him another dollar and planted himself in one of the comfortable lobby chairs to wait. He watched with interest as club members came and went. Mr. Malloy had taught him to watch for details, and he studied the way these privileged men conducted themselves. The way they moved and spoke, the way they addressed each other and the help. He might need to know these things if he ever got to be a millionaire like Mr. Malloy.

Gino didn't think he could ever be as rude to the help as these men, though, not even if he was a millionaire.

To his surprise, both Luther Northrup and Cornelius Raymond got off the elevator and came toward him. They looked like they'd dressed in a hurry, and neither looked happy to see him, but he smiled just the same and rose to greet them.

"What do you want with Luther?" Raymond demanded, although Gino noticed he kept his voice low so none of his wealthy friends would hear.

"I thought I'd come by and let him know what we've found out so far about Miss Northrup's death."

The two men exchanged a look, but plainly, neither of them could decide how to deal with him.

"Is there a quiet place we could talk?" Gino asked.

"Your room is bigger," Raymond told Northrup, who nodded.

"Upstairs," Northrup said and headed back to the elevator.

Gino figured he was supposed to follow, so he did, with Raymond coming along behind.

As the elevator operator took them up, Gino began to have second thoughts about coming to see the men alone. Like Mr. Malloy had said, one of them could be a murderer, and they both seemed pretty angry that he'd had the effrontery to track them down at their club. He hadn't really expected that.

The elevator operator let them off on a floor with a long corridor with many doors opening off it and nobody else in sight. Gino had a few sobering thoughts about what could happen with no one around to hear and then swallowed his apprehension. He wasn't afraid of these rich boys, even if one of them had killed a girl.

Or so he told himself.

Luther led the way and opened one of the doors with a key he pulled from his pocket. They entered a comfortably large, if Spartanly furnished, room with a sitting area at one end and a bedroom at the other. The sitting area had two upholstered chairs with a table in between. A small, square dining table sat against the wall with two wooden chairs pushed beneath it. The bed at the other end of the room was unmade and clothing was strewn around. Gino wondered idly if they had maid service to clean up after the residents.

Luther pointed at the upholstered chairs and went to grab one of the wooden chairs for himself. Gino sat down, surprised to find the chair comfortable and waited for Raymond to take the other seat. Luther set the wooden chair down in front of him with a thump and straddled it, leaning his arms on the back. Then he tried to intimidate Gino with a glare. "All right, detective boy, tell us what you came to tell us."

Gino managed not to laugh in his face. "There's no reason to be rude," he said pleasantly. "I thought you'd be anxious to find your sister's killer."

Luther flinched a little at that. At least he understood that he *should* be anxious. Gino glanced at Raymond and saw he was angry, too, but in a quiet, more dangerous way.

"Just tell me who he is," Raymond said.

"I'm afraid we don't know who the killer is yet, but—"

"No, tell me who the other man was, the one who gave her that ring."

"You think she had another suitor?" Gino asked in surprise.

"How else do you explain it? She kept refusing

to give me an answer to my proposal and she was hiding a ring that someone else gave her."

"It seems simple to me, too," Luther said. "But maybe it's too simple for you, detective boy."

Gino managed not to laugh again. Luther really was humorous, trying to be tough. "Actually, it's not simple at all. We do know who gave her the ring, though."

"Why wouldn't Malloy tell me, then?" Raymond snapped.

"Because he didn't know then. We just found out."

"So are you going to tell us or not?" Luther asked.

Gino waited a beat, pretending reluctance before he finally said, "Miss Wilson gave it to her."

Their expressions were comical, but Gino simply returned their amazed stares calmly.

"Miss Wilson?" Raymond said after a long moment. "Is that the woman she was rooming with?"

"Yes, she owns the house."

"Why would she give Abby a ring?" Luther asked.

Now they were getting into treacherous territory. Gino would have to take care. "Because she had grown very fond of your sister."

"That doesn't make any sense," Raymond said. "Women don't give rings to other women."

"Apparently, they do. Miss Wilson admitted it."

"But why?"

Gino considered what he should say and the fact that he was alone with two men who might take offense on behalf of Abigail's reputation. "From what she said, the same reason a man gives a woman a ring."

They needed a moment to figure it out.

"That old bat!" Raymond cried in outrage. "How dare she . . . ?" He gestured helplessly.

Luther cursed. "You've got a lot of gall, coming in here and talking about my sister that way," he snarled.

"I'm not saying anything about your sister. I'm just telling you who gave her the ring."

"But she took it," Raymond said through gritted teeth. "And she wore it when she wouldn't take one from me."

"Maybe she had to," Luther argued. "You don't know what went on in that house. Maybe she was afraid not to."

"Why would she have to take it, and why would she have to wear it?" Raymond demanded. "Why would she have to do anything? All she had to do was send for me. I would've taken her out of there."

Raymond seemed to expect Gino to answer him, and of course he didn't have any answers at all. "She, uh, Miss Northrup, that is. She liked teaching. Maybe she was afraid of losing her job."

Raymond made a rude noise. "Women don't need jobs. She could've married me. I would've taken care of her. She knew that."

"And she hadn't said anything in her letters about Miss Wilson acting strange?" Gino tried. "Or being afraid of anybody?"

Raymond's glare was murderous. "Do you think I would've left her there for one minute if she had?"

Luther's glare was just as murderous. "I've had just about enough of you slandering my sister's good name, detective boy. I think you should leave."

Gino was only too willing to oblige him.

Not wanting to wait for the elevator, he took the stairs.

10

Mr. and Mrs. Northrup were expecting them, since Frank had telephoned that morning to ask permission to call on them. The Northrups were anxious for word that their daughter's killer had been caught, or at least a bit of encouraging news, so they were more than willing to grant Frank and Sarah a visit.

They sat in the Northrups' formal parlor, drinking tea—or pretending to, in Frank's case. The Northrups looked like they hadn't been sleeping well, and they moved slowly, as if their grief weighed them down somehow. Mrs. Northrup occasionally dabbed at her eyes with her handkerchief.

Frank told them about finding the letters from Cornelius Raymond in Abigail's room.

"We didn't know he had proposed to her, of course," Mr. Northrup said with a sigh of regret over what might have been.

"I could understand why she wouldn't accept him, though," his wife said. "She loved teaching so much, and I guess she wasn't ready to give it up."

"Do you think she would have married Mr. Raymond eventually?" Sarah asked.

The Northrups exchanged a glance.

"Getting married is such an important decision," Mrs. Northrup said. "And I never even imagined Abby was in love with Cory. I also never got the idea he was in love with her either, for that matter. She was fond of him, I suppose, but you'd like to see some genuine affection between a couple, too, wouldn't you?"

"I would," Sarah agreed. "Did she ever mention having affection for someone else?"

Mrs. Northrup frowned as she considered. "Dear me, if she did, I don't know who it could have been. She certainly didn't meet any suitors at the Normal School, I know."

Frank and Sarah had decided not to mention the ring or Abigail's relationship with Miss Wilson unless it was absolutely necessary, so Frank moved on.

"I took the liberty of emptying Abigail's desk at the school. I brought those things with me in case there's something you wanted to keep."

"That was very thoughtful of you, Mr. Malloy," Mrs. Northrup said, tearing up again. "I don't know if we would have even thought of it."

"I found more letters in her desk. They were from some of her old classmates and from Miss Raymond, but we also found a few letters from France." They had decided not to mention that some of them had been carefully hidden. "Do you know who might have been writing to her from France?" Frank asked.

"Probably some of the friends she met last summer," Mrs. Northrup said. "We had arranged for her to stay with different families while she was there, so she could practice her French. She had such a wonderful time."

"Couldn't you just look at the letters to see who they're from?" Mr. Northrup asked. "We certainly wouldn't mind if you read them."

"They were in French," Sarah said. "We're trying to find someone who could read them for us."

"Oh, of course," Mrs. Northrup said. "But couldn't Professor Pelletier help you with that?"

"We didn't want someone who knew her to read them, in case there's something in them she wouldn't want anyone else to know," Sarah said.

"I can't imagine what that would be," Mrs. Northrup said, a little offended at the thought that her dearly departed daughter had secrets.

"Abigail had told Miss Raymond that she'd discovered a scandal of some kind at the school," Frank quickly explained. "We don't know if that had anything to do with her death or if these letters are any part of it, but if there was a scandal and it's mentioned in these letters, we don't want to embarrass anyone if there's no reason."

"Oh, I see," Mrs. Northrup said, although she plainly didn't.

"Who are you going to show them to?" Mr. Northrup asked.

"We've got someone from our agency working on it," Frank assured him, surprising a suspicious-sounding cough from Sarah. What did she think, that he'd say his mother-in-law was hunting down a French expatriate?

Frank had little left to tell them after he explained that none of the students or teachers had seen anyone in the gazebo with Abigail. He wasn't going to mention that Miss Billingsly had hated Abigail for stealing Miss Wilson's affections or that Luther had been painfully jealous of his sister and might possibly have wished her dead or that Cornelius Raymond might have been overcome with fury when Abigail told him she was leaving him for a woman.

"We've had a difficult time finding Cory Raymond to speak with him," Sarah said, rescuing Frank when he ran out of safe information to share with them. "Mr. Donatelli went to his place of business here in Tarrytown, but they said he is rarely there."

The Northrups exchanged a knowing look.

"Yet another reason Cory wasn't a good match for Abby," Mrs. Northrup said. "He hasn't shown much interest in his father's business, I'm afraid, although when the time comes, he may well accept his responsibilities."

Frank wasn't so sure, but it wasn't his business or his son. "I understand he spends a lot of time in New York."

"Yes, he . . . he sees Luther there, I think," Mr. Northrup said.

"They belong to the same club, I believe," his wife said.

Mr. Northrup probably couldn't help his expression of disapproval. "I believe they do. They both enjoy athletics." The way he said the word *athletics* left no doubt of his low opinion of it.

"They're young," Frank said, but that didn't cheer Mr. Northrup. "I understand your son is quite accomplished in gymnastics."

"So he tells me," Mr. Northrup said without enthusiasm. "But gymnastics is not a skill that will help him in business."

Frank decided not to mention that Luther had been offered a job at the club, teaching other young men skills that wouldn't help them in business either.

"Could you give us the names of the families Abigail stayed with in France?" Sarah asked. "Then we'll at least know if these letters Mr. Malloy found are from them or someone else."

"I can't imagine who else would be writing to her, but I'll be happy to give you the names," Mrs. Northrup said. "They're in my book. If you'll excuse me for a moment . . ."

Sarah said, "I'll go with you."

Frank watched her go, glad she'd given him a few minutes alone with Mr. Northrup. When the women were gone, he said, "Did Luther and Abigail get along well?"

Northrup looked up in surprise. "As well as any siblings do, I suppose. Why . . . ? Oh, dear God, you don't think . . . ?" The color had drained from his face and he stared at Frank in horror.

"No, I don't have any reason to think that Luther had anything to do with Abigail's death," Frank lied hastily. "I just . . . He mentioned that he's not much of a scholar, and we know Abigail did very well in school, so I was wondering about them."

"Luther would never apply himself in school. He may have been a bit jealous of all the attention Abigail received, but he only had himself to blame for not doing well himself."

Frank nodded, as if he understood. "It's hard for boys to settle down sometimes. I didn't have much use for school either, and I've done pretty well in life. You expect Cory Raymond to be successful, even though he's not showing any signs of it now. Why couldn't Luther be successful, too?"

Northrup looked a bit surprised. "I suppose you're right. I didn't have much love for school myself, now that I remember. I just . . . Well, you expect so much from your son, don't you?"

Frank thought of his son, Brian, who had been born deaf and with a clubfoot. He'd thought the boy a hopeless case until Sarah had opened his eyes. "We should expect a lot from them, but maybe not too much."

"I think I know what you're saying. I've also just been thinking that Luther is the only child we have left. I don't suppose it would hurt to be kinder to him."

Frank agreed. He only hoped he didn't have to come back here one day and tell Mr. Northrup his son had killed his daughter.

Mrs. Northrup took Sarah down the hall to a pleasant room that she recognized as the family's parlor. It had been closed during the funeral, so Sarah looked around, admiring the framed photographs of Abigail and Luther as children that sat on the mantle, while Mrs. Northrup rummaged in her desk for her book of addresses.

Luther had always been a handsome boy, large but not awkward. Abigail had grown into her looks, starting out rather plain with her pigtails and short skirts.

"This one has always been my favorite," Mrs. Northrup said. Sarah hadn't realized she had come up beside her. She indicated a photo of Luther and Abigail as prepubescent youths, fairly bursting with promise. "It's the last one they had made together." She brushed away a tear. "Here are the addresses."

Sarah took the paper Mrs. Northrup handed her and glanced at it. Some of the addresses looked familiar. "Thank you. It was very generous of you to send her to France."

"We aren't wealthy enough to send her on a real European tour, but we thought she deserved a few months in the country she's loved ever since she first learned about it in school. She would read French novels for fun, when other girls were reading ladies' magazines."

"You said she wanted to go so she could learn to speak French better."

"Oh yes, and she did. I was very surprised when she told me she was embarrassed when she first got there. She thought she spoke the language rather fluently, but she said they laughed at her accent and could hardly understand her at first. Can you imagine? After all the years she studied."

"And her professor at the Normal School is French himself," Sarah marveled. "You'd think he would have helped her with that."

"You would, wouldn't you? But maybe he's from a different part of France. Maybe they have different accents there, like we do here."

"Maybe they do," Sarah said, but she was thinking that even with our different accents, we can still understand each other. "Where did she stay when she was there?"

"Paris, of course—she was there for a whole month. Then she went to Nice. She wanted to see the south of France. And then she spent a few days in a small town in Bourgogne. I can't pronounce it, but it's on your list. It wasn't a place people usually go, but she was adamant she wanted to see it."

Gino came over to the house that evening, after supper. His mother insisted he eat a meal with his family at least a few evenings a week, but he was anxious to hear how things had gone with the Northrups and to report on his visit with Luther Northrup and Cory Raymond.

Sarah had brought Maeve up to date on the case when she and Malloy had returned from Tarrytown earlier. Now the children were asleep and Frank's mother had retired to her rooms.

"I warned you about being alone with those fellows," Malloy said when Gino had told them about his uncomfortable encounter with the two men at their club.

"I don't think they would've killed me," Gino said when he'd finished his tale, "but I hadn't thought about them beating me up just because they were annoyed."

"At least you found out this Raymond fellow apparently didn't know who his rival was for Abigail's affections," Maeve said.

Malloy grinned. "Or so he said."

"You always have to make everything complicated," Maeve complained.

"Everything is already complicated," he replied cheerfully. "I'm just trying to sort it out."

"I think the most important thing I learned is that either one of these fellows might've become violent if they got mad enough at Abigail," Gino said. "And we know from what Miss Raymond told Mrs. Malloy that Abigail could be very annoying."

"They might also be the ones most likely to meet Abigail in the gazebo," Sarah said. "I've been giving that some thought because it seems odd she'd be meeting someone outside in the middle of winter when she had a perfectly warm office she could've used."

"That's true. Why wouldn't she have met with them in her office?" Maeve asked.

"Because the young ladies go into a tizzy if they see a strange man walking around the building," Malloy said.

"Well, we know they do *now*," Sarah said, "and after Abigail was murdered, who can blame them? But would they have been upset to see a strange man before that? Is there some sort of rule about men coming into the building?"

"Nobody said anything about any rules when Mr. Malloy and I came in to question people," Gino said. "Although he's right about the girls being in a tizzy."

Maeve rolled her eyes. "Girls always go into a tizzy when they see Gino."

"Not *all* girls," Gino said meaningfully.

Maeve ignored the provocation, of course,

making Sarah smile. The two of them were such fun to watch.

"Mrs. Northrup gave me a list of the people in France who hosted Abigail when she was there, but none of the addresses match the one on two of the letters Malloy found hidden," Sarah said to bring them back to the subject at hand.

"Do you think she had a secret lover over there?" Gino asked. "Maybe he came to America to find her, and she told him she was in love with somebody else and he killed her."

"It's certainly possible," Sarah said, "but nobody seems to have heard of this mysterious young man, much less seen him."

"Which probably means he doesn't exist. I guess you haven't heard anything from Mrs. Decker either," Gino said.

"Not yet," Sarah said. "Finding someone who knows French well enough to read the letters is only half of it. The person also has to be discreet, just in case there really is some kind of scandal mentioned in them."

"So that could take a while," Maeve said. "Meanwhile, who do you think killed her?"

"After the way they acted today, I'm thinking it was Luther or Raymond," Gino said.

"Why?" Maeve asked. "Just because they scared you?"

"They didn't scare me," he lied. "They just made me a little nervous. I think one of them probably did it because they're young men. In my experience, young men are most likely to have bad tempers and use violence when things don't go their way."

"That's true," Malloy said, "and whoever killed Abigail was really mad at her."

"I might agree with you except for one thing," Sarah said. They all turned to her in surprise. "I've been thinking about this a lot. When I showed Miss Wilson the ring yesterday, she was surprised, but not for the reason I would have thought. Remember, she and Abigail were the only ones who knew its significance. We guessed it might be an engagement ring, but after Cory Raymond told us he hadn't given it to her, we didn't know what to think. I took a chance in showing it to Miss Wilson, and she was suitably shocked, but not because I had it or had thought to show it to her. She was shocked to learn that Abigail was wearing it when she died."

"Why would that shock her?" Gino asked.

"That's what I've been trying to figure out. What does it mean if she didn't know Abigail was wearing the ring she gave her? And that Miss Wilson was surprised to learn she was?"

"Oh, that's easy," Maeve said. "A girl might accept a gift from a suitor, but the only way he'd know it meant something to her is if she wore it. So maybe Miss Wilson wasn't sure why Abigail had accepted it or what her real feelings were."

"Because no matter what, Abigail couldn't wear the ring openly," Malloy said. "Not in that house, at least, where Miss Billingsly would see it and probably guess where it came from."

"Or anywhere, really," Sarah said. "People at the school would see it and ask about it. And her family, too."

"And she couldn't very well pretend some young man gave it to her," Maeve said. "That would make Cory Raymond mad, and he'd want to know who it was."

"And so would her brother and her parents," Gino said. "And everyone else she knows."

"So that's why she wasn't wearing it openly, but apparently, Miss Wilson didn't know she was wearing it at all, because she seemed especially upset when she realized Abigail was wearing it when she died."

"That's interesting," Maeve said. "Did you ask her why?"

"Unfortunately, I didn't have a chance, because that was exactly when Miss Billingsly burst in and Miss Wilson asked me to leave."

"But if she did kill Abigail," Maeve said, "imagine how terrible she'd feel knowing Abigail was wearing the token she'd given her. I'm guessing she would break down if you pressed her and maybe even confess, if she did it."

"Where did you get the idea it's that easy to get

somebody to confess to murder?" Malloy asked with some amazement.

She shrugged sheepishly and Gino chuckled.

"I'm afraid it doesn't matter if it's easy or difficult," Sarah said, "because I doubt Miss Wilson is going to even speak to us again after today. If she did kill Abigail, we'll have to find out some other way."

To everyone's surprise, the telephone rang, its shrill blast making them all jump even though it was out in the hallway.

"Who would be telephoning us at this time of night?" Malloy grumbled, going off to answer it.

"Maybe it's Miss Wilson," Gino told Maeve with wide-eyed innocence. "Maybe she's ready to confess."

Maeve swatted him.

Malloy had left the parlor door open, and they could hear his side of the conversation as he shouted into the mouthpiece to make himself heard. Unfortunately, his side consisted of one- or two-word responses that gave no clue as to who was on the other end or why they had chosen to disturb the family at this late hour.

Maeve turned to Sarah. "What are you going to do next?"

Sarah sighed. "I hope Malloy has an idea, because I don't."

"I still need to check on alibis for Luther and Raymond," Gino reminded them.

"Oh yes, you ran off before you could ask them," Maeve said with a smirk, and he pretended to swat her in return.

"And don't forget the letters from France," Sarah said, smiling again at their teasing. "We might find something interesting there."

"Maybe we should pay your mother a visit tomorrow," Maeve said to Sarah.

"If you're thinking we need to encourage her, I can assure you, she's already working as hard as she possibly can to get those letters translated. It's the most interesting thing she's done in a month."

At last Malloy ended the call, and Sarah's heart dropped when she saw his expression as he reentered the parlor. She instinctively rose to her feet, and she was vaguely aware that Gino and Maeve had, too.

"What is it?" she asked.

"It's Miss Wilson. She's been murdered."

The lobby at the Normal School was eerily quiet when Frank entered the next afternoon. Of course, it was Sunday, and no classes were in session, but he figured the news of Georgia Wilson's murder had spread by now, so the students would be making themselves scarce. Some had probably even gone home.

President Hatch was the one who had telephoned Frank last night to tell him about Miss

Wilson's death, and they had arranged to meet in his office today. Frank wasn't sure why Hatch wanted to meet with him, but Frank certainly wanted to find out as much as he could about Miss Wilson's death, because he was sure it had something to do with Abigail's. Two women who lived in the same house being murdered within ten days couldn't be a coincidence.

The door to the president's office suite stood open, and no one sat at his secretary's desk. He knocked on the doorframe. "Hatch?"

President Hatch appeared in the doorway to his inner office. "Mr. Malloy, thank you for coming. Please, come inside."

When Frank had taken a seat in one of the chairs provided for guests, Hatch sat down in his own chair and sighed deeply. "This is a disaster for the school."

"It's pretty serious for Miss Wilson, too," Frank said blandly.

Hatch's body jerked. "I didn't mean . . . Of course, you're right. We're all grieving for the poor woman. I only meant . . ." He winced, since they both knew what he'd meant.

"You're worried about the safety of the students and the female faculty," Frank said, offering Hatch an easy explanation.

"Yes, yes, that's it. There's obviously a madman on the loose. We need to catch him and stop him before he harms anyone else."

And before parents start permanently removing their daughters from the Normal School, Frank thought, but he said, "How did you find out about Miss Wilson's murder?"

"I thought I told you last night. I received a message at my home. They'd sent a police officer to fetch me because . . . well, apparently, Miss Billingsly told them to."

"Why would she have done that?"

Hatch shrugged. "I guess because in an emergency, she would normally have sent for Miss Wilson, but under the circumstances, I suppose I was the only other authority figure she could think of."

Frank supposed that made sense. "You said they found the body outside, near her house?"

"Yes, she'd gone out earlier, I understand, and someone walking home found her body lying in the alley behind the house."

"How was she killed?"

Hatch's face twisted with distaste. "They said she was strangled."

Not the same way Abigail had died, but it was another impulsive way to kill someone when no weapons were at hand. "How was she strangled?"

"Good God, man, do you have to be so ghoulish?"

Frank supposed it would seem that way to Hatch. "I need to know how she died. That will tell me if only a man could have done it, or if a woman could have killed her as well. If she was strangled with someone's bare hands, for example—"

"Yes, yes," Hatch snapped, waving away his explanation with both hands while the color drained from his face. "I see. The police said the killer used a scarf of some kind."

"A scarf? Was it hers?"

"I don't know, but it seems likely, doesn't it?"

Not necessarily, but he wasn't going to bother discussing that with Hatch, who already looked like he might faint. He'd have to find out where they'd taken her body and who had done the autopsy. If they'd done one at all, of course. He hated not having the authority to order one, the way the police would. He decided to ask Hatch something less upsetting. "Why did she go out? Was she meeting someone?"

"I don't know. Miss Billingsly was quite distraught, as you can imagine, and she couldn't answer any questions."

"Was she drunk?"

President Hatch gaped at him, appalled. "Really, Mr. Malloy, I don't know where you'd get an idea like that."

"From seeing her drunk before," Frank said. "But never mind. How about their maid? Bathsheba, I think her name is. What did she have to say?"

"Nothing helpful, but what can you expect,

after all, from a colored maid? She told me and the police both that she had no idea where Miss Wilson was going or why. She said the ladies don't confide in her, and I saw no reason to doubt it."

Frank saw a lot of reasons to doubt it. Hatch was a bigger fool than Frank had already taken him for if he thought a colored maid wouldn't know what was going on in her own house. He'd bet all of his new fortune that Bathsheba knew at least something that would be helpful. She wasn't going to say anything that might harm her ladies, though, certainly not to the police. Or even to Hatch, probably. Hatch was the one who'd neglected to have a female professor at a school for women for the first twenty-some years. Bathsheba wouldn't have a higher opinion of him than Frank did. "Why did you send for me, Mr. Hatch?"

Hatch sighed again. "Mr. Malloy, I know you've been hired by Miss Northrup's parents to look into the circumstances of her tragic death. I'm wondering if there is any reason I couldn't hire you to look into the circumstances of Miss Wilson's death as well."

Frank leaned back in his chair and studied Hatch for a long moment. Finally, he said, "Why would you do that? Aren't the police going to investigate?"

"I did discuss it with them. Or rather, with the

detective they sent over last night. He didn't seem very interested in the case, just as the police hadn't seemed very interested in Miss Northrup's death. He said it was probably a robbery gone bad and Miss Wilson had no business being out in the streets alone after dark and a lot of other things that made me think he wasn't particularly anxious to find out who killed her."

Frank figured the detective would've been much more interested if Hatch had offered a reward, but they both knew Hatch wouldn't have done that because he didn't really want the police investigating at all. "I don't suppose I need to remind you that you don't want the press involved either."

"No, you do not, and that is another reason I would like your assistance with this matter, Mr. Malloy."

"Mr. Hatch, I must warn you that we've already uncovered some, uh, situations that could be considered sensational if the press discovered them, too."

"I assumed that would be the case, Mr. Malloy, because that is always the case when someone is murdered, which is why I want to hire you. I want to have some control over the investigation and how much information is given to the police and ultimately to the newspapers. I want to protect the Northrups from scandal, just as much as I want to protect the Normal School.

But I also want the killer identified and caught, because his existence is just as dangerous to the school as any hint of scandal would be."

"You're asking an awful lot, Mr. Hatch."

"And I'm willing to pay for it, Mr. Malloy, but I think you are an honorable man who also wants to protect the reputation of these ladies and save the Northrup family any unnecessary heartache."

Frank wondered when he'd become an honorable man. He certainly hadn't been one when he first met Sarah Brandt. The process had been gradual, too, sneaking up on him and taking over before he even suspected. Whenever it had happened, though, Hatch was right. He'd already shielded the Northrups as much as he could, and he would continue to do so. "I can't make you any promises, Mr. Hatch, but I'll do my best."

Sarah and Gino had traveled up to Morningside Heights with Malloy and then separated from him. While Malloy went to the Normal School, Sarah and Gino went to Miss Wilson's house to offer what comfort and assistance they could to her friend.

And of course to see what Miss Billingsly had to say about Miss Wilson's death, if possible.

The shades were all tightly drawn when they reached the house, and black crepe hung on the knocker.

"Do you suppose they're still here?" Gino asked.

"Where would they go? I think they're just trying to discourage visitors."

But no one answered their knock the first time. Sarah tried a second time, using a little more force. Finally, a curtain in the front window twitched a bit. Sarah waited a few minutes, to give whoever was there time to get to the door, and when nothing happened, she pounded on the door with her fist. "We aren't leaving," she called.

At last the door opened a crack, and Bathsheba gave them a murderous glare. "We ain't receiving visitors."

"We aren't visitors and you know it," Sarah said. "We're here to help. Miss Billingsly is going to have to deal with the police and funeral arrangements and possibly even the press. Is she up to that?"

"Mr. Hatch say he gonna take care of everything."

Sarah gave her an understanding smile. "Mr. Hatch telephoned my husband last night and is meeting with him right now. That is how he's taking care of everything."

Bathsheba sighed wearily, then opened the door all the way. "I expect you oughta come in, then."

Unlike the last time Sarah had called, this time Bathsheba took Sarah's coat and Gino's, too.

"Don't know why you need him with you," she muttered.

"There's a murderer on the loose," Sarah said.

"You afraid he might get you?" Bathsheba scoffed.

"No, but we thought you and Miss Billingsly might be concerned, since two of the four women who lived in this house have now been murdered."

This time Bathsheba did register some genuine emotion, but to Sarah's surprise, it was anger. "You don't think this killer is interested in either of us, do you?"

"I have no idea, since I don't know why Miss Wilson and Miss Northrup were murdered. But if *you* know, we'd be very grateful if you'd tell us."

"We don't know nothing about it. Why can't you people leave that poor soul alone in her misery?"

"You mean Miss Billingsly?" Gino asked.

"Who else am I gonna mean? She been grieving all night long. Neither one of us hardly slept a wink."

"I don't suppose she'd speak with us," Sarah said. "Even if she's not involved in whatever caused the murders, she may know something that will help us figure out who did it."

"She not in any shape to talk to anybody. She can't hardly talk sense."

"Then she needs to get hold of herself and soon."

"Why?" Bathsheba asked coldly. "Just to help you out?"

"Yes, to help us catch a killer who murdered two people who lived with her. You *are* anxious to catch this person, aren't you?"

Bathsheba couldn't very well deny it, but she still wanted to protect Miss Billingsly. "I'm telling you, she ain't well."

"If you mean she's been drinking, we'll take that into consideration. Do you think I should go up to her?"

Bathsheba glanced at Gino. "She ain't dressed proper. It'd take some time to get her presentable enough to come downstairs."

"I'll go up, then. Would you mind entertaining Mr. Donatelli while I talk with her for a little while?"

Gino, bless him, gave Bathsheba his most appealing smile. She snorted, but she said, "If he don't mind sitting in the kitchen. I'll take you upstairs first, Mrs. Malloy. It'll be better if I tell her you're here and take you in to see her."

For the second time, Sarah went up the stairs, and again she followed Bathsheba to the back bedroom, the one that had been Abigail Northrup's. She remembered that after Abigail died Miss Billingsly had moved out of the room she'd shared with Miss Wilson all those years.

They stopped at the closed door, and Bathsheba said, "Wait here while I tell her."

Bathsheba slipped inside, leaving the door open a bit. Sarah could see the room was dark. The shades were drawn here, too. Bathsheba crooned to her charge, soft words of comfort Sarah couldn't make out.

"Did I dream it or is she really dead?" Miss Billingsly asked on a wail.

More crooning from Bathsheba.

"Did I do it, Bathsheba? Please tell me I didn't do it!"

11

"Don't you be silly now, Miss Estelle," Bathsheba said. "You never woulda hurt Miss Georgia. You loved her too much." Sarah noticed the maid had said this loudly enough for her to hear. "Now, listen here, you got a visitor. That nice Mrs. Malloy come to see you. She and her man are gonna find out who been causing all this trouble for us."

"Why is she here? I don't want to see anyone."

"I know, sweet pea, but she needs your help."

"I can't help anybody. I can't even help myself." She was blubbering now, and Sarah managed not to sigh. She hated making people weep.

"Course you can. You can do all kinda things now. Miss Georgia, she'd expect you to do what you can."

"But what can I do?"

"We won't know till you try, now, will we? That Mrs. Malloy, she just outside. She gonna talk to you a spell."

"But I'm not even dressed."

"Mrs. Malloy don't care, now, do you, Mrs. Malloy?"

Sarah recognized this as her summons. She stepped into the darkened room. "No, I don't care a bit."

The room smelled stale and faintly of liquor. She smiled, hoping she looked friendly and not threatening. Miss Billingsly made a sound of distress and pulled the covers up to her throat.

"Bathsheba," Sarah said, "why don't you make us some tea. Has Miss Billingsly eaten anything today?"

"No, ma'am, she ain't."

"And some toast, too."

"Yes, ma'am."

Bathsheba hurried out, and Miss Billingsly made another little distressed sound.

"Thank you so much for seeing me," Sarah said, as if she'd had a choice. Casting about, she saw a chair at the dressing table and pulled it over next to the bed. Miss Billingsly cowered a bit as she sat down, but Sarah pretended not to notice. Miss Billingsly wore a plain nightdress and her hair hung down her back in a braid. Her eyes were red-rimmed and bloodshot, but maybe that was just from crying. Sarah purposely didn't look at the half-empty bottle of sherry on the nightstand.

"I was very sorry to hear about Miss Wilson. That must have been a terrible shock."

Miss Billingsly eyed her suspiciously, but Sarah noticed she'd stopped clutching the covers as if afraid Sarah was going to snatch them away. "I . . . I couldn't believe it was her at first."

"Were you the one who found her?"

"Oh heavens, no! I don't think I could've borne it. It was Mr. Stevens. Coming home from work. They live on the next corner, and he goes through the alley because it's shorter."

"It must have been dark back there. I'm surprised he saw her."

"She was . . ." She had to swallow. "She was lying right in the middle. He nearly tripped over her, he said." Her voice broke and she sobbed a few times.

"What was she doing in the alley?"

Miss Billingsly stopped in mid-sob. "What?"

"I was wondering why a woman alone would have chosen to walk down the alley in the dark."

"Oh, I see. Yes, you're right. That would be strange, wouldn't it?"

"Can you think of any reason she would? I mean, do you use the alley in the daylight?"

"Yes, we do. So you think it . . . it wasn't dark yet when she . . . when it happened?"

"That's certainly possible. What time did she go out?"

"I don't know exactly. Bathsheba can tell you. But it was in the afternoon. We don't have classes on Saturday, so we usually go someplace together . . . or at least we used to. But that wouldn't be proper when we were still mourning poor Abby, would it?"

"But Miss Wilson went out somewhere without you yesterday."

Miss Billingsly frowned. "Not on a social call. I'm sure of that. She wouldn't do that."

"Did she give you any idea where she was going?"

Miss Billingsly shook her head. "She was very mysterious. She said she had an appointment, but she would be home for supper. And then . . . she wasn't."

Sarah was trying to remember exactly when darkness would have fallen last night. Winter days could be dark by four thirty or five o'clock, and in the heavily shadowed streets, it came even earlier. "Would she have normally walked down the alley when she was coming home?"

"If she was coming from that direction, I suppose so." Miss Billingsly had stopped crying and was concentrating very hard on what Sarah was asking her. "It was cold and she was probably in a hurry, so she'd take the shortest route."

She might have been in a hurry because she was being pursued, too. "What's in that direction?"

"What do you mean?"

"Is that the way she'd come home from the Normal School?"

"No."

"Can you think of someone she might've met who lives in that direction?"

"I . . . Lots of people. Many of the teachers at the school live in the streets behind us."

So no help there. Sarah managed not to sigh.

"Had she said anything to you about Miss Northrup's death?"

Her lip quivered, but to her credit, she bit down on it and kept her composure. "She's hardly spoken to me since . . ." She drew a shuddering breath. "Since I accused her of killing Abigail."

"Why did you say a thing like that? Did you really believe it?"

"I . . . I was so jealous, you see. Georgia and I . . ." She pressed a fist to her lips to hold back her tears.

Her despair was painful to witness, and Sarah took pity on her. "I know how much you loved her, and she loved you, too."

This time she smiled, a painfully mirthless parody of a smile. "She loved me until she saw Abby. Georgia always said nothing could separate us. She owned this house, and we had our work, and we'd be together as long as we lived. Then Abby came, and she was so young and so smart and so pretty . . ."

Sarah wanted to say something to comfort her, but she knew nothing could. She waited until Miss Billingsly had calmed herself again. "Can you think of any reason someone might kill both of them?"

She considered the question for a long moment. Then her eyes grew wide with horror. "You mean me, don't you? I'm the only one who could've wanted both of them dead!"

"Are you really?" Sarah asked, refusing to be baited.

This stunned her into silence.

"Are you really the only one who wanted them both dead?" Sarah repeated mercilessly.

"I didn't want them dead at all," she cried. "I just wanted everything back the way it was before. I know I'm not pretty. I never was, but Georgia didn't care about that. She loved my mind. She loved the discussions we'd have long into the night. She loved talking with me about our students. She loved going to museums with me and talking about what we saw. We shared everything until Abby came."

"Are you saying you didn't resent Abigail?"

"Of course I did. I saw the way she looked at Georgia. She worshipped her. Nobody could resist a love like that. I didn't even blame Georgia, or at least not very much."

"You must have been angry when Abigail came here to live, though."

"I was, but Georgia said it wouldn't make any difference between us. Abby was a child. Georgia was going to be a mentor to her, and we would be an example to her of how females could live their lives without men interfering."

"And you believed her?"

"I wanted to believe her, because if I didn't . . ."

"If you didn't, you'd have to leave her."

Miss Billingsly's eyes filled with tears. "I

couldn't leave. This is my home. Where would I go? What would I do?"

Sarah couldn't help thinking of all the women whose husbands abandoned them for a younger, prettier woman. Miss Billingsly would have done what they did: survive somehow. At least Miss Billingsly had a profession. She wouldn't have found herself penniless on the street as many women did. Sarah wasn't going to point that out, however. Instead she said, "So you killed Abigail to protect yourself."

"What?" Miss Billingsly cried, stiffening in shock. "How can you say such a thing! I could never hurt her. I could never hurt anyone!"

"Even someone who had ruined your whole life?"

That stopped her, but only for a few seconds. "Mrs. Malloy, I didn't kill Abigail and I didn't kill Georgia. What would that have gained me? When Abby died, Georgia didn't come back to me, did she? If anything, things were worse between us. I couldn't even comfort her because she thought I was glad Abby was gone."

"But you couldn't have known that until after Abigail was dead. Maybe you believed that with Abigail out of the way, you'd get her back."

She was wagging her head before Sarah even got the words out. "I didn't kill Abby, Mrs. Malloy. You've got to believe me."

"Then, who did?"

261

"I don't know! I thought—" She slapped a hand over her mouth as if to hold back the rest of her words.

"What did you think?"

She lowered her hand slowly, and Sarah could almost see her tears drying in the heat of her anger. "I thought Georgia had killed her."

"You did?" Sarah asked in genuine surprise. "Why?"

"Because . . . they had a terrible fight the night before. I don't know what they were arguing about, but they were both very angry. They didn't even speak to each other that morning before we all left for school. So when Abby turned up dead . . ." She gestured helplessly.

"Do you still think she did it?"

"I don't know, but if she did, then who killed her and why? It doesn't make any sense!"

She was absolutely right. It didn't make any sense at all.

Gino had waited patiently in the hallway for Bathsheba to return. She'd said something about sitting in the kitchen, but he knew better than to presume. She seemed a little surprised to find him still standing there, but she motioned impatiently that he was to follow her, so he did.

The warmth of the kitchen enveloped him, a welcome change from the frigid streets and drafty hallway.

"Sit yourself down," she said without the slightest trace of hospitality. "I expect you want some coffee. Or tea. Which is it?"

"Whatever is easier," he said, still smiling.

"I'm makin' tea for Miss Estelle. You can have some of that."

He waited while she filled the kettle and set it on to boil. Then she sliced some bread, and when she was finished, she laid the knife down and brushed her hands over her apron and looked around absently, as if she were at a loss as to what to do next.

"Maybe you'd sit with me while we wait for the water to boil," he said.

She gave a little huff, as though she was disgusted, but she pulled out one of the chairs and sat down. Then she gave him a long, considering look. "A fine-lookin' man like you, I reckon you get just about whatever you want in this world, don't you?"

"Oh no, ma'am. Well, I guess it's a little better now. When I was an Italian on the police force, all the sergeants were Irish, and all they ever did was make life hard for me. Until Mr. Malloy came along, that is."

"Least you got a job with the police. You don't see no colored fellows in that uniform, do you?"

"No, ma'am." Gino couldn't even imagine that, but he supposed the Irish cops had never imagined having Italians on the force either. "I expect it'll happen someday, though."

"Not in *my* day," she said. "Now, tell me what you think I know that'll help you catch whoever been killing my ladies."

"How did Miss Wilson happen to be out in the alley? Or was that really where they found her?"

"Oh, that's where they found her, all right. Our neighbor, he was walking down the alley on his way home, and he nearly stepped on her. It's right dark back there, so he didn't see her at first. He started shouting, and I went out to see what was going on, and . . ." She clamped her jaw shut and looked away, unwilling to cry in front of him.

"And how did she happen to be outside in the dark all alone?"

Bathsheba swallowed hard and turned back to him. "She went out in the afternoon, while it was still daylight. Said she had an appointment, but she'd be home for supper."

"Did she say who her appointment was with?"

"She don't tell me her business, and I didn't ask, though I wish now that I had."

He was sure she did. "What time did she leave?"

"Oh, around three o'clock, I'd guess."

"How did she seem? Was she nervous or anything?"

Bathsheba's forehead wrinkled in concentration. "She seemed determined."

"Determined?"

"Yes. Not nervous, I'm sure. She . . . Her mouth, it was all pinched up." She puckered her lips to demonstrate.

"Like she was angry and not wanting to show it," he guessed.

"More like she was angry, but not at me, so she was holding it back to be polite."

"Who would she have been angry with?"

"Not Miss Billingsly, if that's what you're thinking. I told you before, they never had a cross word, not even when Miss Northrup moved in."

Gino nodded as if he understood, and he was pretty sure he did. "But Miss Billingsly was upset when Miss Northrup moved in, wasn't she?"

"Sure, but what could she do? This is Miss Georgia's house. If she want, she can tell Miss Estelle to just find some other place to live."

"So Miss Billingsly never got mad about it?"

"She was hurt, but she was too much of a lady to say anything, not like that Miss Northrup."

Gino's nerve endings twitched, but he knew better than to express too much interest in her provocative statement. "You already told Mr. Malloy that Miss Northrup argued with Miss Wilson. Was it more than that?"

Bathsheba shifted a little in her chair. "Well, now, like I said, she didn't yell or scream or anything like that, but she let Miss Georgia know what she was thinking. That last day . . ." She looked away as if she'd lost her train of thought.

Gino waited, and when she didn't continue, he said, "Did she argue with Miss Wilson on that last day?"

Bathsheba sighed wearily. "The night before. She . . . Well, she wanted to do something that Miss Georgia told her not to do. She said . . ."

"What did she say?" Gino prodded gently when she hesitated. "It could be important."

Bathsheba winced. "I couldn't hear all they was sayin', you understand. I don't listen at keyholes."

"Of course not," he said with perfect sincerity.

"But I couldn't help hearing. They was right in there." She motioned to the parlor.

He nodded.

"Miss Northrup, she say she gonna tell President Hatch something. She say he gonna be shocked and he gonna have to take some action."

"What kind of action?"

"I don't know."

"What was she going to tell him?"

"Don't know that neither, and she wouldn't tell Miss Georgia either. Miss Georgia was real upset. Said she could cause a scandal that might ruin the school's reputation. Miss Georgia say she should think about all the people who'd get hurt."

"But she wouldn't say what it was?"

"No, not even when Miss Georgia begged her."

"Did she convince Miss Northrup not to tell?"

She shook her head. "Miss Northrup, she the

266

most hardheaded . . . Miss Georgia couldn't tell her nothing. Nobody could. She knew what was best, and she was gonna do it no matter what."

"And you're sure Miss Wilson wasn't able to change her mind?"

"Not unless she did it after they left here that morning. Miss Georgia, she couldn't hardly even look at Miss Abigail at breakfast. And Miss Abigail, she so smug, I couldn't hardly stand to look at her neither."

But Abigail hadn't told Hatch. Or had she? Could the college president have killed her to avoid a scandal? What could she have possibly known that would be so important? "I know Abigail didn't say, but do you have any idea what Abigail was going to tell Mr. Hatch?"

Bathsheba looked at him for a long moment, as if weighing his right to hear her theories. Finally, she said, "I think you know enough about what goes on in this house to guess."

"She actually thinks Abigail was going to tell Hatch about Miss Wilson and Miss Billingsly having a . . ." Gino gestured helplessly when he realized he had no way to describe the relationship between the two women.

"A romance?" Sarah suggested with a smile. The three of them had returned home so they could share what they had learned without fear of being overheard, and were sitting in the parlor.

She turned to Malloy. "Could that have gotten her killed?"

"People kill other people for stupid reasons sometimes, but Hatch is really terrified of scandal and rightly so. Parents are already taking their daughters home. If they found out there was a scandal in addition to two murders . . ." He shrugged.

"So maybe Abigail told Hatch about the *romance,*" Gino said, "and he killed her to keep her quiet. Then Miss Wilson figured it out and accused him, and he had to kill her, too."

"That's a good theory except for one thing," Malloy said. "Don't you wonder why Hatch wanted to see me today?"

"I thought he just wanted to tell you about Miss Wilson's murder," Gino said.

"He did, but he also wanted to hire me to investigate it."

"Oh," Gino said, obviously disappointed. "Which means he probably isn't the killer."

Sarah patted his hand to comfort him.

"Unless he's very clever and thinks he can trick me into deciding it's somebody else," Malloy said.

"If he's clever, he wouldn't do a stupid thing like that," Sarah said, earning a grin from Malloy. "Do you think Abigail told him something that day?"

"He didn't mention it, but I'll need to go back and ask him, I guess, just to make sure."

"And why would he have gone outside to meet with her?" Gino asked. "He's got an office where they could talk without being disturbed."

"She might've met with Miss Wilson or Miss Billingsly outside, though," Sarah said.

"Why not use her own office or theirs?" Malloy asked.

"She shared her office with Pelletier, and she wouldn't want him to walk in on them," Sarah said. "The other women probably share their offices as well."

"So you think Miss Wilson might've tried once more to make Abigail change her mind?" Gino asked.

"Or even Miss Billingsly, if she figured out what Abigail was going to tell Mr. Hatch," Sarah said. "Except I don't think Miss Billingsly could've done it. She's so fragile, I think she would've gone to pieces if she'd actually taken someone's life."

"Maybe she's just pretending to be fragile," Malloy said. "Maybe she's even just pretending to be drunk."

Sarah gaped at him. "I never thought of that! We expect females to be emotional and even hysterical, so we never question it when they are."

"Do you think she could be pretending?" Gino asked Sarah.

She tried to recall all of her encounters with Miss Billingsly. "I don't know her well enough to be sure, but I do know my mother says a female should always know how to faint convincingly in case she needs to get out of a difficult situation."

"Did Miss Billingsly faint?" Malloy asked with interest.

"Not yet," Sarah said with a grin, "although she did fall down rather well the very first time we met her."

"Yes, she did," he agreed with a grin of his own.

"We thought she was drunk," Sarah told Gino. "Which reminds me, at the time I thought she'd been drinking because she was mourning Abigail, but now we know she hated Abigail and was probably glad she died. Today, she confessed that she thought Miss Wilson had killed her, though, which *would* explain why she was drinking."

"Because she was afraid Miss Wilson would be arrested, I guess," Gino said.

"That seems logical, but why did she think Miss Wilson killed her?" Malloy asked.

"Because of the fight they had the night before," Sarah said.

"But Miss Billingsly said she doesn't know what the scandal was that Abigail was going to reveal," Malloy said.

"She claims she doesn't, but we just have her word for that. She might've guessed or Miss Wilson might've told her at some point."

"This is all a lot of guessing," Gino complained.

"And we're forgetting all about Luther Northrup and Cornelius Raymond."

"Should we still be thinking about them, though?" Sarah asked.

"Why wouldn't we?" Gino asked right back.

"Because they might've killed Abigail, but they don't have any reason to kill Miss Wilson."

"Unless . . ." Malloy said, leaning back in his chair.

"Unless what?" Sarah prodded.

"Unless Miss Wilson did kill Abigail."

Sarah tried to make sense of this, but Gino was ahead of her, probably because he was an impulsive young man himself.

"If Miss Wilson did kill Abigail—and now we know she could've had a good reason to—then Abigail's brother and lover would know they didn't do it, and from what I told them yesterday, they could've figured out Miss Wilson did."

"And one or the other of them killed Miss Wilson in revenge," Sarah added.

"Maybe both of them together," Gino said, "although that's kind of far-fetched, even for this case."

"So we don't think Luther or Raymond killed Abigail?" Malloy asked.

Sarah exchanged a frown with Gino, who shrugged. "I guess one of them might've done it, but then why would they kill Miss Wilson?"

"Maybe one of them killed Abigail but was

mad because Miss Wilson had drawn her into sin or something," Gino said.

"That might be a little far-fetched, too," Malloy said, grinning, "even for this case."

"But it's still possible. You said yourself, people kill people for stupid reasons. So how do we sort this out?" Sarah asked.

"Tomorrow, Gino goes back to the athletic club and asks Luther and Raymond for their alibis for yesterday and the day Abigail was killed," Malloy said.

"Can I take a bodyguard?" Gino asked in mock terror.

"You're right, you shouldn't go alone. We'll both go, then."

"What about Mr. Hatch?" Sarah asked. "Don't you need to find out if Abigail ever met with him?"

"I'll go to the college to see him when we've finished with the boys at the club," Malloy said.

"And if one of the *boys* did kill Abigail or Miss Wilson, won't he lie about where he was?" Gino asked.

"Which is why you'll be checking their alibis while I talk to Hatch."

"Do you need me to do anything?" Sarah asked.

"No, thank heaven," Malloy said. "You've done more than enough already. For some reason, I thought having a detective agency would mean you wouldn't be involved in the investigations anymore."

Sarah had to smile at that. "Do you expect me to sit at home and be bored?"

"Maybe you should be a midwife again, Mrs. Malloy," Gino said, earning a scowl from Malloy.

"I do miss my old vocation," Sarah admitted. "But I don't miss being called out in the middle of the night and being away from home for days at a time."

"Maybe the ladies could come to you," Gino suggested with a wicked grin. "You've got enough room here for them."

"Sarah is perfectly happy being a wife and mother," Malloy said in what he probably thought was the last word on the subject.

"How very progressive of you, Malloy," she said.

Malloy turned to Gino. "That's not a compliment."

"Are you going to join a club?" Gino asked Frank as they entered the New York Athletic Club the next morning.

"I'd have to find one that would take me," Frank said. "Micks aren't welcome most places, you know."

"Mr. Decker's club accepts Jews."

Frank gave him a look. "Jews with lots of money."

"You're a Mick with lots of money," Gino said.

"I'm not sure that makes any difference," Frank said, thinking it probably did. The question was whether he really wanted to join a club or not. He certainly didn't plan to sit around smoking cigars and reading the newspapers all day. He could do that at home.

Well, maybe not smoke cigars, but he didn't like smoking cigars anyway.

"Mr. Donatelli," the fellow behind the counter said by way of welcome. Frank was glad to see Gino had made an impression. "What can I do for you today?"

"I'm looking for Mr. Raymond and Mr. Northrup, as usual," Gino replied.

Frank noticed the fellow was sizing him up and trying to reconcile his Irish face with the tailor-made suit.

"How about Mr. Vander Hooten?" the fellow asked cheerfully.

"If he's here, I won't refuse to see him," Gino replied just as cheerfully.

"I don't think he's come in yet, but Mr. Raymond and Mr. Northrup are here. Shall I tell them you'd like to see them?"

Frank pulled a fiver out of his pocket. "Why don't you let us surprise them?"

He eyed the bill hungrily, but he didn't take it. "I could get in a lot of trouble."

"Nobody will ever know. We'll say we snuck in if anybody asks." Frank laid the bill on the counter.

"You know where to go?" the fellow asked Gino, who nodded. He picked up the bill and slipped it into his pocket with practiced ease. Then he went to assist a member who had just come in, leaving Frank and Gino to their own devices.

Gino headed for the elevator, and Frank followed. The operator greeted them respectfully and took them up.

"You think they're still in bed?" Frank asked.

"I got here later than this the last time, and they had to get dressed before they came down."

The corridor with the sleeping rooms wasn't nearly as fancy as the lobby. In fact, it was actually drab, as if the club didn't have to cater to the men who stayed here. Maybe they didn't. Maybe just being away from their regular home was enough.

Gino stopped in front of one of the doors and pounded several times. "Mr. Northrup?" he called. "Message for you."

He gave Frank a grin, and Frank nodded his approval. They waited patiently, because they could hear some promising noises from inside the room. After several minutes the door opened, and Luther Northrup stood there blinking at them. He wore a set of balbriggans with pearl buttons. His hair stood up in a few odd places, and his face was creased from sleep. "What the . . . *you?*" he said at last.

"Sorry to bother you so early, old man," Gino

said, pushing his way past Northrup into the room. Frank followed.

"What do you think you're doing, coming in here like this? I didn't invite you."

"We just need to ask you a couple questions, Northrup," Frank said. "It won't take long."

"And who are you?" He turned to Gino. "Who is he?"

"Frank Malloy. He's the one investigating your sister's death."

He squinted, as if trying to bring Frank into focus. "Oh yeah, I remember you now, from the funeral. You said you were a professor."

"No, I didn't. You just thought I was. Now we need some information from you about Abigail's murder."

"I already told this fellow, I don't know anything about it."

Frank started walking toward Northrup, so instinctively, Northrup started backing up. Frank walked him right up to one of the easy chairs at the end of his room and forced him down into it. "We just need to know where you were the day your sister died."

Northrup blinked stupidly. "What?"

"You heard me. What were you doing when you found out she was dead?"

"Oh. I . . . I was practicing on the bars."

"You were drinking?" Frank demanded angrily.

"No! The parallel bars," he explained frantically.

"He's a gymnast," Gino explained. "They swing around on these bars."

"Why?" Frank asked, not bothering to hide his amazement.

Gino shrugged.

Frank sighed and turned back to Northrup. "Were you swinging on these bars all day?"

"No, I was doing other things, too. I swam in the morning."

"Swam?" It was the dead of winter. "Where did you swim?"

"Here. We have a pool."

"On the roof?"

"No, in the basement."

"You have a pool *inside?*"

Gino leaned over and whispered, "Let me do this." He gently pushed Frank aside so he could glare directly down at Northrup. "What did you do after you swam?"

"I don't know exactly. I was in the exercise room. I think I jumped rope for a while and lifted weights and—"

"Were you here all day?"

"Yes, until my father telephoned me to tell me about Abby."

"Did anybody see you?"

"Lots of people saw me."

"Who?"

"I don't know. I didn't pay much attention."

"Well, you better try to remember because we

think you weren't here. We think you left and went up to the Normal School to see your sister, and you got into an argument with her and you killed her."

"What?" he cried in horror. "I never! I'd never raise a finger to Abby!"

"Then tell me who can vouch for you being here all that day."

"I don't know!" he fairly screamed, but then he remembered something. "Rudy. And Pete. And the other fellows who work here. They keep records. They know which members are here every day. They can tell you."

But they wouldn't tell Frank, not even for a bribe. "Get dressed. You're going downstairs with us to ask them to give us the names."

Northrup pushed himself to his feet, his expression sulky and rebellious, but before he could even take a step, someone pounded on the door.

12

"Grandmother is here!" Catherine cried, bursting into Sarah's private parlor.

Elizabeth Decker followed her in. Sarah greeted her mother and settled her on the sofa. "Where's Maeve?"

"I told her I'd look after Catherine for a while so she could have some time for herself," her mother said, gathering the child into her lap.

"I thought perhaps you had some news for me," Sarah said, sitting down beside her.

"I do. I've found someone I think can help us."

"Someone who speaks French?"

"Someone who *is* French," her mother said, "although she's rather elderly. She may turn us down because of that, but if so, I'm hoping she'll at least know of someone else in the city who could do the translation for us."

"You haven't spoken to her yet?"

"I haven't even met her yet, although I got my friend to write to her, telling her I'd be calling on her."

"Who is it? How does your friend know her?"

"She's Millicent Avery's mother-in-law. Of course her name isn't Avery anymore. It's de Béthune, or something like that. Her parents married her off to a French count, I think. He was penniless, of course, and he married Millicent for her enormous dowry that he used to return his family's estate to its former glory. The usual story, except he died when they'd only been married a few years, so Millicent came home. She didn't like France very much, I gather, and without her husband, well, I guess she had no incentive to stay. She has a son, however, and her mother-in-law wanted to see him grow up, so she came to America with them."

"I wonder how Millicent felt about that," Sarah said.

"Apparently, they get along very well. At any rate, Madame de Béthune will be able to read your letters and, hopefully, translate them for you."

"And an elderly French lady isn't likely to care about a scandal at some female college."

"Exactly," her mother said. "Now, I've promised Catherine that we'd spend some time together, but after luncheon, you and I can call on Madame de Béthune and find out if she'll help us."

Frank answered the pounding on Luther Northrup's door to find Cornelius Raymond. He was unshaven and still tucking in his shirttail, and his hair stuck up at odd angles.

"Good morning," Frank said with just a touch of irony. "Won't you come in?"

Gino frowned, but Luther looked very relieved to see his friend.

"What's going on here?" Raymond demanded when he was inside.

"We were just asking Luther some questions," Frank said. "I assume the young fellow down at the front desk told you we were here."

Raymond gave Frank what he probably thought was a murderous glare. "Of course he did. He was concerned about Mr. Northrup's well-being."

"Did he think we were going to beat him or something?" Frank asked, thinking he might demand his five-dollar tip back.

Raymond straightened a little and adjusted his suit coat, probably realizing what a comic figure he cut. He'd forgotten his vest completely and his shirt had no collar. "I don't know what he thought, but he suggested I might want to join you."

"That was very thoughtful of him," Frank said, enjoying Raymond's discomfort. "You saved us a trip. We were going to call on you next."

"They want to know where I was when Abby died," Luther said rather plaintively. "They think I killed her."

"How dare you?" Raymond snarled.

"We dare because both of you had good reasons to be angry with Abigail," Frank explained patiently, "and both of you seem to have nasty tempers that could get out of hand."

"What reason did I have?" Luther demanded.

Frank considered Luther for a long moment until he fairly squirmed. "I think you've been

281

angry at Abigail your entire life for all the times she proved she was smarter and better than you are."

Luther flinched as if Frank had slapped him, and Frank turned to Raymond.

"And you were angry at Abigail because she wouldn't give you an answer to your proposal. You'd expected her to accept immediately and be grateful for the offer, didn't you?"

Raymond shook his head. "I . . . I . . ."

"And when you demanded to know why she wouldn't accept, she told you she was in love with someone else. Maybe she even told you that person was a woman. Maybe your pride couldn't take such an insult, so you grabbed the first thing you saw and attacked her with it."

Raymond was still wagging his head, but he'd gone pale and his eyes were wide with terror. "I never touched her! I didn't even know about"—he swallowed loudly—"about that *woman* until *he* told me." He gestured toward Gino, who'd been watching the whole thing with avid interest.

"We only have your word for that," Gino said.

"Oh, you can believe me," Raymond said. "If I'd had any idea she was involved with a female, well, I would never have made her an offer in the first place!"

Frank could easily believe that. "Then you won't mind telling us where you were the day Abigail was killed."

That stopped him.

"Tell him," Luther said softly. "It doesn't matter now."

Raymond gave him a murderous look, but he said, "I was visiting a . . . a young lady."

Luther made a choking sound and Raymond flushed.

"Does this 'young lady' live in a brothel?" Frank asked.

Raymond looked as if he might explode, but Luther said, "Yes, she does."

"Don't most people visit brothels at night?" Gino asked, earning a glare from Luther.

Frank had been thinking the same thing.

"The young lady is very popular," Luther reported, his eyes shining with suppressed mirth. "If you want her complete attention, you have to go in the daytime."

Frank didn't think Luther deserved to take such pleasure in his friend's embarrassment. "So you knew the man who wanted to marry your sister was in love with a prostitute?"

Luther looked up in alarm. "I didn't . . . I mean, they weren't married yet, were they? Where's the harm?"

For a moment, Frank remembered fondly how the police were practically expected to give suspects the third degree. That privilege would've come in handy just then and maybe taught Luther Northrup a valuable lesson. Instead, he turned his disgust on Raymond, who quickly jumped to his own defense.

"I'm not in love with her! One doesn't fall in love with a prostitute!"

"One just spends his afternoons with her," Frank said. "Were you with her Saturday afternoon, too?"

"Saturday?" Raymond echoed in confusion.

"He surely was," Luther reported with that gleam again.

"Were you?" Gino asked with interest.

Raymond grunted a yes.

"What time did you get there?" Frank asked.

"I don't know," he said through gritted teeth. "Sometime in the afternoon."

"And what time did you leave?"

"Probably around seven."

"That seems early for a Saturday night," Gino said. "The evening's just getting started."

"He doesn't like to see other men take her upstairs," Luther reported gleefully.

Raymond looked as if he'd like to rip Luther's head off.

"And are you one of the men who took her upstairs after he left?" Frank asked Luther.

Luther's amusement evaporated when he saw Raymond's expression. "Of course not! I don't even go to that place."

Frank didn't bother to ask how he happened to know so much about it if he didn't. "Then you weren't with Raymond on Saturday afternoon. Where were you?"

"I . . . What does it matter?"

"Because that's when Miss Wilson was killed."

"Miss Wilson?" Luther echoed in confusion.

"The woman who gave Abigail the ring."

Both Luther and Raymond stared back in shock.

"She's dead?" Luther asked.

"Murdered people usually are," Frank said.

"Murdered?" Raymond said. "And you think one of us did it?"

"Even if you didn't kill Abigail, you both had a reason to kill Miss Wilson," Frank said. "You might've even thought Miss Wilson killed Abigail and you were just getting revenge."

"That's crazy!" Luther insisted.

"That's ridiculous," Raymond said at the same time.

"Luther, you haven't told me where you were on Saturday afternoon," Frank said.

"I . . . I was at home, or at least on my way," he said with obvious relief. "My father sent me a telegram and told me to come home because my mother wanted to see me. She . . . she wanted to talk about when Abby and I were little. It was . . . terrible." He rubbed his eyes at the memory.

"And when did you come back to the city?"

"Last night. I stayed over Saturday night and went to church with them. They wanted me to stay longer, but I told them I have a job now. That's not a lie. I accepted a position here at the club."

"You'll need to go downstairs with Gino and tell them to give you a list of everyone who was in the club the day Abigail died."

"They won't like that," Luther said. "If you talk to all those people about me, I'll lose my job."

"I don't have to talk to all of them. I just need a few of them to say they saw you here that day. You can look at the list and tell me who you remember saw you." He turned to Raymond. "And I'll need the name of the brothel and the young lady you see there."

"They won't tell you anything," Raymond grumbled.

He was probably right, but Frank said, "I'm not the police. Luther, get some clothes on. Gino, take him downstairs and get those names. Raymond, write down the information about the brothel and then I'm done with you."

"You should get a carriage," her mother said as they rode through the city streets in hers.

"Malloy is talking about getting a motorcar," Sarah said.

"Good heavens, do you think he really will?"

"Actually, he keeps saying other people want him to get one but he's not going to."

"Which makes you think he wants to get one."

"Of course. He seemed a little surprised when I said I wanted to learn to drive it, too."

"Would you really?"

"I think so. I might change my mind when I've tried it, but I do want to try, at least."

"I'd be terrified," her mother said. "They go so fast."

"But they're much easier to keep than a carriage. You don't have horses to feed and care for, and you don't need a driver."

"So you'd drive Malloy around the city?" her mother asked with a smile.

"I think that's what he's afraid of, but I'm sure Gino would drive him if it comes to that. Now we need to decide what we're going to tell Madame de Béthune."

"I was going to leave that up to you, dear. That's why I brought you along."

"Why, thank you, Mother," Sarah said, genuinely pleased. "I'm a little worried that an elderly lady might be distressed when we tell her someone was murdered."

"She might, but on the other hand, that's also a compelling reason to figure out what the letters say."

"What do we do if she doesn't want to help us?"

"We ask her if she knows anyone else in the city who can," her mother said.

"You make it sound so easy."

Her mother smiled. "If it were easy, you wouldn't have needed my help."

The de Béthunes lived in a lovely town house a

few blocks from Sarah's parents on the Upper West Side of the city. A maid admitted them and escorted them to a parlor decorated in a decidedly French style, where two ladies awaited them. Sarah vaguely remembered Millicent Avery de Béthune as someone she had known in her youth, a time that often seemed like another world. Millicent greeted her warmly and introduced her mother-in-law, who turned out to be not as elderly as they'd been led to believe.

Madame de Béthune spoke with only a slight accent and her voice was musical. She wore a gray cashmere gown trimmed with silver lace that matched her shining silver hair. A small woman, she seemed almost fragile next to her robust American daughter-in-law.

Millicent wore a stylish Prussian blue taffeta gown that only accentuated her plumpness, but her sweet, smiling face and deep dimples were captivating.

"Your letter was so mysterious, Mrs. Decker. We hardly knew what to make of it," Millicent said when they had dispensed with the formalities and she had served them tea.

"But perhaps that was your intent," Madame de Béthune said with a smile. "You create a mystery so we must see you in order to solve it."

"You have found us out," Sarah's mother said, delighted.

"And now that you have gotten your wish to

meet with us," Millicent said, "you must grant our wish to know exactly why you needed to see us. Or rather to see my *belle-mère*."

Sarah's mother nodded to her, giving her permission to begin her explanation.

"I'm sorry to say that the reason we need your help is because a young woman was murdered almost two weeks ago."

Millicent gasped and Madame de Béthune murmured something in French and crossed herself.

"I didn't want to distress you," Sarah hurried on, "but you needed to know why this is so important. She was an instructor at the Normal School of Manhattan. She had just graduated from the school herself and had been hired to teach there, which was quite an honor. She was, from all reports, an outstanding young lady beloved by many."

"Perhaps you know that Sarah's husband is a private investigator who serves a few select clients," her mother said.

"Oh yes," Millicent said. "We've heard all about Mr. Malloy from my father. What an interesting life you must lead, Sarah."

Sarah didn't bother to bite back her grin. "I do, especially when I'm helping him with one of his cases. The parents of the young lady who died have hired Mr. Malloy to find out who killed her."

Both of the Madame de Béthunes leaned forward expectantly.

Sarah took a deep breath, hoping she would not disappoint them. "The young lady—her name is Abigail—she taught French at the Normal School."

"She is from France herself, yes?" Madame de Béthune asked.

"No, she is thoroughly American, but apparently, she was a very good student, good enough that the college hired her to teach it. Her parents were very proud of her, of course, and as a gift, they sent her to visit France for a month last summer."

"Ah," said Madame de Béthune, "and there she learned she does not speak the *français* very well at all."

"That's true," Sarah said, astonished. She hadn't even thought to mention that detail. "How did you know?"

"Many Americans think they know how to speak the *français*, but . . . I know I speak the English with an accent."

"But you speak it very well," Sarah's mother said.

Madame de Béthune waved away her compliment. "I have had years to practice, but I can hardly make myself understood when I first come to America."

"So you're saying that Americans have the

same problem when they go to France," Sarah said.

"*Oui*, and Americans are very patient to those who do not speak their language, but the French are not so kind."

"Not all Americans are patient," Sarah's mother said sadly.

But Sarah was remembering something. "Abigail's mother told me the people she stayed with in France laughed at her when she first got there, and they could hardly understand her."

"I had the very same problem when I married Claude and moved to France," Millicent said. "Sometimes I think people pretended they didn't understand me, just to be mean."

Madame de Béthune patted her hand. "This is what occurs when Americans teach other Americans to speak the *français*. Is this why you have come today?"

"Oh no," Sarah said. "That has nothing to do with why we're here. I was just explaining to you how Abigail had happened to visit France and why she knew someone who sent her letters from there."

"Ah, a romance perhaps?" Madame de Béthune asked hopefully.

Sarah and her mother exchanged a look. "We have no idea. We only know that she received these letters . . ." She waited while her mother pulled the letters from her purse. "We also know that she told a friend of hers she had discovered a scandal at the college."

Madame de Béthune's eyes lit up. "A scandal? What kind of a scandal?"

"We don't know that either," Sarah said, certain now they had found exactly the right person to help them. "And these letters may have nothing at all to do with the scandal or Abigail's death."

"But they may have everything to do with it, and you will not know until you know what they say," Madame de Béthune said.

"And that is why we need your help," Sarah said. "I know this is asking a lot of someone we've just met—"

"*Pas du tout*," Madame de Béthune said, her delicate hand waving away her concerns.

"Which means 'not at all,'" Millicent said.

"I will be happy to help you," Madame de Béthune said. "But I will need a few days."

"Of course," Sarah said. "You are doing us a great favor, so take all the time you need. And as I said, it may come to nothing."

"Or we may find the *scélérat* who killed this poor girl."

Sarah only hoped she was right.

Much to Gino's disappointment, Frank left him at the club with Luther while Frank found a hansom cab to carry him down to the Tenderloin to find the brothel that Cornelius Raymond frequented.

The district was lousy with houses of ill repute that ranged from fairly elegant to sordidly shabby. As he'd expected, Raymond's favorite was one of the more elegant ones.

The place was locked up tight this early in the day. Frank's determined knocking finally roused a colored maid who informed him they weren't yet open for business.

"I'm not here to do business. I need to speak to the madam."

"She won't be happy," the maid informed him.

"I don't expect her to be."

She left him standing in the foyer for so long, he finally found himself a seat in the parlor. The room was richly furnished but cluttered now with empty glasses and bottles and a few stray articles of feminine apparel scattered here and there. It reeked of cigar smoke.

After nearly half an hour, a furious middle-aged female appeared. She'd dressed in a perfectly respectable gown that she could have worn to church if she'd been so inclined. He supposed she usually did dress that way. Her hair had been done up in a remarkably elaborate style that looked a little odd. He needed a moment to realize it was a wig, and she'd put it on crooked in her haste.

He rose to his feet, and she eyed him up and down. "You don't dress like a copper."

"Detective Frank Malloy, at your service, ma'am."

"At your service," she snorted. "That's what I'm supposed to say to you, you twit. Now what could you possibly want at this ungodly hour of the morning?"

"I'm investigating the murders of two females, and one of the men suspected of the crimes claims he was here when each of the women was murdered."

"And why should I help you?"

Frank pulled out a five-dollar bill and held it up. She was not impressed. He added a second one to it, and she nodded.

"If your man said he was here, he must've been, then. Men don't usually claim to be in a whorehouse unless they really were."

She was right, of course. "I don't suppose you could confirm that Cornelius Raymond was here on Saturday afternoon and on the Wednesday before last."

She gave him a pitying look. "I don't normally admit I know any man who might've come in here, you realize."

"Of course. I'm not working on a divorce case, though. This man wants you to say he was here."

"Then he was here."

Frank sighed wearily. "Except I only want you to say he was here if he really was."

"Mr. . . . Malloy, was it? I don't pay no mind to when customers come and go. Every day is pretty much like another one here. Even the girls couldn't tell you who they saw when. They don't pay attention and why should they?"

Why, indeed? Nobody who visited a place like this wanted people to remember. Except Cornelius Raymond, of course. "But he does come here?"

"Corny? Sure. He's smitten with our little Lila. She has a particular *speciality* that he likes," she added slyly. "I don't suppose you'd be interested—"

"I don't suppose she'd vouch for him," Frank said gruffly.

"She'll do anything you want her to if the price is right," the madam said.

He should've known he was wasting his time here. And his money. He crossed the room and handed the bills to the madam. "Thanks for your help."

She cackled, stuffing the bills into her bodice. "Anytime."

Hatch's secretary looked up in alarm when Frank entered her office. He figured she was even more spooked now that Miss Wilson had been murdered. At least she relaxed a little when she realized who he was.

"Did you have an appointment, Mr. Malloy?"

"No, but I'm sure he'll see me if he's in."

Alice jumped up from her seat. "I'll check."

She obviously knew he was in, but she had to

ask if he'd see Frank. Frank felt bad that he didn't really have any news to report, but that couldn't be helped.

Alice returned in a few moments and escorted him into Hatch's office. The instant the door closed behind her, Hatch said, "Do you have news already?"

Frank shook his head. "But I did hear something you ought to know, and I have a question for you."

Hatch's face fell, but he invited Frank to sit down. "What's the question?"

"I found out that Miss Wilson and Miss Northrup had an argument the day before Miss Northrup was murdered. It was about something Miss Northrup had learned, some piece of information. She had decided to tell you what it was, and Miss Wilson didn't want her to."

"What was it?"

"No one seems to know. My question is, did she meet with you the day she died and did she tell you whatever it was?"

Hatch thought this over for a long moment. "She didn't meet with me. She may have asked for an appointment. You can check with Alice about that, but if so, she didn't keep it. And you don't have any idea what she wanted to tell me?"

"I don't know for certain, but I do have a suspicion. She described it as a scandal of some kind."

"Dear heaven, I hired you to *prevent* a scandal." Hatch was genuinely distressed, as Frank had expected.

"I'm doing my best, Mr. Hatch, but I have to tell you, we've discovered some things about Miss Wilson and Miss Northrup that would be considered, uh, sensational if the press found out about them."

Hatch frowned, but he seemed more annoyed than alarmed. "Do you mean the romance between them?"

"As a matter of fact, yes," Frank said in surprise. "What do you know about it?"

"As little as I have to," Hatch said. "Oh, everyone knows Abigail had a smash on Miss Wilson. Do you know what a smash is?"

"Yes, it, uh, came up when we were questioning your students."

"Many of the girls develop strong feelings for the female teachers. They usually outgrow them in time, but Abigail did not. Instead she developed a romantic friendship with Miss Wilson."

This was something new. "What's a romantic friendship?"

Hatch shrugged. "Women are highly emotional creatures, as I'm sure you know. They tend to feel things more deeply than we do."

"Including friendship?"

"Exactly. Some females become as devoted to each other as lovers. These friendships often take the place of romantic relationships with the opposite sex."

"Especially with women who don't attract suitors or husbands."

"You seem familiar with the concept, Mr. Malloy."

"I told you, we've learned a lot about Miss Northrup and Miss Wilson."

"And you said what you'd learned might be considered sensational."

"Yes. You mentioned romance and—"

"Mr. Malloy, I hope you aren't going to suggest there might be something improper about the relationship between Miss Wilson and Miss Northrup," Hatch said coldly.

"And what would you say if I did?" Frank said, fascinated by the turn of the conversation.

"I would say you would be doing a disservice to two ladies of spotless reputation who did not deserve to have their good names slandered. No one wants that, I'm sure."

"Not even if the stories are true?"

"Not even then. You see, Mr. Malloy, this matter was settled long ago in a very public way."

"The matter of Miss Wilson and Miss Northrup's friendship?" Frank asked, confused.

"No, the question of possible impropriety between ladies who are intimate friends. You see, there was a legal case in England about forty years ago. It was a girls' boarding school, not so very different from our situation here at the Normal School. One of the students accused the two ladies who ran the school of engaging in improper behavior with each other. It seems they would share a bed late at night, when all the students were asleep, and they were overheard to say some, uh, questionable things to each other that indicated . . . well, improprieties. As you can imagine, the parents withdrew the students immediately. All of them. The school closed and the reputation of the two ladies was ruined, so they sued the accusing parent for slander."

"They did?" Frank asked in amazement.

"Of course. And they won, in spite of testimony from several of the older girls about their behavior. The judges, you see, knew perfectly well that respectable females experience no desire for sexual relations and submit to them in marriage merely as a means of procreating. And to please their husbands, of course. That being true, it's difficult to understand why either of these ladies would have been interested in such activities at all. In addition," he continued, stopping Frank's interruption with a raised hand, "sexual relations can only be conducted if one of the participants has a male member in order to complete the act. In the case of two ladies, there is no male member, and therefore, there can be no act of sexual congress."

Frank stared at Hatch, trying to judge whether

he was serious or not. "Do you really believe all that?"

"I have chosen to believe it, because if a parent asks me a question about the subject, this is what I will tell him. You see, Mr. Malloy, I am determined to avoid even the faintest suspicion of improprieties. Even though the English ladies won their lawsuit, their school was ruined and no parents would ever entrust their daughters to them again. That will not happen here."

Frank saw it very well. Hatch was prepared to do anything necessary to save his school. "You understand that if these women were murdered because of their . . . their romantic friendship, and the killer goes on trial—"

"—the newspapers will turn it into a circus. I can understand that very well. Your job is to prevent that."

"Prevent what, exactly?" Frank asked, growing more and more annoyed with Hatch with every word he spoke. "Prevent word of their romantic friendship from getting out or prevent the killer from being caught?"

"I thought you understood that I want the killer caught so he cannot harm anyone else."

"Anyone else at the school, in particular," Frank said.

"I'm most concerned about our staff and students, of course, but I'm willing to protect the general population as well," Hatch allowed.

"That's generous of you."

Hatch ignored his sarcasm. "I thought I made it clear to you that I wanted to avoid a scandal of any kind as well. I'm sure the Northrups share my concern. They won't want their daughter's good name tarnished in any way."

"So I'm back to my original question: What if the women were killed because of their romantic friendship?"

"When you find out who killed them and why, I think you will need to consult with me and the Northrups to determine what action we should take."

"And are you prepared to let the killer go free in order to protect the school from scandal?"

"You are ahead of yourself, Mr. Malloy. That is a decision I cannot possibly make at this time. And please, don't bother me again until you have something to report."

Frank thought he'd bother Hatch whenever he needed to, but he wasn't going to give the man warning, so he took his leave without another word. In the outer office, he found Alice had been waiting for his return. She jumped up again and closed Mr. Hatch's office door. At first, Frank thought she was simply being considerate of her employer's privacy, but then she came up to him and whispered, "Did you find out who did it?"

"Not yet," Frank said and watched her shoulders slump. "Can you tell me if Miss

Northrup tried to meet with Mr. Hatch on the day she died?"

Alice's eyes widened. "I'd forgotten all about that. She did! She came here early that morning and asked to see him."

"And did she?"

"He wasn't in yet. I told her she could wait, but she had classes to teach, so she made an appointment for . . . Let me check."

She hurried around to her desk and opened a book that lay on the corner, flipping pages until she found the one she wanted. "Yes, she made an appointment to speak to him at three o'clock that day." She sighed. "I guess Tobias found her in the gazebo before that, and I never thought of it again. Is it important? That she had an appointment, I mean?"

Frank gave her a smile, the kindest one he could manage. "It makes me pretty sure President Hatch didn't kill her."

Alice made a startled sound and covered her mouth with both hands. When she lowered them, she was smiling back.

13

Gino felt a little foolish. He shouldn't have acted so disappointed when Mr. Malloy told him he wouldn't need his help at the brothel. He didn't want Mr. Malloy to think he was interested in going to a brothel. It was just that he'd never been inside one before. This had seemed like the perfect opportunity to see what it was like without any complications or embarrassment. Instead, he was left to deal with a disgruntled Luther Northrup.

Getting the brothel's name and address had been the work of a moment, and then Raymond and Mr. Malloy had both left them.

Luther groaned and rubbed his face with both hands. "I was supposed to start work today."

"Then start. You can take me to Rudy first, though."

"I need to get dressed."

"Then do it."

Gino plopped himself down in the other chair, making it clear he had no intention of letting Luther out of his sight. Luther pushed himself to his feet and plodded back to the other side of the room and began to rummage around. Gino didn't actually watch the young man stripping out of his long underwear and putting on the snug-fitting outfit that seemed to be a uniform for the staff here. Still, he couldn't help noticing how muscular Luther was, just like the fellows he'd known in the army who spent a lot of time in clubs like this. Maybe he should look into this athletic business. He wondered idly if they allowed Italians to join.

When Luther was dressed and had shaved and carefully slicked back his hair, he turned to Gino with a resigned sigh. "Let's go."

Luther didn't bother to summon the elevator. Instead they descended the several flights of stairs more quickly than Gino would have, had he been setting the pace. He was a little breathless when they reached the lobby, although he couldn't help noticing that Luther wasn't winded at all.

Ledbetter looked up guiltily when he saw Gino, but he smiled at Luther. "You're starting today?"

"That's right," Luther said. "Say, Rudy, could you give my friend here some information? He'll tell you what he needs."

Ledbetter's smile faded when he glanced at Gino again. "Sure," he said, not sounding sure at all.

To Gino's dismay, Luther slipped away without another word, obviously anxious to separate himself from Gino's shady dealings. Gino knew better than to appear dismayed, however. Instead, he turned his wrath on Ledbetter, who certainly deserved it. "Thanks for sending Raymond up. Saved us from having to find him."

"I . . . I figured . . . You're welcome," Ledbetter managed.

From Ledbetter's expression, Gino judged that the lessons Malloy had taught him about how to intimidate someone had taken. "I figure you're still working off Mr. Malloy's tip, so you'll get me what I need for free. I need a list of the members who were here on these afternoons." He gave Ledbetter the dates.

But instead of going to a log book, the way he had when Mr. Malloy asked him if Luther had been at the club on a certain day, Ledbetter just frowned. "You mean the ones who just came in for some exercise or a meal?"

"That's right."

"We don't really keep records of that. Members come and go whenever it suits them, and they might leave by a side door when they're finished, so even if I saw them come in, I wouldn't know when they left."

"But you knew Northrup and Raymond had spent particular nights here," Gino reminded him.

"We keep records of that because we charge extra for the sleeping rooms. We put the charges on their bill."

Gino managed not to grind his teeth and glanced over at the door through which Luther had disappeared.

"I can't let you go in by yourself," Ledbetter said nervously. He obviously didn't want to displease Gino again, but he also didn't want to lose his job. "You have to be escorted by a member."

"Donnie!" a voice called, and Gino looked up to see Fred Vander Hooten, who had just come in from outside. "Back again?"

"Just the man I came to see," Gino lied, forgetting his grievances with Ledbetter. "Do you have a few minutes?"

"Sure. I was just going up to have some breakfast. Have you eaten?"

So once again his old army friend had rescued him. Gino was more than happy to have a second breakfast, and over coffee he told Vandy that he was back to find out more about Luther Northrup.

"A second woman has been murdered," he explained.

"How awful!" Vandy said. "Do you think the two deaths are connected?"

"Oh yes. The second woman also taught at the college with Abigail Northrup, and Abigail was renting a room in the woman's house."

"Then they must be connected. Say, you don't think Luther is involved, do you? Luther wouldn't kill his own sister, surely."

Gino shrugged off his concerns. "I don't think so, but my boss . . . Well, you know how it is. He says we have to be careful and check his alibi."

"Alibi? What's that?"

"It means where he was and what he was doing at the time and can anybody vouch for him."

"How exciting," Vandy said, although Gino didn't find it the least bit exciting. Rich men must have really boring lives. No wonder Mr. Malloy started the detective agency. "When does he need somebody to vouch for him? Maybe I can do it."

Plainly, he'd be terribly disappointed if he couldn't. "Well, I know he was in the city when the women were killed, but I need to know if he was here or not when the women were actually murdered. That's what he claims, at least. That would be Saturday afternoon and a week ago Wednesday, the day Miss Northrup died."

Vandy was terribly disappointed. "Wasn't here on Saturday. My cousin got married, don't you know? And I wasn't here the day the Northrup girl died either. I know Northrup was here when the word came, though, if that's any help. Everybody was talking about it the next day, how he turned white and had to sit down when he heard the news. Must've been an awful shock."

Gino hoped it was. "I guess I'm going to have to ask Northrup who he remembers seeing on those days, and then ask if they remember seeing him, too."

"That could be a little embarrassing for him," Vandy said. "I wouldn't want somebody checking up to make sure I didn't kill somebody, especially my own sister. What will people say?"

"I know, but we need to make sure—"

"Say, I know! I could help you," Vandy said. "Nobody'd think a thing of it if I started talking about Northrup's troubles. Everybody's been doing it. I'll tell them there's been a second murder, and that'll get the talk started again."

"But you can't just ask anybody in the club. You need to know who might've actually seen him. Let's find Northrup and get him to tell us who he remembers was here on those days."

"Good idea," Vandy said. "But . . . what if he can't remember?"

"Then he'll still be a suspect."

Frank realized he remained an object of curiosity among the young ladies at the Normal School. Apparently, a lot of them were still in residence and attending classes, or at least wandering around the building and gossiping in small clusters. The mood was somber, since they'd heard by now of Miss Wilson's murder, and he guessed that had been the main subject under discussion, at least until they saw him descending the stairs from Hatch's office. They seemed to have a lot to say about him after he passed each group. He reached the lobby and stopped, wondering if he should try to see anyone else while he was here, although he wasn't sure who might have something to tell him, since Miss Wilson's death had taken place somewhere else.

"Mr. Malloy, sir," a voice called.

Frank turned around to see Tobias hurrying toward him across the expanse of the lobby.

The janitor nodded when he reached Frank. "Thank you for stopping, sir. I just wanted to say I was right sorry to hear about Miss Wilson. She was a real nice lady."

"I'm sure she was."

Tobias glanced around to make sure nobody was close and lowered his voice. "I saw you was upstairs meeting with Mr. Hatch. I'm wondering, is you going to help find out who killed Miss Wilson, too?"

"That's very observant of you, Tobias. As a matter of fact, Mr. Hatch did ask me to help with that."

"Do you figure the same person done killed both of those ladies?"

"It's possible, but it's also possible different people did it."

Tobias nodded, as if he'd suspected that very thing. Then he glanced around again. Still satisfied that nobody was near, he said, "I saw her . . . Miss Wilson, that is. I saw her and Mr. Pelletier talking on Friday."

"Talking?"

"Well, she was upset, like. Not yelling or anything. Ladies like Miss Wilson, they don't get all emotional, at least not in public. But I could see whatever she was saying to Mr. Pelletier was important."

"How was he acting?" Frank asked with interest.

"Real serious. Didn't look like he said much, but seemed like he was trying to calm her down."

"That's interesting. Thank you for telling me, Tobias. Do you know where Mr. Pelletier is?"

"Well, now, I don't rightly know. He was teaching Miss Northrup's class and his own this morning, but I think he done left. Probably didn't feel like sitting around here, what with Miss Wilson dying like that and everything."

Frank would love to find out what Miss Wilson had been discussing with Pelletier the day before she turned up dead. "Do you happen to know where Mr. Pelletier lives, Tobias?"

"Oh no, sir. That ain't no concern of mine, but Miss Alice upstairs, she can tell you that directly," Tobias informed him with a satisfied smile.

Pelletier wasn't at home either, so Frank found the office of the coroner who had taken Miss Wilson's body. It was on a side street in Morningside Heights. Frank wished she'd been taken to Doc Haynes or at least to someone he knew would have done a thorough autopsy, but the police here hadn't found that necessary. Or else Miss Billingsly had chosen not to defile her friend's body. But the city was full of men calling themselves "coroners" who were really undertakers and did nothing more than embalm bodies, and some weren't even particularly good at that. Miss Wilson had been sent to one of them.

Frank was just grateful that Hatch knew where she'd been taken.

A ragged youth slouched on a chair in the corner of the small office of Jerusalem Moody, coroner. The place was dirty and the boy was dirtier. He jumped to his feet when Frank entered.

"Can I help you, sir?"

"Is Mr. Moody around?"

"No, sir. He went out to pick up a body."

"Well, then, maybe you can help me. I'd like to take a look at Miss Wilson's body. She's the lady who was strangled on Saturday."

The boy frowned. "You said you want to look at her?"

"Yes." He considered giving the boy his business card but decided he might not be able to read it. "I'm a private investigator. I've been hired to find out who killed her, and I need to take a look at her neck to see how she was strangled."

"Oh." The boy looked confused.

"Is there some reason why I can't see her?"

"Oh no, sir, I don't think. See, we usually charge, if somebody wants to fiddle with one of the bodies, but I don't think there'll be a charge for what you want. If looking is all you want, that is."

311

"Fiddle?" Frank asked, wondering if the boy meant what he thought.

The boy just shrugged. "She's in the back."

The back room was much larger, and three bodies lay on tables, in various stages of embalming. Miss Wilson's seemed to be complete. She lay in repose, covered by a dirty sheet.

"We're just waiting for her clothes to come. Don't know when the funeral is yet," the boy said.

Frank went over to where she lay. She looked very small and insignificant, as most dead people did. Her hair was a tangle and would have to be arranged, and her cheeks were a bit more sunken than he recalled, but all evidence of her dying struggle had been erased from her expression. He pulled the sheet down a bit to examine her neck.

He could see the marks where she had been strangled. Hatch had said the police told him a scarf had been used. He could see that. A cord or something thin would have left one even mark. This was more like a mass of small lines where the various folds of the scarf dug into her skin. The marks were a solid mass across the front of her neck, too, which meant she'd been strangled from behind.

This was interesting, because she would have been caught by surprise. Her killer might have even been walking with her and simply dropped back a few steps before pulling out the scarf and looping it over her head. He reached under the sheet and pulled out one of her hands.

"She put up a fight, looks like," the boy said.

Frank agreed. The nails had been trimmed, but they'd obviously been broken in the struggle. Two were ragged below the quick.

"Did she have any skin under her nails?"

The boy gaped at him in surprise. "We don't look for that. Why would we?"

Frank sighed, missing the experienced hand of Doc Haynes. "Because that would mean she'd scratched her attacker." Frank would then look for marks on a suspect's face or hands. But in this weather, the killer could've been wearing gloves that would've protected his hands, and if he was behind her, it's unlikely she could reach his face in the few moments before she lost consciousness. "Did she have any bruises anyplace else?" he asked, reluctant to look at her naked body himself.

"No, sir. Just that on her neck and her fingers."

Frank pulled the sheet back over her. "Do you have her clothes? The ones she was wearing, I mean?"

He did, but they told him nothing except that she'd lost control of her bladder as she died.

"Did you find out anything?" the boy asked when he stepped away from the table.

"Just that she might've been killed by a man or a woman and either somebody she knew or somebody she didn't."

"That don't seem like much help," he said.

Frank sighed. "It isn't."

"You should have put your office in our house," Sarah told Malloy when Gino and Maeve joined them that evening in the parlor to discuss their findings from the day. Mrs. Malloy was putting the children to bed.

"I didn't want the business to interfere with our family," he said with a sheepish smile. "So what did you learn today, Gino?"

"Only that checking Luther's alibi is going to be harder than we thought." He explained the problem with tracking members and told them of his friend's offer to help.

"Do you think he can do any good?" Malloy asked.

"He can do at least as well as I could, maybe better," Gino said. "I can't get into the club without a sponsor, and the members don't know me, so they aren't likely to answer my nosy questions even if I can manage to ask them. Vandy can do whatever he likes and nobody'll think anything of it."

"That's true, if he takes it seriously."

"I think he will. Did you have any luck with Raymond's alibi?"

Sarah thought Gino was smirking a bit, and when she looked at Malloy, she was sure he was blushing.

"Not a bit."

"What was Raymond's alibi?" she asked.

When Malloy didn't reply, Gino said, "He was visiting a brothel. Both times."

"That cad!" Maeve said. "And all the time he was begging poor Abigail to marry him!"

"I'm liking Cory Raymond less and less as the days go by," Sarah said. "And you say his alibi isn't good?"

"It may be," Malloy said, "but I'm told that at the brothel they don't pay much attention to when their customers come and go or even which days they show up."

"So his lady friend couldn't vouch for him?" Gino said, still smirking.

"His *lady friend,*" Malloy said with more than a trace of irony, "would be willing to say anything he wants her to, true or not."

"Oh," Sarah said.

"So you see the problem," Malloy said.

"That means both of them are still suspects," Maeve said.

"For at least one of the murders, yes," Malloy said. "And maybe both. I also had a chance to see Hatch this afternoon. I asked him if Abigail had told him anything about a scandal. He said she hadn't, and that he hadn't even seen her the day she died."

"And you believed him?" Gino asked.

"Not until I asked his secretary if Abigail had

met with him that day. Turns out she tried to see him first thing that morning, but he wasn't in, so she'd made an appointment for late afternoon."

"And by then she was dead," Sarah said. "Did he have any idea what kind of scandal she might have discovered?"

"No, and when I mentioned to him that we've discovered some things about Miss Wilson that people might consider scandalous, he told me a very interesting story." Malloy told them about the two women in England who had sued for slander. He tried to be discreet, in deference to Maeve, but she was the one who asked the most questions, so by the time he was finished, they all felt a little uncomfortable.

"So Hatch wouldn't have cared even if the scandal Abigail was going to tell him about was Miss Wilson and Miss Billingsly's affection for each other," Maeve said.

"I never could accept that anyway," Sarah said. "It sounds to me as if Abigail had genuine affection for Miss Wilson herself. She was even wearing the ring Miss Wilson had given her. Why would she have wanted to hurt her in any way?"

"Unfortunately, she's not here to tell us," Malloy said. "But I think you're right. And if that wasn't it, what else could it have been?"

"We still have the letters," Sarah said. "And the good news is that Mother found someone to read them for us." She told them about their visit to Madame de Béthune.

"How long do you think it will take her to read them?" Gino asked.

"She asked for a few days. I didn't want to rush her, since she's doing us such a huge favor."

"Of course," Malloy said. "Waiting is hard, though."

"Especially when we don't have any idea why these women were killed and if anybody else is in danger," Maeve said.

No one spoke for a long moment as the truth of Maeve's words sank in.

"What else can we do while we're waiting, though?" Sarah asked.

"Oh, I forgot to mention that when I was at the college today, Tobias told me he saw Miss Wilson talking to Pelletier and she looked upset," Malloy said. "I don't know that it had anything to do with her death, but I figured I'd ask Pelletier about it. At least he can tell me what was on her mind that day."

"Did you see him?" Gino asked.

"No. He wasn't at the school, so I got his home address. He lives in one of those bachelor apartments, but he wasn't home either. I'll try to run him to ground tomorrow afternoon when his classes are finished."

"I can check with Vandy to see how he's doing with Luther's alibi, I guess," Gino said.

"And I'll take Catherine for a walk," Maeve said, making everyone laugh.

"Sarah, it looks like you can attend to your own business for a change," Malloy said with a smile.

"Finally," Sarah said.

"What are you planning to do today?" Maeve asked Sarah as they lingered over coffee in the breakfast room that morning. Malloy had gone to his office, Mrs. Malloy and Brian had left for school, and Catherine had wandered off to the kitchen to visit with their cook, Velvet.

"I was thinking I could check with some more of the maternity homes today and see if any of them will take that poor girl at the Mission."

"When is her baby due again?"

"I'm guessing three or four months. Most of the homes don't have room to house the women longer than a month or two before the birth, and I can't stand the idea of putting her out of the Mission until then."

"How do the other girls feel about having her there?"

Sarah had been worried about that herself. "I haven't had the courage to ask Mrs. Keller. I know if she was having difficulty, she'd send for me, but they must be wondering why we've suddenly decided to break our rules for her."

"She was very clever to keep her condition

a secret until she'd wormed her way into Mrs. Keller's affections," Maeve observed slyly.

"Maeve, that's a terrible thing to say," Sarah tried, but Maeve only grinned.

"You know it's true. Do-gooders are the easiest people in the world to fool because they always assume everybody is as good as they are."

Sarah sighed. "I think your background has ruined your innocence."

"Being raised by a grifter, you mean? Of course it did. But you know I'm right."

"Unfortunately, I do," Sarah said. Had she ever been innocent enough to take everyone at face value? She supposed she had, but that was a very long time ago now. "I guess I do know Hannah deliberately misled everyone in order to have a safe place to live, but who can blame her?"

"Not me. And if she's that clever, she just might be able to take care of herself and her baby when the time comes."

"I hope so," Sarah said. "This world isn't very kind to unmarried girls and their children."

"It isn't kind to anyone unless you have a lot of money."

Sarah didn't even flinch. "Which is why I feel obligated to do what I can to make it a little kinder."

The doorbell rang, echoing in the massive foyer. The sound of Catherine's small feet running from the kitchen followed, along with the more sedate footsteps of their maid, Hattie.

"Who could that be?" Maeve asked. "It's early even for Mrs. Ellsworth."

"For an instant I thought it must be a birth," Sarah said. "It's hard to get used to not being summoned at all hours to bring a baby into the world."

"Do you miss it?"

"I don't miss the sleepless nights, but I do miss the deliveries. There's nothing more exciting than a new life."

"Too bad you can't just do it now and then for fun or something."

"That would mean turning women away when it wasn't convenient for me, though. I couldn't do that."

"There must be something—" Maeve began but stopped when Hattie appeared in the doorway.

"Mrs. Frank, there's a telegram for you." She had carried it in on a small silver tray, the way she'd been taught by a previous employer. She held the tray out for Sarah.

"Who's it from?" Maeve asked when Sarah had torn it open. Reading the message was short work.

"It's from Irene Raymond."

"Raymond? Isn't she the lover's sister?"

Sarah smiled. "We don't know he was Abigail's lover."

"He wanted to be, though. What does she say?"

"She wants to meet with me."

Maeve's eyes widened with anticipation. "Does she say why?"

"Of course not. You can't say much in a telegram, but I'm sure it's important."

"What are you going to do?"

Sarah gave it some thought. "Well, since I didn't really have anything planned, I think I'll take the train up to Tarrytown."

"Are you sure that's where she is?"

"It's where she sent the telegram from. I'll telegraph her back what train I'll be on. If she wants to meet me at the station, she can. If not, I'll go to her home."

"I'm guessing she won't want you to go to her home."

"That's what I'm thinking, too."

"Do you think she's figured out who killed Abigail?"

"I hope so, but maybe she just wants to convince me her brother didn't do it. Or maybe she has another reason completely."

"I wish I could go with you. I could ask Mrs. Ellsworth to take Catherine today," Maeve said with a hopeful smile.

Sarah shook her head. "I don't think that's necessary. This will probably be a waste of time. I just hope whatever she has to say is worth making a trip to her."

"If she was considerate, she would've come here," Maeve said.

"So you could go with me easily," Sarah said. "But I'm guessing she can't get away without some kind of explanation to her parents."

"And she probably doesn't want to tell them she's going to meet with you."

"I'm sure she doesn't. So I guess I need to change into a traveling suit and get to the station so I can find out what she wants to tell me."

Sarah was beginning to wish she had waited for a reply to her telegram, just to be sure Irene Raymond would meet with her after she'd made the long train ride up here. Her concerns ended abruptly, however, when she saw Irene waiting for her in the station.

"Thank you so much for coming, Mrs. Malloy," she said by way of greeting. "I've been so worried about what's going on, but I don't dare go into the city. My parents are absolutely terrified for me after what happened to Abigail."

"That's certainly understandable," Sarah said. "Do they know that I'm here?"

"No," she said quickly, glancing around as if afraid one of her parents might have suddenly appeared in the station. "I mean, I didn't tell them. I think they'd like to forget that Abigail is even dead. They don't want her name mentioned. It's just too painful."

"That's too bad."

They stood, staring at each other for a long

moment. Sarah wasn't sure what she was supposed to do next, and plainly, Irene hadn't thought that far ahead either.

"We should probably find someplace where we can talk," Sarah finally suggested.

"Oh yes, of course." She glanced around again, but the station offered nothing in the way of comfort except some wooden benches for waiting travelers. Besides, it was drafty and noisy from the trains and the travelers bustling through.

"I wouldn't mind some refreshment," Sarah said by way of suggestion.

Irene brightened instantly. "I'm so sorry! I didn't think. There's a ladies' tearoom just down the street."

"That would be perfect."

The two of them left the station and walked the block and a half to the tearoom. Unescorted ladies were often not welcome in restaurants, so places like this had become common in the city for ladies who needed a warm drink and a bite to eat while they were shopping. The place was small and tastefully furnished, offering tables for two or four. Sarah and Irene chose one near the back, away from the other customers, and ordered tea and some sandwiches.

When the waitress had gone and Irene still said nothing, Sarah said, "Did you have something you wanted to talk to me about?"

Poor Irene did seem awfully distressed. "I've

just been thinking about Abigail so much, ever since the funeral. I've been trying and trying to figure out why anyone would want to hurt her. I was hoping you'd have some news by now, I suppose."

Sarah's hopes sank. She'd entertained the notion that Irene might have some new information for her. "I do have some news, but it isn't good, I'm afraid."

"Oh dear, what is it?"

"Have you heard about Miss Wilson?"

"No. What has she done?"

"She was murdered on Saturday."

Plainly, this was the last thing Irene had expected to hear. She gasped, and the color drained from her face. "That's impossible!"

"I wish it were. It happened in the alley right outside of her house, apparently."

Tears flooded her lovely eyes. "How horrible. Who is doing this and why?"

"I was hoping you'd have something to tell me about it."

Her horror became fear. "Me? I don't know anything. I've been stuck here without any news for days. I didn't even know about poor Miss Wilson. Oh, and Miss Billingsly. She must be beside herself. How will she stay in that house alone now?"

Sarah had no idea, but that wasn't her concern. "Have you spoken with your brother recently?"

"Cory? Not really."

"I guess you haven't seen him," Sarah said, remembering he was in the city yesterday when Malloy and Gino questioned him.

"Oh, he came home yesterday, but I haven't . . . He's been in a foul mood ever since Abigail died. He doesn't want to talk to anyone."

He might have told Irene about Miss Wilson, Sarah thought, and wondered why he hadn't. "Did your parents know Cory had proposed to Abigail?"

Now she was disconcerted. "Uh, no, I don't think they did."

"Because Abigail's parents didn't know. They were surprised to hear it, too. They had no idea Cory had fallen in love with her, and they didn't think she was in love with him."

"They . . . they hadn't told anyone," Irene tried.

"But did Abigail really return his affection? After all, she was wearing a ring someone else had given her."

"Oh, Mrs. Malloy, you're just being mean now. You know Abby didn't want to marry Cory."

"I didn't intend to be mean. And you're right, I did know that, but I had to make sure you did. Why do you think he wanted to marry her?"

"You mean besides being in love with her?" she asked with a sad little smile.

"We both know he wasn't. What was his real reason?"

Irene sighed and her eyes grew moist again. "Cory is . . . Well, he isn't like Luther. Luther just isn't very bright, so he'll never amount to much. But Cory *is* bright. He could do anything he wanted in life. The problem is, he doesn't want to do anything for more than a day or two and then he gets bored. He's supposed to be learning our family's business from Father, but he hardly ever even goes to the office. He prefers to be in the city doing whatever it is he does there."

Sarah could have told her about the girl at the brothel, but she didn't. "What did Abigail have to do with this?"

"Father has been telling him he needs to settle down, and I think Cory thought if he married Abigail, that would make our parents happy. He'd be married and he could have his own home, and he wouldn't have to pay attention to what our parents wanted anymore."

"Do you think Abigail knew this?"

"I'm sure she suspected. Cory had never paid her any particular attention before, and then suddenly, he was begging for her hand."

"I wonder why she didn't just turn him down and be done with it," Sarah said.

Irene shook her head. "I think she took some perverse pleasure in teasing him. She knew he didn't love her and she didn't believe anything he said, so she was probably getting a little revenge before she turned him down completely." Irene's face suddenly lightened. "So you see, Cory didn't have any real reason to kill Abby. He didn't love her, so he wouldn't have cared if she turned him down. That means he couldn't possibly have done it."

Sarah simply stared back at her. If Abby had just been teasing him and finally admitted it, his wounded pride and his hot temper could have driven him to murder her.

14

Frank was happy to note that his presence at the Normal School today hardly caused a stir. The young ladies were obviously becoming used to seeing him, although they still whispered behind their hands after he passed by. He wondered what Hatch and the other teachers were saying to the students about him and the murders. How did they calm the girls' fears? How did they reassure the parents that the girls weren't going to be murdered after class one day?

He was awfully happy not to be a college president.

Frank found Professor Pelletier in his office, but he wasn't alone. A student sat in the wooden chair beside his desk. She'd been explaining something to him when they heard Frank approaching and looked up.

"Oh," she said, startled.

"*Excusez-moi*, Mr. Malloy, but I am occupied at the moment," Pelletier said. "If you would like to return later—"

"Oh, I was just leaving," the girl said, jumping to her feet with a distinct expression of alarm. "I . . . I can come back later, Professor." She scurried off, being careful to give Frank a wide berth as she passed, as if afraid he would grab her and do something untoward.

"I didn't mean to scare her," he said with a smile.

"The students, they are nervous with all the . . . unpleasantness."

"I'm sure they are. Can I talk to you for a few minutes?"

"*Mais oui*, sit down."

Frank took the chair the girl had occupied.

"What may I do for you?" Pelletier asked.

"I guess you know about Miss Wilson."

Pelletier made a distressed sound and lifted his hand to his forehead. "So sad. So tragic."

"Yes, and for two of the teachers here to be killed so close together, naturally, we think there must be some connection."

"And they lived in the same house. The connection is to be expected, yes?"

"Yes. So President Hatch has asked me to investigate both of the murders."

"He has told us this."

"Good. So I'm trying to figure out what the connection might be between the two deaths, if there's a reason somebody might want both of them dead."

Pelletier nodded, listening closely, almost as if he was afraid to miss a word.

"Someone told me they saw you and Miss Wilson talking on Friday, the day before she died."

Pelletier gave one of those shrugs Frank thought were so silly. "Miss Wilson, she and I would often talk."

"But they said she seemed upset that day, and that you were trying to calm her down."

He frowned, puzzled. "I am trying to remember, but . . ." He shrugged again.

"You see, it might help if I knew what she'd been doing and thinking in the days before she died. It might tell me what the connection was between her murder and Miss Northrup's. So I'd really appreciate it if you could try to remember what she said that day."

"I see. Ah, then let me think." He took a minute, furrowing his brow as he did so. "Oh, now it comes. She was . . . It was nothing. She was make the apology to me. She was sorry to suggest Miss Northrup be hired. If she did not, Miss Northrup would still be alive."

"Why would she apologize to *you* for that?"

Pelletier's smile didn't quite reach his eyes. "I did not want it. She convinced President Hatch."

That sounded a little strange to Frank. Miss Wilson didn't seem like the kind to apologize, because she probably never thought she'd been wrong. Of course, she'd never had her lover murdered before, either. "And what did you say?"

"I tell her we do not know and it is not her fault. This is what you say, even if you do not believe it," he added.

He was right about that, of course, although Pelletier would be a true gentleman indeed to say that to a woman who had forced him to accept Miss Northrup against his will. "That was very kind of you."

"I am glad now that I did, because she is gone."

Was that all it took to clear Pelletier's conscience? "Well, thank you for your time," he said, rising to his feet.

"Did you find anything to help when you look in Miss Northrup's desk?" Pelletier asked before Frank could leave.

"Not really, although whoever returned her keys also returned some letters."

"Letters?"

"Yes. As a matter of fact, some of them were in French."

"Were they? She had friends there, I think, from her trip. She did a tour last summer."

"That's what her mother told us."

"She visited my home when she was there," Pelletier said, his voice a little rough.

"Your home?"

"My . . . the place I was born."

"Your hometown."

"That is it. She was able to tell me about my family, how they are."

"That was nice of her."

"*Oui*. I was pleased."

"She was an outstanding young lady," Frank said, quoting her parents. "She'll be missed."

Pelletier smiled sadly. "She already is."

Sarah had begun to regret her impulse to come to Tarrytown. Malloy would tease her unmercifully when he found out how she'd wasted all this time talking to Irene Raymond, unless she could figure out something useful the girl might be able to tell her.

Their tea and sandwiches had arrived, and that gave Sarah some time to think. Then she remembered, Irene was the one who had first told her about the scandal Abigail had uncovered.

"Miss Raymond, you said that Abigail had discovered some sort of scandal."

"Yes, have you found out what it was yet?"

"No, but maybe you can help us some more. I don't think we know enough about it to figure it out yet."

"I told you, she wouldn't tell me what it was."

"Can you remember exactly what she said when she told you?"

"I told you before, it was something about someone at the school and when people found out, they'd be shocked."

"Do you think it could have involved Miss Wilson?"

This confused her. "Miss Wilson? Why would you think that?"

Sarah debated telling her and realized that with Miss Wilson dead, there was no reason to hesitate. "Miss Wilson is the one who gave Abigail the ring she was wearing when she died."

"Why would she have given Abigail a ring?"

"Because she was in love with her."

She needed a few moments, and Sarah watched her face as the truth dawned on her. "Dear heaven."

"Yes."

"But they were both females," she argued, her eyes begging Sarah to tell her she was mistaken.

"Miss Wilson and Miss Billingsly are both females, and they have lived together for many years."

"But they were friends," Irene said.

"More than friends, I believe."

"You mean . . . they were in love, too?"

"Yes," Sarah said. "And Abigail had come between them. That's the real reason Abigail would never have married your brother."

Irene covered her mouth with both hands and shook her head in silent denial. Sarah sipped her tea and gave her some time to think it through.

After a few minutes of stunned silence, Irene lowered her hands. "I had no idea. You must believe me."

"I do. I was just wondering if this was the scandal she had discovered. It would certainly be shocking."

"But if Abigail was involved . . ." Irene shook her head. "Abigail would never embarrass herself. You must understand. She had to be the best. She had to be the one everyone looked up to. She was always above reproach, and she had no pity for anyone who didn't meet her standards. She would happily have revealed someone else's weaknesses, but not if it reflected badly on her, too. And I think she also would not have lived in that house if she didn't approve of . . . of what was happening there. Mrs. Malloy, Abigail would have packed up her bags and carried them down the street herself if she had to in order to separate herself from something she considered scandalous."

So President Hatch had been correct, even though his reasons for dismissing their theories had been completely different. "Then who else at the college might have been behaving in a way Abigail considered scandalous?"

"I told you, I have no idea! Abigail wouldn't tell me, but she thought it was delicious."

"Delicious?" Sarah echoed in amazement.

"Oh yes, didn't I say that before? She was absolutely delighted over whatever it was that she had learned, and she was going to take great pleasure in exposing this person."

"But who did she hate at the school? Whose downfall would she have celebrated?"

Irene only shook her head. "No one that I knew

of from my time there. Of course, I wasn't there when she was a teacher. Other teachers were jealous of her, you know, but that just meant they hated her, not the other way around. Abigail wasn't petty. She only cared about important things."

"But it's possible someone at the school had earned her bad opinion recently."

"Anything is possible," Irene said, "and since someone killed her, it seems very likely."

Sarah could think of only one more question, one more element of the case that they hadn't figured out yet. Would Irene know anything about it?

"Do you know anything about the trip Abigail took to France last summer?"

Irene rolled her eyes. "Oh yes. I heard every glorious detail from her when she returned home."

"Did anything happen there that she might have wanted to keep secret?"

"What do you mean?"

"I mean she received some letters from there. She apparently kept most of them in her desk at the school, but she had hidden three of them. We were wondering why."

"I don't have any idea. What did they say? Didn't you read them?"

"They're in French, so we had to find someone to translate them for us."

"You should have asked Professor Pelletier. I'm sure he would have been happy to help. Abigail was always his best student, and he had a soft spot for her, I know. Oh, I just remembered! She did have a secret about that trip!"

"Oh," Frank said, turning back to Pelletier. "I almost forgot. Do you know of any reason why Miss Northrup might've hidden some of the letters she got from France?"

Suddenly, Pelletier's whole expression sharpened. "No, I do not. Why do you ask?"

"Because I found some letters that had been hidden," he said simply.

"These letters, where were they hidden, if that is even true?"

"She had tucked them into one of her books." Which meant that whoever took the letters out of her desk hadn't found them, but Frank wasn't going to mention that to Pelletier.

"Is that really hiding? Ah, perhaps so, to a young lady. But I do not know why she might have hidden some of the letters, as you say. Perhaps the letters themselves will say."

"They're written in French, so I can't read them."

"Ah, *bien sûr*. That is too bad."

"Yes, but you're probably right. They might not have really been hidden. She just tucked them into the book and forgot about them."

"*Oui*, that is most likely. Young ladies are like that. Careless."

Except Frank knew Abigail Northrup was anything but careless.

"Abigail had a secret?" Sarah asked, trying not to get her hopes up. If this was like the rest of the conversation, it would be another waste of her time.

"Yes, she was so excited about it. She finally got Professor Pelletier to tell her the name of his hometown. We had decided he was ashamed of it because he would never say exactly where in France he was from. He'd just say 'a small town in Bourgogne.' Abby knew she was going to France, but she didn't tell him, you see. She planned to visit this town while she was there, and then when she returned, to surprise him with news from his family or whomever she could find who remembered him."

"And did she?"

"Yes, although he wasn't as pleased as she'd expected. Or maybe she wasn't as pleased as she'd expected."

"What do you mean?"

"I mean the town turned out to be just a dirty little place with a crumbling church and a few old houses. She only stayed two or three days, I gathered, and she wouldn't say much about it. Then Professor Pelletier wasn't happy that she'd gone there either. I think we were right, that he was ashamed, and now he was even more ashamed because Abigail knew."

"That's understandable, I guess."

"Of course it is. Their relationship . . . Well, I don't think it was the same after that. She used to talk about him with such respect, and I expected that when she was teaching with him, he would be a . . . a . . . guide or . . ."

"A mentor?" Sarah said.

"Yes, a mentor to her. But something changed."

"Could Professor Pelletier be the one she'd discovered a scandal about?"

Irene just frowned. "Because he came from a poor little town in France? Who cares about that except him?"

"And you said Abigail wasn't petty."

"She would never try to embarrass someone about something like that. She would consider it beneath her. I don't think she ever even mentioned it to anyone but me. I was also the only one who knew why she wanted to go to that town in the first place, so she had to tell me what happened, but only because I pestered her about it. She was probably sorry to have done it at all."

When she finally got home, Sarah had barely had time to greet Catherine and Maeve and change out of her traveling clothes before her mother arrived unexpectedly. The maid brought her straight up to Sarah's private sitting room.

"I'm so glad you're back," her mother said by way of greeting. "I telephoned earlier and Maeve told me you'd gone off somewhere on the train, so I decided to just come here and wait for you to get home."

"I was in Tarrytown, talking to Abigail Northrup's best friend. What's happened?"

"Madame de Béthune sent me word that she has finished with the letters and wants to see us as soon as possible."

"But she said she'd need several days," Sarah said, already on her feet.

"I know, but her note said she found the letters so interesting, she put everything else aside. She thinks she has some good information for us."

"That's wonderful. I'll just need a few minutes to get dressed again."

The Decker carriage was waiting for them, and they somehow endured the excruciatingly slow trip through the city streets. Sarah found herself wondering if a motorcar would make any difference. She supposed the tangle of horses and wagons at every intersection would still make for slow going, no matter how fast your motorcar could move.

When they arrived, at last, the maid took them right upstairs to the formal parlor, where Madame de Béthune and Millicent awaited them. Sarah couldn't help noticing that both of her hostesses were practically glowing with the anticipation of their visit.

"Oh, Sarah, this is the most interesting thing that's happened to me in years," Millicent said when she'd welcomed Sarah and her mother. "I can't believe I'm helping to solve a murder."

"I'm sure your mother would be very proud," Sarah's mother said with just a trace of irony.

Millicent laughed gaily. "You know she'd be horrified, but my dear *belle-mère* shares my excitement, don't you?"

Madame de Béthune smiled her assent. "I thought this would be the work of days, but no. The reading, it was very fast. These letters . . ." She held up the packet that Malloy had found in Abigail's desk. "These letters are nothing. They are from friends saying how is the weather and Mama is well. Nothing." She slapped them back onto the table to show her disdain for them. Then she picked up the three Malloy had found hidden in the book. "These are not nothing. These are *très important*."

"*Belle-mère* read the letters," Millicent explained, "and then she tried to translate them for you. She wasn't sure about some of the English words, however, so she would tell me what they said in French and I helped her choose how to phrase it. We worked on them for most of the morning," she said proudly.

"We never expected you to devote so much effort to it," Mrs. Decker said.

"How could we not," Millicent said, "when a young woman's life was taken?"

"We're very grateful," Sarah said, somehow managing not to insist Madame de Béthune tell them instantly what she'd discovered.

"We wrote out the translations for you," Millicent said, picking up several sheets of paper and finally handing them to Sarah. "I'm afraid the meaning isn't entirely clear to us because we don't know what she had written to these people or how she replied to their letters."

"And we do not know this person that they speak about," Madame de Béthune added.

"But perhaps it will make more sense to you," Millicent said.

Sarah took the papers and glanced at the neat rows of handwriting. "I don't know how to thank you. I don't know what we would have done without your help." Would it be rude to sit here and read the letters? Sarah desperately wanted to, but . . .

"You must read them now," Madame de Béthune said. "You must tell us what they mean."

"And if the information is important," Millicent added.

Sarah gave them a grateful smile. They had thoughtfully dated each of the translations. The first one was from October. It was signed with a woman's name. Much of the letter was "nothing," as Madame de Béthune described it. She was apparently responding to Abigail's letter of thanks for offering her hospitality when she had visited the woman's village.

"Do you know where this town is that she mentions?" Sarah asked.

"We did not," Madame de Béthune said.

"But I looked it up," Millicent said. "I had all sorts of books about France so I could learn about it when I married Claude. We finally found it. It's a little town in—"

"Bourgogne," Sarah guessed.

"How did you know?" Millicent said. "*Belle-mère* said it's no bigger than a flea dropping."

This made all the ladies laugh.

"The girl who died, her best friend mentioned that she'd visited this town. It was the hometown of the professor who teaches French at the school. She wanted to come back and surprise him with news from his home."

Millicent and her mother-in-law exchanged a knowing glance.

"What is it?" Sarah's mother asked.

"Keep reading," Millicent urged Sarah. "I don't want to spoil it."

The letter concluded with the lady telling Abigail the name of some town official who could give her the information she was seeking. He had apparently been unavailable when Abigail was there, but this lady had told him Abigail would be contacting him.

Sarah passed the paper to her mother and started reading the second one.

This one was dated in December and was signed by a man, the same name the previous letter writer had given Abigail in the first letter.

"Do you know the person he names?" Millicent asked.

"Oh yes," Sarah said. "Professor Pelletier is the one who teaches French at the Normal School."

"We had guessed as much. And this village was his hometown?"

"That's what he told Abigail," Sarah said, remembering what Irene Raymond had said just this morning.

"What does it say?" her mother asked when Sarah had finished reading the rest of the letter.

"He says he can't find anyone who remembers a Jacques Pelletier ever living in the village or anyone from the village ever emigrating to America at all, for that matter."

"How strange," her mother said.

"*Oui*," Madame de Béthune said. "In a town like that, a son who went to America, he would be a hero. He would send money home. He would be known to everyone."

"But if his family had died . . ." Sarah's mother tried.

"They would all remember. Everyone," Madame de Béthune insisted. "Read the last letter."

Sarah passed the second letter to her mother and picked up the third. This one was dated two weeks before Abigail died. She must have received it only days before her death. The same official thanked her for the donation to the church and informed her the priest had been happy to check the baptismal records. They had determined that no family named Pelletier had ever lived in that village in the past one hundred years.

"What does it mean?" Sarah's mother asked when she had told her.

"I think it means that Professor Pelletier lied about being born in this village."

"Why would he do that?" her mother asked.

"*Belle-mère* and I have been discussing this," Millicent said. "And we have an idea."

"Did you see? On the letter from the lady," Madame de Béthune said.

Mrs. Decker shuffled to it.

"The last thing she writes," Madame de Béthune said.

"'Your written French is excellent. So much better than when you speak,'" Sarah's mother read. "Why is that important?"

"You say before how the girl who die, she does not speak the *français* so well."

"And you said that's what happens when Americans teach Americans to speak French,"

Sarah recalled. "Except Abigail was taught by a Frenchman, at least once she got to the Normal School."

"A Frenchman who lied about where he was from," Millicent said.

"But maybe he had a good reason for lying," Sarah's mother said.

"What would that reason be?" Millicent asked.

"Maybe he was ashamed of his real hometown."

"Then why would he claim to be from this town?" Sarah asked, almost thinking out loud. "It's no bigger than a flea dropping, and even Abigail said it was a sad place, dirty and poor."

"He claimed it," Madame de Béthune said, "because no one will know of it and no one will go there."

"So no one will ever guess that he isn't French at all," Millicent concluded triumphantly.

Frank found Gino moping in their office, where they'd agreed to meet at the end of the day.

"No luck?" Frank asked.

"I don't know what you'd call luck, but I did see my friend Vandy. He found three fellows who not only saw Luther Northrup at the club on the day Abigail died, but they swam with him in the pool for an hour or more."

"You should be happy. At least we don't have to tell the Northrups their son killed their daughter."

"I suppose that is good news."

"What about the day Miss Wilson was killed?"

"Nobody was sure about that. Her death didn't make any impression on the members, because they never even heard of her, so nobody remembered that day in particular."

"Then cheer up, maybe Luther killed Miss Wilson."

"Very funny. That's not why I'm down. I'm worried. What if we can't solve this case?"

"Do you think you'll lose your job if we don't?" Frank asked with a grin.

Gino gave him a glare. He was getting better at it. "I'm just afraid we'll stop getting clients if we don't solve the cases."

Frank supposed he had a point. "It's much too soon to give up."

"How about you? Did you have any luck?"

"Not much. I caught Pelletier in his office and asked him what he and Miss Wilson had been talking about the day before she died. He claimed she was apologizing to him for getting Abigail hired over his objections."

"Why would she do that?"

"I'm glad I'm not the only one who thought that was strange. He said she'd realized that if Abigail hadn't gotten the job at the college, she would still be alive."

Gino considered this for a moment. "I guess that could be true."

"Unless you believe we all have our time to go,

and she would've gotten run over by a trolley car or something that day if she didn't work at the school."

"You're just trying to confuse me now."

Frank didn't deny it. "I guess we should go on home. I think we've done all we can for today, and it's really getting cold outside."

Before Gino could reply, the telephone rang. Gino reached for it, but Frank scooped it up before he could get it, just to tease him.

"Frank Malloy, Confidential Inquiries."

"Mr. Malloy, is that you?"

"Yes, it is."

"Jacques Pelletier here. Please forgive, but you say about some letters you find. They are in French, you say, and I am too stupid to offer to read them for you. I think of this when you are gone."

"That's very nice of you to offer, Professor."

"You have the letters, no?"

"Yes, I do," Frank said, stretching the truth just a bit.

"We can meet, and I can do this for you."

"When would you like to meet?"

"This evening? There is a tavern near the school." He gave the name and address. "I can meet you there. We can have a meal together."

"I can be there in an hour or so. Thank you, Professor. This is a big help."

"That was Pelletier," Gino said when Frank had hung up.

"Yes. When I saw him today, I told him about finding the letters. He said he didn't think the ones in the book were really hidden. He thought maybe Abigail stuck them in there and forgot or something."

"That's possible, I guess."

"And now he's offering to translate them for me."

"That's nice of him."

"I thought so, too."

"Why didn't you tell him we already have somebody doing that for us?"

Frank smiled. "Because I'm curious. I told him in his office that the letters were in French and I couldn't read them. I expected him to offer to translate them for me, but he didn't. He claims he didn't think of it then, but that would be strange, wouldn't it?"

"Yes, it would."

"So I'm wondering why he waited until later to suggest it."

"Does it matter?"

"I don't know. But I'm going to ask him when we meet."

The winter sun had completely deserted the city by the time the carriage delivered Sarah and her mother back to the Malloy home. They had been discussing Professor Pelletier the entire way, trying to figure out if Madame de Béthune's theory could possibly be true.

"More than one person told me how the French made fun of Abigail's accent when she was there," Sarah said.

"That doesn't prove anything," her mother argued right back. "And even if all of this is true and this Pelletier person is only pretending to be French, who would care?"

"I'm sure the people at the Normal School would care. They've been bragging for years that they have a real Frenchman teaching the students. The parents and probably the students as well would be furious, and Pelletier would be a laughingstock."

"And lose his job, too. But would someone commit murder over something like that?"

"Don't forget that Abigail's murder was apparently an impulse. Whoever killed her just happened to see the screwdriver lying there and grabbed it. This person probably hadn't intended to do anything to her at all except talk."

"I suppose if you intended to murder someone, you would plan a bit ahead of time," her mother said.

Sarah couldn't help smiling. "I think you'd at least bring a weapon of some kind. You simply can't count on finding something effective just lying around."

"Now you're making fun of me."

"I'm feeling brave because I know you don't have a weapon, Mother."

"You underestimate me. I always have a hatpin."

"Thank you for the warning. I won't make that mistake again."

"But seriously, Sarah, I'm still not convinced."

"I'm not completely certain myself, and even if I were, we don't know any reason he might have killed Miss Wilson, too."

"Unless she figured it out and confronted him about it," her mother said.

"Now you're trying to prove Pelletier is guilty."

"I know. What a muddle."

"It is, but this is the most promising information we've gotten so far. I can't wait to tell Malloy. He'll be a good judge of whether it rings true or not. I can't believe we didn't even consider Pelletier a suspect until now." They'd pulled up in front of Sarah's house. "Will you come in for a while?"

"I should get the carriage home. It's too cold to leave the horses standing outside for any length of time."

Another good reason to get a motorcar, Sarah thought. She thanked her mother again for finding Madame de Béthune and wished her good night.

The house was quiet long enough for Sarah to take off her coat, but by then the children had realized that someone had come home. Catherine and Brian came clattering down the stairs from the nursery with Maeve right behind them. Sarah spent the next few minutes hearing about their day. Mrs. Malloy came out of her rooms to interpret for Brian, although Sarah was pleased to realize she could understand a good bit of what he was saying with his American Sign Language. The whole family was making good progress.

When the children had settled down, Sarah helped Maeve herd them back upstairs.

"How did your visit with the French lady go?" Maeve asked after the children had run on ahead.

"Very well. We found out some interesting information."

"I can't wait to hear all about it."

"And I can't wait to tell Malloy what we've learned. Is he home yet?"

"No, he's not. He telephoned to say he wouldn't be having supper with us tonight."

"Why not?"

"He's meeting someone for dinner."

"Did he say who it was?"

"Yes, that Professor Pelletier."

15

Frank hadn't been sure what to expect, but the tavern Pelletier had sent him to was a perfectly respectable place where family men obviously went to drink without worrying about being robbed or getting into a fight. A rotund German and his equally stout wife ran the place, and they poured him a beer almost before he sat down at one of the tables.

Business was slow tonight. The dropping temperatures were probably keeping people home. He'd expected Pelletier to be waiting for him, but he saw no familiar faces at all among the handful of customers. Frank sipped the beer, but decided he wanted coffee to warm him up instead. He told the waitress he was waiting for someone and that they'd order dinner when his friend arrived.

Earlier customers had left newspapers behind, so he occupied himself by scanning them, stopping every now and then to read a story. Each time the door opened, he looked up, expecting to see Pelletier, but the man never appeared.

"I think your friend is not coming," the German said after a while. "Maybe the cold is too much for him."

"Maybe it is." Frank's stomach growled,

reminding him Pelletier had promised they would eat. "In any case, I'm tired of waiting for him. Can you bring me some supper?"

The dish being served that night was a thick stew, so Frank enjoyed a bowl of it, along with another beer. When he was finished, he checked his watch and realized over two hours had passed since he'd told Pelletier he'd meet him in one hour. Pelletier had only been coming from a few blocks away, so he had either been detained or changed his mind about coming.

Frank had traveled all the way up to Morningside Heights for a second time that day in the bitter cold and this time for nothing at all. He paid his bill and bundled up, pulling on gloves and winding a scarf around his neck. Then he set out for the unpleasant trip home.

Although it wasn't late, the streets were fairly empty, probably because of the cold. People would be sheltering their horses as best they could and huddling in their homes until the morning sun brought the temperatures back up a bit. Frank paused a moment outside the tavern and looked up and down the street, just in case Pelletier happened to be running down the street in a frantic effort to catch him before he left. But he saw no one running or hurrying or even the least bit interested in him.

With another sigh, he started down the street toward the nearest El station. He'd taken only a few steps when he heard someone calling. He stopped to listen. There it was again.

"Malloy!"

The call was weak, as if the person were sick or injured. He looked around, trying to decide from what direction it had come. The cold and the buildings distorted sounds.

"Here," the voice called again. "Across the street. Hurry, please."

This was definitely someone hurt. Frank headed across the street, moving carefully over the cobbles so he didn't twist an ankle and fall in the darkness. The shadows lay thick in front of the storefronts, closed now, their windows black.

"Where are you?" he called, his words making tinny echoes.

"In here. Can't walk," the voice called.

It seemed to be coming from the alley that ran between two of the stores. Could it be Pelletier? Had someone waylaid him on his way to their meeting and tried to kill him as well?

"Pelletier?" he tried.

"*Oui*, please help!" He sounded desperate.

Wishing for a light, Frank entered the alley, moving slowly and stepping carefully. The meager light from the streetlamps faded quickly as he moved down the narrow passage. "Where are you?"

He jumped at a skittering sound before he realized it was a rat racing away from him. The stench of garbage and dung clogged his nose, making him wish he hadn't eaten so much stew. "Where are you, Pelletier?"

Just as he took another step, he heard a slight scraping behind him. Before he could turn, something swept quickly, softly, across his face and tightened around his neck.

Sarah let herself back into the house quietly, so Catherine wouldn't hear. She didn't want the children to know she'd been out and wonder why.

Maeve jumped up from where she'd been sitting beside the telephone in the foyer. "Any word?"

"I sent a telegram to Gino's parents' house, but the telegraph operator told me it was foolish to wait for an answer that might not come. They'll bring it right over if it does. I gave them a nice tip and promised an equally large one for a delivery."

"I've been telephoning the office every fifteen minutes, but there's still no answer."

"No, I'm sure Gino left, and he probably went home. He'll telephone as soon as he gets my telegram, I'm sure."

"Or finds Mr. Malloy, if he knows where he was meeting this professor," Maeve said. "Or come over here, if he doesn't. We're probably worrying for nothing. If they're meeting for a meal, they'll be in a public place, after all."

"But Malloy won't know he might be meeting with a murderer," Sarah said.

"And the professor doesn't have any reason to

harm Mr. Malloy," Maeve pointed out reasonably.

"You're right, of course," Sarah said, taking off her coat and hat and gloves and savoring the warmth of the house.

"Mrs. Malloy and the children already ate supper while you were out, but Velvet is keeping ours warm."

"I don't think I could eat a bite," Sarah said.

"Just try. It'll give you something to do while you're waiting, at least."

Their cook was only too happy to dish up their supper, and Hattie served them in the breakfast room because Sarah didn't want to sit in the giant dining room with just the two of them. She managed only a few mouthfuls. She noticed that Maeve didn't seem very hungry either.

"Are you sure this professor is the killer?" Maeve asked.

"Not positive, of course, but the more I think about it, the more I think we missed some important clues. Irene Raymond had told me that Abigail said she'd discovered a scandal. It concerned one person at the school, and people would be shocked. She also said that President Hatch would have to take some action."

"If this professor was just pretending to be French all these years, then that would fit everything she said."

"I know. I feel like such a fool for not realizing it before."

"How could you, though? Without the information in the letters, I mean. Abigail herself didn't take any action until she got the final letter. You said that was only a few days before she died."

"It had to have been. That would fit with all the other things we know, too. She had an argument with Miss Wilson the day before she died. She was going to reveal something scandalous about someone at the school, and Miss Wilson was trying to stop her."

"Did she tell Miss Wilson what it was, do you think?"

"Miss Billingsly and Bathsheba didn't think so, and Miss Wilson might've thought she was the one who was going to be humiliated."

"Imagine how upset Miss Wilson would've been to think that Abigail was going to betray her."

"She must have been terrified," Sarah agreed. "If only Abigail had told Miss Wilson who was really involved. Maybe Miss Wilson could have advised her on how to handle the situation better."

"She could hardly have handled it worse than ending up murdered," Maeve said.

Sarah was just about to agree when the shrill ring of the telephone pierced the stillness of the house.

Frank instinctively grabbed for his throat while his brain scrambled to make sense of what was happening. The figure behind him jerked harder and the constriction on his neck increased, pulling him up onto his toes while his gloved fingers clawed desperately at the fabric at his throat.

He tried to cry out but no sound could escape. Some tiny, still-functioning part of his brain reminded him that this was how Miss Wilson had died. What had he thought she could have done to save herself?

She couldn't have done much, but he was bigger and stronger and he began to thrash around, swinging his elbows to strike his assailant. His elbows hit only air, but his assailant lost his grip for a moment, and Frank caught a gasp of air before the noose tightened again. His toes struggled for purchase on the slick cobbles, desperate for a foothold he could use for leverage. But his slipping jerked his attacker off-balance, too. He staggered, loosening his grip again, and Frank lunged forward, carrying his attacker with him.

Both men fell into the inky blackness with a thud. Pain exploded somewhere, but Frank had no time to register where. His attacker was moving again, trying to escape now, but Frank grabbed a handful of his coat with one hand and drove his other fist blindly into the body, eliciting a grunt of pain.

"Mr. Malloy, where are you?" Gino's voice called, frantic.

"Here!" he replied, driving home another punch. This one went to his attacker's face and something crunched beneath his fist.

Pelletier cried out and tried to fight back, but Gino was suddenly there. He needed a few seconds to sort out who was who in the darkness, but then he ended the fight with a single blow.

"What did you do?" Frank asked when he realized Pelletier had gone limp.

"Blackjack," Gino said.

Hours after Malloy's telephone call informing her he'd be even later than he'd thought, when he had finally returned home, Sarah had installed Malloy upstairs in their private sitting room and allowed Maeve and Gino to join them. She'd stripped him out of his filthy clothes, which were ruined from rolling around in the garbage-filled alley, and bandaged his injured knee and a few other abrasions and brought him a hot toddy. In fact, all of them were enjoying hot toddies as they shared the day's adventures. Sarah was sure that Malloy's encounter with Pelletier had been harder on her than it had been on him.

"So it looks like your French lady was right," Malloy said when Sarah had told them what Madame de Béthune had said. "Pelletier told us everything when we got him to the police station."

"The cops up in Morningside Heights weren't too happy to see us," Gino said. "But then we told them they could take all the credit for arresting Pelletier, so they cheered right up."

"How generous of you," Sarah said.

"As long as Hatch and the Northrups know we were responsible, that's all that matters," Malloy said.

"So how did Pelletier get the idea to pretend he was French?" Maeve asked.

"He'd been trying to earn a living as a tutor and not having much luck," Malloy said. "He'd always been pretty good at French, so he tried getting a job teaching that, but nobody wanted to hire him. Someone at some school made a remark that if he were French, he could get a job easily, since Americans love France so much. But that's only because they haven't been there," Malloy added to Gino and Maeve, making them smile.

"So he started using that phony accent," Gino said, continuing the story. "It was pretty easy, I guess, so long as he avoided real French people."

"But he had to invent some kind of life story, I guess," Sarah said.

"Yes, people kept asking him where he was from, so he chose this little town nobody ever heard of," Malloy said.

"And his plan worked beautifully for years, until Abigail came along," Sarah said.

"He's still furious at her," Gino said. "Do you know what he's the maddest about, though? He's mad because she said he was a bad teacher.

She told him how real French people couldn't even understand her, and it was his fault for pretending to be French and not being able to speak it properly."

"So I suppose she must have confronted him when she got the letters from France telling her they never heard of him in the town where he was supposed to have been born," Sarah said.

"Yes. She was going to go straight to Hatch that morning, I gather, but he wasn't available," Frank said. "She had to wait all day, but I guess her secret was just too exciting and she couldn't help letting something slip to Pelletier."

"Why were they outside in the gazebo, though?" Maeve asked. "They shared an office, so why not just talk there?"

"Pelletier had an idea of what she was going to say," Gino said. "He knew she'd been to the town, after all. And they couldn't have a private conversation in their office. Students were always coming and going, and they couldn't close the door when they were in there together."

"Oh yes, for propriety's sake," Sarah said.

"That's right. They're very strict about that at the school. So he suggested they go outside to the gazebo. Nobody would overhear them there," Gino said.

"I think Pelletier thought he could talk Abigail out of betraying him," Malloy said. "That's what he was hoping, anyway, but she refused."

"Her sense of right and wrong wouldn't allow her to forgive him," Sarah said.

"He claims he didn't mean to kill her," Gino said. "He cried like a baby when he told us that part. He just saw his whole life ruined. He'd lose his career and be laughed out of the city. He was so furious, he doesn't even remember picking up the screwdriver. He said he just wanted to make her stop smiling so smugly at him. And then she was dead."

"Or so he says," Malloy said. "Who knows what really happened, and it doesn't matter. He killed her."

"Did he kill Miss Wilson, too?" Maeve asked.

Malloy nodded.

"But why?" Maeve asked.

"He said she figured out that he killed Abigail," Gino said. "We're not sure how, though."

"It may have had something to do with the ring," Sarah said.

"What ring?" Maeve asked.

"You remember, Abigail was wearing a ring on a chain around her neck when she died. We found out that Miss Wilson had given it to her because she was in love with her. She didn't know Abigail was wearing it until I told her, though. Until then, she probably believed—and feared—that Abigail was going to betray her to President Hatch, but when she found out Abigail was wearing the ring, she realized Abigail loved her in return. That may have gotten her thinking about who else Abigail might know something about."

"She probably didn't even know what it was," Maeve said.

"She would've known Abigail got letters from France and may have figured it out, though," Sarah said.

"Then she made the mistake of saying something to Pelletier," Gino said.

"How did he kill her, though?" Maeve asked.

"He met her at a restaurant to talk," Malloy said. "She must've realized she shouldn't be alone with him if he killed Abigail, but she thought she'd be safe in a public place."

Sarah gave Maeve a meaningful look that made her shrug apologetically.

"Then he followed her home," Gino said. "When she was in the alley behind her house, he threw his scarf around her neck and killed her."

"Just like he tried to kill Malloy," Sarah said with a shudder.

"He never stood a chance with me," Malloy said. "He didn't realize how much harder it would be to kill a man."

Sarah wasn't so sure about that. "I just don't understand why he attacked you in the first place."

"Oh, I guess that wouldn't make sense unless you knew how I lied to Pelletier," Malloy said. "I had told him that afternoon about the letters written in French that I'd found in the book. When he called our office later, he offered to translate them for me. You know, I didn't think of it at the time, but he should have also offered to translate the other letters, but he'd already read them, so he knew there was nothing in them he needed to worry about."

"Didn't you tell him you already had someone reading the letters?" Sarah asked.

"No, because I was curious about why he was being so helpful suddenly. So when he asked me if I had the letters, I told him I did, and he suggested that we meet so he could read them for me."

"But then he didn't meet you," Sarah said.

"No, all he wanted was the letters, and he didn't want to be seen with me, so he waited outside until I figured out he wasn't coming."

"He was pretty frozen by then," Gino remarked.

"I'm sure he was," Sarah said.

"And when I left," Malloy continued doggedly, "he attacked me. He planned to steal the letters and destroy them once and for all."

"And kill another person in the bargain," Sarah said, furious.

"Luckily, Mr. Malloy had his trusty bodyguard to save him, though," Maeve said with a sly grin.

Gino groaned, his humiliation complete.

"It wasn't his fault," Malloy said. "He did exactly what I told him to do."

"You told him to go off and leave you alone to

get murdered?" Maeve asked with fake innocence.

Poor Gino groaned again, and Malloy couldn't help chuckling. "He was in the tavern with me the whole time, and he knew to wait a few minutes before he followed me out, in case Pelletier tried to sneak up on me outside."

"I saw Mr. Malloy cross the street, but I didn't see him go into the alley," Gino hurried to explain. "So when I came out and he was gone, I thought he'd just gotten ahead of me. I hurried off, but when I didn't catch up to him and still didn't see him anywhere, I figured something was wrong and I went back."

"Thank heaven you did," Sarah said.

"Oh, Mr. Malloy had him under control by then," Gino said. "I just used my blackjack on him because I was mad I'd missed all the fun."

"What a sad story," Maeve said. "Two women dead just because a man lied and was ashamed to admit it."

"Murder is always a sad story," Sarah said. "No one ever has a really good reason for it, or at least not a reason I ever think is good enough."

"But at least we found the killer, so Gino doesn't have to worry about going back to the police force," Malloy said, earning a scowl from him.

"Have you sent word to the Northrups yet?" Sarah asked.

"I sent a telegram telling them Pelletier had been arrested and that I'd be coming up to see them in a day or two. I'll telephone Hatch's office in the morning, and then go see him."

"I don't think he's going to be happy to find out what really happened," Sarah said.

"I can't do anything about that. He wanted to avoid a scandal, but he also wanted the killer caught and removed. All things considered, this scandal isn't much at all. The man was a good actor and he fooled lots of people for a long time. It's embarrassing, but I think the school will survive."

"I'm sure it will," Sarah said. "And now I think we should get to our beds. Gino, it's far too late for you to go home, so Maeve will show you to one of our spare rooms. We'll sort everything else out in the morning."

Over the next few days, Sarah read with interest the newspaper accounts of Pelletier's crimes. In these versions, Abigail and Miss Wilson were tragic heroines for having discovered the evil professor's secret. No hint of scandal touched either of them, and they were described in the printed accounts as friends and colleagues. Pelletier was generally considered a fool for committing two murders to cover up such a venial offense as lying to protect his career. President Hatch managed to elicit sympathy for himself and the school, and he actually gave Malloy a bonus for handling the case so well.

The Northrups were still heartbroken over the loss of their daughter, but at least they had managed to protect her memory by hiring Malloy to investigate.

The following Tuesday morning, Sarah sat in her private sitting room, looking through the various newspapers Malloy had brought her. She was happy to see no further mention of Pelletie or the murders. Malloy sat nearby, also perusing the newspapers.

"Did you see this? It's snowing in Florida," he said.

"Really?" She took the paper he offered her. On the front page was a line drawing of a photograph taken on the Florida Capitol's front steps in Tallahassee. It showed legislators having a snowball fight. "That's amazing."

"It's apparently never snowed there before, at least as far as anybody knows."

"I saw something yesterday about the storm. It's supposed to be a really bad one."

"And it's heading for us," Malloy said. "It should start snowing sometime today, they say."

"The snow is always bad, but this terrible cold makes it so much worse."

"At least you don't have to worry about going out to deliver a baby," Malloy said.

"That's true, and they always seem to arrive when the weather is at its worst."

Someone tapped on the door, and their maid, Hattie, came in. "A girl from the Mission brought this message for you, Mrs. Frank."

Sarah took the envelope. Mrs. Keller's note was short and to the point.

"What is it?" Malloy asked.

"That girl at the Mission who is pregnant, Hannah, she's apparently gone into labor."

"I didn't think her baby was due for months."

"It's not. She's having a miscarriage, and Mrs. Keller has asked me to come at once."

"Can't she call another midwife?" Malloy asked.

"I suppose she could, but . . ." She gave him what she hoped was an appealing look.

He sighed. "I know I can't stop you, but I'm going with you at least."

"What on earth for?" she asked in surprise.

"Because of the weather. With this cold and a snowstorm coming, I don't want to have to worry about you being stranded out there somewhere alone."

He was right, of course. Even in a city, a person could be lost, and danger lurked everywhere. "Hattie, please make the girl comfortable. I need to dress and make sure my medical bag is packed." She turned to Malloy. "When is it supposed to start snowing?"

"Oh, the girl said it's been snowing awhile now," Hattie reported.

The city had taken on an oddly festive air with the snowfall. Children were running and sliding and throwing snowballs. Adults were bustling about, shopping to prepare for a few days indoors, if it came to that. It rarely did in the city, where so many hands were available to clear the streets and sidewalks.

Malloy had found them a cab, although the driver wasn't happy about their destination in the slums of Mulberry Street. The girl who had brought the note—her name was Iris—was pathetically grateful she didn't have to trudge back to the Mission through the deepening snow.

The cold was bitter, sharp, and angry. The city had already frozen solid from it, and the snow would make it worse. Sarah thought of all the little street arabs, abandoned homeless children who roamed the city with no shelter. She thought of the poor who lacked fuel for heat. How many of them would die before the snow melted?

Malloy tipped the driver generously, but he still wouldn't wait. He didn't want to sit long in this neighborhood or in this weather. If Malloy wanted to leave, he'd have to find another cab later.

Mrs. Keller welcomed them warmly. "Mr. Malloy, I didn't expect to see you, but it's always a pleasure."

"He wouldn't let me come alone, what with the snow," Sarah said.

"Iris, take Mr. Malloy to the kitchen and give him some coffee to warm up," Mrs. Keller said. "I'll take you upstairs to Hannah, Mrs. Malloy."

"How is she doing?" Sarah asked as they climbed the stairs.

"It's hard to tell. She . . . Well, I think she's been suffering since yesterday, but she never said a word. This morning, one of the girls noticed she was huddled up in a corner and told me. She didn't even want to admit it then, but I could see for myself."

"It's much too early," Sarah said sadly. "The child won't survive."

"I've already told the other girls so they won't be shocked. I think they've been looking forward to having a baby in the house."

"They didn't really think you'd let Hannah stay that long, did they?"

Mrs. Keller smiled. "They were hoping. Girls love playing with a baby, so long as it's not theirs. This way," she added, leading Sarah to the end of the hall. "I put her in my room so she'd have privacy."

The girls slept four or five to a room in order to squeeze as many of them into the house as possible. Hannah had done well to conceal her distress from the others as long as she had.

Mrs. Keller's small room was neat but plain. She had a narrow iron bed, a dresser, and a washstand. Her clothing hung on pegs along one wall. The single window overlooked the rear alley, where snow had blanketed everything ugly about this part of the city in pristine white.

"Hello, Hannah," Sarah said to the girl lying curled into herself on the bed. "How are you feeling?"

"Not so good, Mrs. Malloy."

"I'm sorry about that, but I'll try to make you more comfortable, at least. I'd like to examine you, if you don't mind, to see what's happening."

Hannah just stared up at her with terrified eyes and lay perfectly still as Sarah set her medical bag on the dresser and pulled out her stethoscope. As Sarah approached, Hannah caught her breath. At first Sarah thought she was just frightened, but then she realized the girl was having a contraction. Sarah quickly laid her hand over the girl's stomach to feel what was going on. After a minute, the contraction faded, and Hannah sighed with relief.

"How long has this been going on?"

"Since last night, late. I was already in bed when it started."

"Why didn't you wake me?" Mrs. Keller said. "You shouldn't have laid there all night without telling anyone."

Hannah didn't reply and she seemed to curl even more tightly into herself.

Having Mrs. Keller chide her for not telling anyone she was losing her child wasn't helping,

Sarah decided. "Mrs. Keller, would you get Hannah a nightdress and some clean sheets?"

"Yes, of course." Mrs. Keller hurried out to do Sarah's bidding, leaving Sarah in privacy to ask the questions she needed to ask.

"Are you having any bleeding?"

Hannah shook her head.

"I'd like to use this to listen to what's going on with your baby." Sarah held up the stethoscope. "I'll just press this part against your stomach like I did before. It won't hurt. May I?"

Hannah nodded, her eyes wide now.

Sarah inserted the earpieces into her ears and pressed the bell against Hannah's stomach. She hadn't really expected to find anything. She thought the baby had probably already died, but to her surprise she heard a strong heartbeat.

"What is it?" Hannah asked, obviously seeing Sarah's surprise.

"Nothing. I just . . . It looks like your baby is going to be born soon, but it's much too early. He'll be too small to survive, I'm afraid. I just want you to understand and be prepared."

"How long does it have to be before the baby is big enough?"

"They say nine months, and it takes almost ten months sometimes. Occasionally, a baby survives when it comes after only eight months, but even then, they often don't survive. So you see—"

"This one is nine months."

"What?"

"It got started last May. I know because it was only the one time. The man who lived downstairs in our tenement, he grabbed me one night when I was coming home and dragged me under the stairs. I never told anybody, not even when I knew there was a baby. Especially not then. I didn't know if he'd take it from me if he knew, so I kept it a secret until it was almost time, and then I came here."

Sarah wasn't quite sure what to say, and before she could make up her mind, Hannah had another contraction, which told Sarah that, if Hannah was right about the timing, she was giving birth to a full-term infant and they were much closer to the birth than she'd suspected.

Luckily, Mrs. Keller returned at that moment with the things Sarah had requested. Between the two of them, they got Hannah changed into the clean nightdress and put the fresh sheets on the bed before Hannah had another contraction.

Sarah sent Mrs. Keller for towels and examined Hannah more thoroughly. Sure enough, the baby was crowning.

"I can see your baby's head, Hannah. It won't be long now." Sarah showed her how to grip the bars on the headboard and how to push when the next contraction came.

"Will my baby live?" Hannah panted in between contractions.

"I think so." Sarah knew better than to make promises, because anything could happen, but this baby showed every sign he was going to arrive safely.

Mrs. Keller arrived with the towels just in time. The baby's head emerged, startling an "Oh my!" from her as she set the stack of towels down.

"One more push," Sarah told Hannah, and the baby slid free.

"Good heavens," Mrs. Keller said this time, since the baby was obviously full-size and more than ready to make his entrance into the world. Or rather, her entrance.

"It's a girl," Sarah said, holding her up.

"Is she all right?"

Sarah cleared the baby's mouth and annoyed her enough to make her cry, which Sarah always thought was the most beautiful sound in the world. "She seems to be fine," Sarah shouted over the baby's wails. "She's got all her fingers and toes."

"Why is she crying, then?" Hannah demanded.

"That's how they get their lungs opened up," Sarah said. "She'll settle down in a minute and you can nurse her. She won't cry then."

Later, when Hannah had fed her daughter and the babe had drifted off to sleep, Hannah said, "I'm awful sorry I lied to you, Mrs. Malloy."

"You should be apologizing to Mrs. Keller," Sarah told her.

"I'm right sorry about lying to you, too, Mrs. Keller. I hated like anything to do it, but I didn't know what else to do. I was too scared to sleep in the streets, and it was getting cold . . ."

"There's no need to explain," Mrs. Keller said. "I can understand perfectly. In your place, I'm not sure I wouldn't've done the same thing."

"I don't think I would have," Sarah said, earning a dismayed wince from Hannah. "Because I wouldn't have been clever enough to even think of it," she added to soften her rebuke. "You took advantage of Mrs. Keller's good nature, but you did it to save your baby, so I don't think we can be too angry at you."

"I can't believe you kept your condition a secret all those months," Mrs. Keller said.

"I'm lucky I'm so tall. I used to hate being so big, but not anymore because it helped me hide her." Hannah looked down at the baby sleeping in her arms. "What happens now? To us, I mean. I know we can't stay here."

"You'll stay here until you've recovered," Mrs. Keller said firmly.

"And then we'll find you a place to live," Sarah said. "A safe place. Will your family take you back, do you think?"

"Oh no, not with a babe, and I don't even know where they are now, anyway."

"Then we'll find you someplace else to go. You'll need to get a job, and we'll find a settlement house with a nursery where you can leave the baby while you work."

"They won't take her from me?"

"Not unless you want to give her up," Sarah said.

"You can, you know," Mrs. Keller said. "Raising a child alone is going to be very difficult."

"I know, but she's all I have in the world. I couldn't possibly give her up, not after all I've done to keep her."

"You don't need to think about all that just yet, though," Sarah said. "Right now you should get some sleep."

Sarah and Mrs. Keller tucked Hannah and the baby in and left them to rest.

"You and Mr. Malloy won't be going anywhere just yet either, I'm afraid," Mrs. Keller said as they descended the stairs. "The storm has turned into a regular blizzard."

"Oh no."

"I'm sure Mr. Malloy will be mortified that you'll have to spend the night, but the girls will be delighted. They love having a man to fuss over."

Sarah found Malloy in the parlor, standing at the front window and watching it snow. "You should've left when you had the chance," she said with a grin.

He didn't return her smile. "How's the girl?"

She realized no one had told him. "She's fine

and so is the baby, who is a healthy little girl. She lied about how far along she was."

His troubled expression cleared instantly. "Why did she do that?"

"She was afraid. A girl in that situation has a lot to be afraid of. She thought if she went to a maternity home, they'd take her child."

"They might have."

"So she hid her condition as long as she could and lied about it when she couldn't hide it any longer."

"And if you'd known how close she was to delivery, what would you have done?"

"I would've tried to find a place where she'd get good care but get to keep her baby, although it wouldn't have been easy."

"So the girl is all right? And the baby?"

Sarah hadn't realized what he was worrying about. Malloy had lost his first wife when Brian was born. "They're both perfectly fine."

"And how are you, Mrs. Malloy?" he asked, his eyes narrowing as he studied her face.

"What do you mean?"

"I mean you should see yourself right now."

Sarah touched her hair self-consciously. "Is something wrong?"

"No, something's right. I haven't seen that look on your face in a long time."

"What are you talking about, Malloy?"

"I'm talking about that look you get when you

deliver a baby. It's like . . . Well, you look real satisfied, like you've just done God a favor or something."

"I'm sure that's a blasphemous thing to say," she scolded him.

"I'm sure it is, but it's also the truth. Delivering babies makes you happy."

Sarah sighed. "Yes, it does. I've missed it. But I can't go back to being a midwife."

"Why not?"

She shook her head. "Maybe you've forgotten how babies come at all hours of the day and night and how I'd be called all over the city and be away from home for days sometimes."

"What about those maternity homes?"

"What about them?"

"Is it different there?"

Was it? She'd never thought about it. "I suppose it's easier because the women are right there when they go into labor."

"They must have midwives who live there, too, so they don't have to travel around the city."

"I suppose so."

"And if there was one of these homes where they had midwives and the women could stay and have their babies and keep their babies and get the help they needed—"

"Malloy, what are you talking about?"

"I'm talking about the kind of place this girl Hannah needed and you couldn't find for her, and

I'm talking about a place where you could go to deliver babies sometimes but there'd be other midwives for when you couldn't."

"You're serious, aren't you?" she asked in amazement.

"I might be. I haven't had much to do since we got here except think about this and watch the snow. The snow isn't very interesting."

"We'll have to spend the night," she said.

"I know. The snow's already too deep. We'll have to wait here until they clear the streets tomorrow."

"Good. That will give us plenty of time to talk about this idea of yours," she said, taking his hand.

Author's Note

The Normal School of Manhattan is a fictional creation and is an amalgamation of Hunter College (formerly the Normal College of the City of New York) and Barnard College. The first colleges for women opened after the American Civil War. The loss of so many men in the war left a surplus of women with no hope of finding a husband and the need to support themselves. The colleges gave women the skills to have productive careers as teachers and social workers.

In the nineteenth century, unmarried professional women often shared living quarters and developed deep friendships with their peers. Author Henry James wrote about such a relationship in his novel *The Bostonians*, and as a result, these relationships became known as Boston marriages. Because of the social mores of the era, the exact nature of each of these relationships is known only to the people involved, but we can speculate that at least some of the women were lesbian couples. The legal case in England that President Hatch relates to Frank is a true story that illustrates the thinking of the time period very well.

The snowstorm described at the end of the book is the Blizzard of 1899, which did bring snow to Tallahassee, Florida, for the first time in recorded memory. It froze the port of New Orleans and created a record low temperature for Miami: 29°F. New York City received sixteen inches of snow, but the worst snow fell between North Carolina and Virginia.

And before you ask, French Letters really was a brand name for condoms in the nineteenth century and became another name for them, much like Kleenex is often used for tissue.

I hope you enjoyed this book. Please visit my website at victoriathompson.com and leave me a message or follow me on Facebook at facebook.com/Victoria.Thompson.Author and Twitter @gaslightvt. I'll be sure to let you know when new Gaslight Mysteries are published so you don't miss a single one.

Center Point Large Print
600 Brooks Road / PO Box 1
Thorndike, ME 04986-0001 USA

(207) 568-3717

US & Canada:
1 800 929-9108
www.centerpointlargeprint.com